Bob Judd has been praised for capturing the thrilling atmosphere of international motor racing in his novels—which he researched by renting a car and driving at Le Mans, Silverstone, Brands Hatch, Mexico, Indianapolis, and Daytona. After writing about racing and automobiles for over twenty-five years, Bob Judd has become an acclaimed mystery writer as well, using his knowledge of the sport to create the exciting novels featuring former race-car driver Forrest Evers . . .

BURN: When a friend dies in the flames of a burning car at the Phoenix Grand Prix, Forrest Evers takes the ultimate risk to find the real story . . .

SPIN: Forrest Evers is living the high life in Monaco—but a fatal track accident at Silverstone forces him to get behind the wheel and race to conclusions about the driver's mysterious death . . .

CURVE: A beautiful woman asks for Forrest Evers's help in escaping her husband—a cocky young Italian driver. But before he knows it, he's caught in a web of crime and corruption . . .

CURVE

Bob Judd

Originally published as *Monza*

BERKLEY PRIME CRIME, NEW YORK

Originally published as *Monza*.

This Berkley Prime Crime Book contains the complete text of the original hardcover edition.
It has been completely reset in a typeface designed for easy reading, and was printed from new film.

CURVE

A Berkley Prime Crime Book / published by arrangement with the author

PRINTING HISTORY
Macmillan London Ltd. edition published 1991
Berkley Prime Crime edition / November 1994

ISBN: 0-425-14466-6

Berkley Prime Crime Books are published by The Berkley Publishing Group,
200 Madison Avenue, New York, NY 10016.
The name BERKLEY PRIME CRIME and the BERKLEY PRIME CRIME design are trademarks belonging to Berkley Publishing Corporation.

PRINTED IN THE UNITED STATES OF AMERICA

10 9 8 7 6 5 4 3 2 1

Author's Note

Sooner or later, some scholar is bound to notice that I have lifted the plot of *Curve* from a long and gorgeous Victorian poem, ''The Ring and the Book'' by Robert Browning (first published in London in four volumes over the winter of 1868–69). The scholar will also complain that I have taken shocking liberties with Browning's story.

Well, yes, I have. Shocking. But as Browning was the first to point out, it wasn't really his story either.

Browning stole the plot from a bundle of yellowing seventeenth-century newspaper clippings covering a murder case in Rome in 1698. Although ''stole'' is probably too harsh a word. Browning didn't really ''steal'' the story, he gave a bookseller in Rome one lira for the clippings.

When Browning published ''The Ring and the Book'' some critics complained that his poem ruined the best novel never written. No doubt *Curve* will finish off the job. But then *Curve* is not really a novel either. It's much closer to one of those grand old Italian thrillers with music; it's really more of an opera.

"Living well is the best revenge . . .
until you think of a better idea."

CURVE

Chapter 1

Black is the best dream colour.

Wall to wall limbo black.

I was dreaming that soft black with no light, no place, nobody and no nothing except the darkest and sweetest sleep, when I heard a door crash in the distance. I was thinking of opening my eyes when hands of surprising strength grabbed an arm and a leg and pulled me away from the sheets. For a fraction of a second, in mid-air, I thought I was still dreaming until I hit the floor face down.

Not a dream.

My reactions are reasonably quick and I was just opening my eyes, pushing up from the floor when I was kicked in my side on one side and kicked in my ear from the other side, snapping my head sideways. Then I was grabbed by the shoulders and stood on my feet and pushed into the wall with enough force to make my nose bleed. The voices behind me were men screaming in Italian, a touch of panic in the high notes. I could not remember where I was.

My side bloomed red pain and I could not breathe. The wall in front of my face seemed shiny and red like film. They were saying "bastard," "you fucking bastard," "you rotten son of a bitch."

The thick metallic taste of blood in my mouth made me feel a breath away from throwing up. If only I could take a breath, I remember thinking, I could do something about

1

this. But taking a breath was a full-time occupation.

Another thumping of boots on the wood floor announced the arrival of another group of angry men. There seemed to be two groups of men with two points of view. Both in a rage. I turned my head to see who they were and a tap behind my ear brought peace. As I slid down the wall I remember a kick in my back but it didn't hurt a bit. All the way down the wall to wall to wall black.

Bounce, bounce, bounce my toes were bouncing, scraping the skin off the top of my feet as they dragged down stone steps. I focused on my dragging feet and became aware of the shouting around me, the sound of a crowd, the flashes of light from cameras and the tendrils of sharp pain that led from my ear and my back and my legs to my stomach where they joined in a hard concentrated ball of pain. And then I looked up and that part of it came back to me, where I was.

High above the lobby of the Castelnuovo, a row of small Gothic windows with peaked arches sent shafts of sunlight down through the smoke and confusion. There were several Poliziotti in front of me and no doubt more behind, and a Poliziotto on either side was half carrying, half dragging me down the stone steps. I tried to get my feet underneath me, to support my weight and stop scraping off skin. Supported by two men who were shorter than me, I felt like a drunk riding a bicycle, wobbly with bent knees.

When the crowd of men and women in the lobby below saw us they let out a huge roar and a blaze of flashing lights. The front door where Rossella and I had walked through in the early morning had been flung open and a tide of people were trying to surge through it. Their faces were angry, screaming. I tried standing upright so at least I could walk down the stairs and I realized I was virtually naked and my hands were handcuffed behind me. I felt another wave of nausea but it passed. The cold metal prod in the back of my neck, I assumed, was a gun.

The stairway led into the middle of the entrance hall. When we reached the bottom, we stopped, faces staring at me from all sides. I was standing upright now, taller than most of the crowd and I could see over them through the door and out to the square where there were hundreds of people and police cars and vans with flashing lights. In the distance, an ambulance, its siren a faint scream, its blue lights flashing helplessly, was trying to get to the edge of the crowd and out through the gate. If it was making any progress, I couldn't tell.

Our way was blocked by a dozen Carabinieri, the Italian State Police, in high black boots, a red strip down the side of their trousers and hats from an old Marlon Brando motorcycle movie.

"Bene, OK," the one with the most scrambled eggs on his hat said, "we'll take him from here."

"You are obstructing Poliziotti and I must ask you to move aside so we may take our prisoner into custody," said one of the Poliziotti in front of me in that flat, official, memorized-from-a-manual voice.

"You couldn't find your ass with both hands. This is a state case and I'm not letting you dogbrains fuck it up."

"Please, you will step aside. This is our jurisdiction. You must have a warrant of jurisdiction signed by a judge. You don't have a warrant of jurisdiction signed by a judge, get the fuck out of our way."

As they continued their learned discussion, a short elderly lady in black poked her dark wrinkled face between the shoulders of two Carabinieri. She looked me in the eye for a moment and then she spat at me. Some of it landed on the Poliziotti alongside me and he automatically swung his fist in her direction. But equally automatically, her face was gone so the Poliziotti settled for second best and gave me a jab in the side, dead centre where I had been kicked and I wondered if seeing the stone walls glaze red was a symptom of kidney damage.

After several minutes, the Carabinieri won. I was their prize, most likely because they outnumbered the Poliziotti two to one. The Carabinieri formed a tight circle around me and using their truncheons as prods began to push forward towards the door. In a way I was glad for their protection. The faces that peered at me were screaming "Pig," "Bastard," "Pimp," "Monster" and I had the feeling that without the circle of Carabinieri around me, waving their sticks and guns, the crowd would have happily kicked and torn me to death. Some were obviously reporters and photographers, trying to get a story, shouting questions I couldn't hear above the din. But most of the crowd had the everyday look of village people, the men in short-sleeved shirts and some in those grey nylon jackets that shopkeepers wear, and some with ties. There were women in house dresses or suits with padded shoulders, and children flinging small sharp stones. They were so angry, so ferocious I almost forgot I was nearly naked.

As we moved through the front door the ambulance in the distance finally broke through the crowd in the square and moved cautiously out through the gate and disappeared. For a few moments I could hear the ambulance siren rise and fall over the shouts of the crowd. Then it was gone.

In shock, the blood slows, the breath and the brain slow down and the body retreats into itself to lick its wounds. I must have been suffering from a mild form of that because my mind was moving so slowly as they pushed me into the grey van. It is too bad I never acquired the habit of sleeping in pyjamas, I remember thinking, because then I would have pyjamas to wear. Followed by an equally inane thought that my gold nylon bikini briefs were what you'd expect a male stripper to wear. I'd never worn them before, and I hadn't expected to wear them in public. They were a joke. An old silly, dumb joke. They had been the last pair of briefs in my drawer, shoved in the back since Susan gave them to me years ago, when we were married and when we still made jokes. The gold nylon bikini briefs were the only knickers left in my drawer because Zilna the Cypriot fascist had the flu and nothing in my flat in London had been washed or cleaned for three weeks.

The crowd was jeering, pointing fingers at me. What had happened, and what was happening seemed to be of such stunning force that I didn't even question it. I remember thinking that my hands hurt, but I didn't ask why. I didn't ask why this was happening to me or what had happened to Rossella. Rossella, I thought.

And it was only then, when they shut the van door, and the siren went on and the driver started honking his horn nonstop, and I looked at the two teenage men in uniform opposite me, glaring at me, it was only then that my mind started to work again.

Not that it helped.

It seemed distant, hazy like some country on the other side of the world and some other time on the other side of the dial. Some other life. But it was only the night before, wasn't it? It must have been the night before.

I remembered that it had been a still night and we had seen the stars overhead. In the mountains we could smell cedar and pine from the forests and the sound of our passing boomed off the village walls in our wake.

But the memory always lies. A few golden strokes with a broad brush and you think, sure, that's the way it was. While behind the golden strokes the details lie hidden in the dark. And the details are everything.

When I thought about it the details came back slowly, reluctantly, one by one.

When I thought about it I remembered patches of rain, and sometimes, in the middle of a bend, water running across the road, the car suddenly snapping into the beginning of a spin, wanting to shoot over the edge. I remembered holding it out on the edge for an extra beat or two for the exhilaration, and accelerating at the same time, downhill. And then the stars would reappear overhead. And Rossella would look at me with the glad smile of a schoolgirl released from the convent, on her way home for the holidays. Which, in a way, she was.

Later there was a flash of an ancient house moving left to right at eighty miles an hour followed by a guardrail. Then, coming over a rise, the lights pointed toward the night sky then quick-swivelled down to see the road disappear thirty yards ahead, right. Hard on the brakes, turning in, following the headlights sweeping around the corner, waiting for news of the road up ahead. The black road, when it swung around to centre in the windscreen, was lumpy with patches and old frost heaves, crowned high in the middle and not much wider than the car. It crested fifty yards away then disappeared. Trees on both sides of the road arched overhead. From second at 85 mph into third, accelerating again, the speedometer showing 105, the headlamps making paths into the night sky.

And this is the part that brought it all back. Rossella putting her hand on my thigh just above my knee as we hurtled towards the crest, her four warm fingers on the inside and her thumb along the top of my leg, gripping tightly.

I remember I shifted up into fourth, her face relaxed and smiling, looking straight ahead into the darkness and shouting happily over the din that she loved this. She said she loved the feeling of control, feeling in my leg the control I had over the car. "It is the first time," she said, looking away from the road and holding me in those immense blue eyes, "it is the first time I have felt safe for five years."

"I feel so safe with you," she said.

Part 1

Chapter 2

Pianoro is a village of small vineyards and fruit farms patching the hillsides and valleys behind Bologna. At the end of summer the air is clear and fragrant with peaches and apples and the vineyards are fat with grapes.

Piano like soft. Oro like gold.

The day had begun hot and dry in London. Yet another unseasonably hot day in yet another unseasonably hot season. Kensington Gardens were brown and the *Independent* had a front page photo of a dusty farmer in a dusty field. In the early afternoon, Ken flew me down to Bologna from Luton in his jet, telling me for the fifty-third time that I had reached the stage in my career as a Formula One driver when I really should invest in "my own transport." He means a jet.

Formula One drivers have jets the way executives have attaché cases. It's part of our outfit. With sixteen races around the world plus test days and celebrity days everywhere in between, you can save yourself serious time skipping the hassle at the airport. Your flight is never delayed due to incoming aircraft or a pilots' strike. Your flight is always waiting for you whenever you drive in, and it is warmed up, ready when you are, Mr. Evers.

With an income swelling past the million-dollars-a-race mark, a successful Formula One driver can afford two jets if he feels like having a backup at home in the garage. But

I looked at the numbers. A Lear or an Avianco would be fun and it would mean I could bring some friends along, no extra charge. Whip down to Ischia after the race. Take a lady for a ride. But the numbers still say that unless you lease your jet while you're not using it, unless you can keep it up in the air at somebody else's expense, you'll lose two to five hundred thousand a year on maintenance, depreciation and fees. But if you lease it out, it's not yours then is it? It's just another financial complication.

I'd rather pass the hours of boredom and moments of terror of piloting a jet to somebody with less imagination and more training. In a Formula One car my mind races just ahead of the projectile, splitting the oncoming world into tiny, specific, thousandth of a second portions. In a jet, the empty sky fills me with despair for the time it will take to cross the empty sky to the lumpy cloud on the horizon, which may or may not contain a doctor zonked out on goof balls in a little single-prop Cessna, staggering along three miles off his designated path and into mine. So unlike a normal Formula One driver I hitchhike when I can and fly scheduled for the longer hauls. But then I am not a normal driver.

Normal Formula One drivers have the nervous, under-fed look of jockeys in the parade ring before the Gold Cup. I am too tall, too broad across the shoulders and I lack the balletic grace of the best of them. Every year the cars shrink a little more, and I am squeezed tighter, knees up in the cockpit, bruising my shins and my thighs on the bulkhead and my forearms on the sides of the damn carbon-fibre tub.

But this year looked, no, not looked. This year was, really was sensational. Over the winter Ken and our head designer, Max, had sold Max's automatic transmission to a Japanese and Australian consortium for several hundred million dollars payable over the next decade. Included in the deal were several million annually for the Arundel Formula One team. Marlboro McLaren spends nearly a hundred million pounds a year to race their two cars. And they get their engines free from Honda. We were restricted to a budget of a mere thirty-five million. It wasn't enough, there is never enough. But it was enough to go racing. We had a wind tunnel, an autoclave to produce our own carbon-fibre chassis, our own backup test driver, three aerodynamicists, and a staff of thirty-nine designers, engineers, mechanics, a public affairs department and the mark of every truly successful modern independent entrepreneurial company, a full-time tea lady.

We were a long way from Fiat's budget for Ferrari, and we didn't have the boost that Williams gets from Renault but we were running shoulder to shoulder with leaders towards the championship. For the first time in the five years I had been driving for Ken, Team Arundel was a contender. Guido had won at Spa the week before and I had come in fourth. So now Guido and I were tied for fourth in the points for the driver's championship. And Team Arundel was third in the manufacturer's championship. We had a chance.

The team, Guido, myself, we all had a chance.

The heat that had seemed so strong in London paled in the blaze of light at Bologna's Aeroporto di Borgo Panigale. Stepping out of the plane, down the ramp in the dazzling light, a silver Lancia waited ten yards away. A syrup of heat waves rising off the tarmac made the car look transparent and floating. The tarmac was soft and sticky and warmed my feet through my soft Italian loafers. Little Ferrari badges on the car told us that this was the Lancia with the Ferrari V-8. The one that costs £20,000 more than the 2-litre turbo and goes 2 mph slower. Such is the power of the prancing horse in Italy. The driver, a man with a beautifully tailored white suit and a perfect silver haircut knew the way, and the air-conditioning worked. We settled back in the dark grey leather seats.

If you have to work on a Friday evening, I thought, this is the way to do it. I hadn't wanted to come, but Ken had insisted, "for the good of the team."

We began to climb out of the suburbs of Bologna, and up into the hills, the early evening light warming the sides of the old burnt yellow and umber houses turning them gold. Ken, the long legs of his six foot seven inch frame sprawled like a go-kart driver, had been silent since we had left the airport, no doubt rehearsing just how he should phrase it. "I wish," he said when he turned to me, "I do wish you'd try a bit harder."

It was a conversation we'd had before. "He is not an easy man to like," I said.

"No," ken said, looking out at the scenery again, "he is not an easy man to like. But Guido does bring quite a bit to the team."

Indeed he did. To Team Arundel Guido DiSanto brought Italian tyre, wine, computer and fashion sponsors with their serious budgets and their marketing plans. He brought half a million new fans, members of the Guido DiSanto Fan Club, formed by his manager and a PR firm when Guido won the European Formula Three Thousand championship the year before. He brought pole positions in Phoenix, Imola, and Spa. And now, with the win at Spa, he was bringing glory as well as fame and fortune to Team Arundel. According to the racing journalists he brought a "much-needed breath of fresh air" to the team. He gave us "a new lease on life," he brought "panache," "daring," and "the kind of commitment that we haven't seen since the young Ayrton Senna arrived on Toleman's doorstep." None of the above endeared him to me.

But I would try. For Ken and for the team. And because I am a professional. Besides, this was Guido's day. And as the luck would have it, what was going to be a pleasant reception was now going to be a full-bore celebration of Guido's victory at Spa. Champagne followed by dinner. At Guido's fifteenth-century Castello di Pianoro. For Guido's sponsors a chance for their management and their sales force and their most important customers to meet the Formula One team that swallowed so much of their cash, and gave them so much time and space in the media around the world. To shake hands with Guido and, er, whatsisname, the other driver.

Up into the hills in the summer evening. Where the air was cooler and the colours even more golden. We rounded a corner, and turned left, drove through the immense and rusting wrought iron gates, the fat tyres of the Lancia crunching freshly spread crushed stone in the drive, the car's shadow flicking in and out of the tall cedars that lined both sides of the drive. We pulled up by the front door, and got out into the warm evening air. A quick visual cruise of the parking lot revealed a small fleet of the big Alfas and Lancias you'd expect from successful Italian corporate businessmen, as well as the Ferraris, Lamborghinis and Jaguars for the high rollers. It also seemed that there were two chauffeurs for every car. I thought that it was a sign that the Italians are big on security on their own home ground and turned back to the yellow stone castle. It had the slightly run-down, been in the family for years look so loved by the Italians and the British. And I had to admit, it was beautiful.

The castle stood out on a promontory, commanding the valley. In the honeyed light, its tower and Gothic windows were half hidden behind thick dark cedars. Surrounded by orchards and vineyards, with the valley below and the mountains behind, the castella looked like the kind of family edifice that is either handed to you in a will along with the responsibility of being the Duke, or you sacrifice a lifetime building an empire in frozen foods or petroleum to achieve. At twenty-eight, Guido appeared to be doing well. Even for a Formula One driver.

He was standing with his back to us, talking to a group of men dressed in the baby pastels of designer resort wear. Without looking up Guido waved for us to come over.

Chapter 3

Guido was holding court. I wasn't really up to playing courtier, as in grinning and hanging on his words, so I took a mental step back.

His face looked like it belonged on a much bigger man, almost like an oversize mask; large, black eyes set wide above high cheek bones, a wide, deep-purple mouth with a thick lower lip and a long Arabic nose. His hair was long, straight, and black. You wouldn't call him handsome, but he had a kind of magnetism, an intensity you could feel. He was by far the smallest in the circle of men standing on the worn stone steps of his home, but they paid him deference, nodding their heads, listening, agreeing. He had a rasp in his voice and the habit of rising up on his toes when he talked. Giving him that all important extra half-inch.

"Attitude," he was saying, jabbing his cigarette in the air for emphasis, "the whole thing is attitude. Number one you gotta feel you own the track. Number two, you gotta make the other guy feel you own the track. You come up behind a guy to pass, you drive through him." He gestured with his hand, knifing the air. "Make him move over. It's not his track, it's your track. You don't come up behind him and turn your turn signal on, 'please, can I pass now?' There's no turn signals on a Formula One car. You drive through him." He eased back down the half-inch onto the soles of his shoes, looking from face to face, looking for approval in their faces and getting it. He noticed Ken, his eyes hitting Ken around belt level and moving up. "Oh, yeah," he said. "I want you to meet my team manager, Ken Arundel. Be nice to him, he owns the team."

Ken smiled down the distant British smile he keeps for state occasions and shook hands, one by one, as Guido named the names. "Carlo Bonventre, the chairman of Vini Cristalli. Angelo Farulli, General Manager of Farulli Tyre and Rubber Company, Francesco Pagano, Managing Director of Pagano Computers." Guido went on, "Guafreducci Fasolino, Fasolino Men's Fashions, Luigi Lucchesini, Luce Glass and Ceramics . . ." These were the new generation of self-made Italian men. Smart, aggressive and sophisticated international businessmen who felt disdain for the Americans and the British and were on equal terms with the Japanese. When Henry Ford was talking to Gianni Agnelli about a merger between Ford and Fiat in Europe, Henry was telling him how it would be. How he, Henry would run the show. Nobody ever told Henry Ford what to do. Agnelli pointed out that the cars and trucks, the Fiats, Ferraris, Alfas and Lancias were a mere ten per cent of the Fiat empire. His little empire. Was Henry really serious . . . did Henry really think that he could give Agnelli orders?

The handshaking had come around full circle to me. "Oh yeah, excuse me, I almost forgot," Guido said, "Forrest Evers, my number two driver." He stopped for a moment rising up on his toes again. "I got a lot to learn from him. One day, some young blood's gonna come along and try to push me off the track. I don't know how I'm gonna handle that. Maybe that's something Forrest can show me."

Ken's eyebrows lifted as if to object, and his hand was on my shoulder to restrain me, but Guido was already ushering the group inside and the moment had passed. Team Arundel did not have a number two driver. Team Arundel had two number one drivers. Our contracts were specific, and they were clear. Guido was looking impatient, standing in the doorway, up on his toes, beckoning for us to follow.

It was his day.

We followed Guido through the ancient entrance hall, its faded yellow walls hung with old dark paintings, Italian lords and ladies perched on horses. The floor was marble, its vast geometric pattern of the sun and its rays worn down by countless entrances and exits over the centuries.

We moved slowly through the tall, dim room and into the ballroom. The contrast was stunning. From medieval aristocracy to wall to wall scarlet carpet. Wall to wall disco music. Carpet so red, the chins and faces in the room had a reflected pink glow. Disco music so loud you had to shout to talk. My feet sank in but didn't touch bottom and there was a scent of carpet glue. There must have been a hundred people in the ballroom, counting the waiters with glasses of champagne on silver trays, and there was room for a hundred more. The walls had been freshly painted bright green and the floor to ceiling windows framed with several acres of new white nylon. Overhead three glass chandeliers the size of limousines blazed with light. And theatre-size speakers pointed down at us from the four corners of the ceiling. Guido stopped in front of us and turned, spreading his arms. "What do you think?" he said in Italian. "Before it was gloomy, you know, depressing. You get it? Red, white, green? Colours of the Italian flag, Bella Italia. I hope you don't mind, Signor Farulli, it's Pirelli carpet. You make Farulli carpet, I'll rip it up, put down Farulli carpet."

Signor Farulli looked down his long nose, sighting in on a bright red fluff ball, "I think for now, Guido, Farulli sticks to tyres." He looked back up at Guido, "Very soothing colour, tyres. Black." Then his thin face broke into a wide grin of widely spaced teeth. "But I tell you. You win some more races for us and if you want, I'll give you red tyres."

"Hey, Dottere Evers, you don't have a glass of our champagne." This was Carlo Bonventre looking at me with concern. He was about thirty-six, tall, good looking in a thin-faced way. He could have passed for a male model;

voluminous trousers, a white billowing shirt with no collar like you see on the decks of the yachts in whisky ads. "Here," he said, "let me get you a glass of our Cristal di Cristalli. It's better than the French champagne. Not so much gas." He pursed his lips in disapproval of the French. Then smiled again. "I want to propose a toast." His long thin hand with a silver bracelet on a tanned wrist extended in my direction, holding a glass of sparkling wine. He had a kind of casual grace that seemed almost feminine.

"Normally I don't drink, Signor Bonventre," I said. "But if you are proposing a toast . . . " I said raising the glass in his direction.

"You speak good Italian. Too good to have learned it from Guido."

"I'm out of practice. I went to school in Milano when I was a boy. My mother thought it would improve me."

I thought of the gloomy winter days of perpetual fog in Milan when I was seven. A dumb stranger, unable to speak. On the holidays, the other boys went off to estates on Lake Como, the sun on the Amalfi Peninsula, villas in Tuscany and Sicily. They would come back tanned and grinning. I came back from dripping London with my deep grey London pallor. I hold the Milanese fog totally responsible for my gloomy nature. On the other hand, that was years ago, and I know almost nothing of Italy now. I don't know why, for example, there is a note of viciousness creeping into the love songs on the radio. Or why there is, just under the glittering surface, such despair.

"Your mother was right," he said. "Italy improves everybody. Hey, excuse me everybody," he said raising his glass. "Stop the goddamn music. I have a toast to make." Heads turned in our direction and the DJ turned down the disco to a dull thump. "I want to propose a toast to the next Champion of the World, Guido DiSanto."

It was too much. Cristal Di Cristalli is indeed a beautiful wine. Crisp, balanced, refreshing. And the room was hot. And just a sip from the tall frosty flute would have been delicious. And Guido was the host. And he had won at Spa. And he did have a shot at being the next world champion.

But so did I. I can be charming at the dinner table, and I will take my portion of humble pie with medium grace. But there comes a time when enough is too much. As the room filled with "bravos" and the murmurs of praise, I set my glass down on a passing tray. A gesture unseen, I think, by anybody in the room except Signor Bonventre who interrupted his smile for an instant to fix me with his eyes and then turned to whisper to a short dark man at his side. His smile returned, full watt, and he took another sip of wine as the applause subsided and the sales managers and distributors crowded around Guido to shake his hand and tell him how great he was.

"Forrest, ole buddy." A familiar American voice made me turn around. "Howya doin'?"

"Not too bad for a number two, Jack."

"Yeah, I heard him say that. A real prick with ears. So next time blow his doors off." Jack Boyce had on his usual open friendly grin. You often saw Jack where wealth and automobiles crossed paths. Jack was handsome, in a rugged, round-faced, boyish way. Jack was sincere. Jack knew all the right names, and Jack was on his way to all the right places. Jack was Vice-Presidential material. Jack was a used car salesman.

Except that's not fair to Jack because Jack didn't really sell used cars. Jack brokered "investment opportunities," "appreciating assets," and "substantial acquisitions." Jack was the curator of "hollow rolling sculpture." His "portfolio" included names like Bugatti, Ferrari, Cisitalia, Pegaso, Blower Bentleys and Aston Martin Zagatos. Sometimes we called him "Quayle," just to piss him off.

"It's a great feeling when you win your first Formula One race," I said. "When you cross that finish line first, and they wave the chequered flag, you are the best in the world and your feet don't touch the ground for a week."

"Yeah, well, they're all a little up in the air 'cause Guido won. You know how the Italians are. If he falls off at Monza they'll be calling him a bum."

"Thanks for the soothing words."

"Christ you are feisty. What happened to you at Spa?"

"You want to hear how my anti-roll bar control stuck? How I was ploughing through the corners like. . . "

"No I don't want to hear about your roll bar. Or the Bull pin on your Heffling shaft. In Formula One you get one winner followed by twenty-five excuses."

"And how my front tyres overheated and went off."

"You gonna let me tell you about your new car."

"Jack I have more cars than I know where to park."

"Won't hurt to let me tell you about it."

"I don't want to hear it. Every damn car company in the world says they want me to drive their new Gizmo. What am I going to do with another car? Stick it in a garage and look at it twice a year?"

"It won't cost you anything. I'll give it to you."

"Jack, you wouldn't give a Dinky toy away. What are you up to?" Jack sells his cars for what people used to pay for Picassos. And for all the use most of the collectors get out of their "investment" they might as well hang it up on the wall.

"You have to give it back in two weeks."

"OK, Jack, what is it?"

"Didn't you see it on the way in? It's parked right outside."

"I didn't see anything special."

"You probably thought it was a plain old 308. It's the original Boxer. You know the 365 BB? Just been completely rebuilt. Here's the keys." He held out a black leather fob with the prancing horse, keys dangling.

"Put your keys back in your pocket, Jack. I'm flying back to London with Ken."

"What have you got to go back to London for? An empty flat? Pay your bills? Listen, take the car for a couple of weeks, drive it I don't know where. Wherever. You gotta come back down to Italy anyway. I know you have a practice session at Vallelunga in a couple of days and Monza is next weekend after that. Why bust your nut flying back and forth, ole buddy? Take a holiday. Take somebody with you. I'll pay the expenses.''

"Jack, I don't want the car and I don't want a holiday, but what I don't understand is why you want me to drive it. You worried there's a bomb in it?''

"Very funny. Let me tell you a little secret, Forrest. Ferraris are a dog on the market right now. In fact everything is a dog on the market. Nothing is selling, nobody's buying. This is a nice one, but I'd have to discount it to sell it.''

"Needless to say, you don't want to do that.''

"Needless to say. But if you drive it for a couple of weeks, then I can sell it as Forrest Evers' very own personal car. Should bring an extra 25 per cent.''

"I don't think my driving the car would bring you an extra hundred lire from this lot. Why don't you offer it to Guido?''

"Because he'd wrap it around the tree. Or sell it and tell me it was stolen. Besides I don't want to sell it here, I got a buyer in London.''

"You already told somebody you'd sell them 'my' Ferrari?''

"Take the keys. It's cheaper than a rentacar.''

Chapter 4

The scent of Bolognese cuisine made me grin like a cat with a canary in his dish. Ah, the good stuff, I thought, my spirits lifting. No relationship whatsoever to the grim drool Britain calls Spag. Bol. The air was perfumed with fresh basil, and oregano. Lemon, garlic, olive oil, butter, and langoustines.

Dinner was in a long high hall. As I went in I was idly calculating how much 25 per cent of the value of a Ferrari Boxer would be. I was up thirty-five thousand pounds (no wonder Jack was willing to pay my expenses—could I spend thirty-five thousand in two weeks?) and scanning the place cards at the head table until it dawned that I would not be at the head table. So I set off to cruise the room for the little card that said Forrest Evers. Honoured guest. Team-mate. Hero driver who has come all the way this evening from far away Gran Bretagna. Winner of four Formula One Grand Prix. Holder of five offshore bank accounts. World Championship Contender.

The Forrest Evers chair had been chosen with care and was where I should have suspected it would be, at the last table in the far corner, banged on the back by the kitchen door.

It was such a petty insult. A public insult, but still a petty one. And there was nothing I could do about it without being even more petty myself. But why, after all, should I care? Wasn't I a sophisticated man of the world? Above this adolescent rivalry. Bring on the humble pie, waiter. And the local lovelies. Living well is always the best revenge. Until you think of a better idea.

By the time the fresh tortellini stuffed with ricotta and rughetta arrived, I learned that the heavy lady on my left was a food writer for a newspaper in Bologna who didn't give a damn about racing drivers but was going to review the dinner for her paper. She gave her plate her total undivided attention and she did not like interruptions. On my right was a small dark man who eyed me suspiciously and spoke a dialect from southern Italy that I couldn't understand.

At the head table, raised on a platform, Guido had seated himself in the middle with his chair slightly raised to compensate for his height. At least, I thought, I didn't have to talk to him.

I made another stab at polite conversation with the bosomy lady. I envied her freedom to make her pasta disappear with a few deft flicks of the wrist. I could look, I could sniff and I could taste, but two, or oh what the hell, Evers let's go whole hog wild, and have three. Three tortellini were my limit. My penance for a wealthy life is monk-like abstinence. Liquor slows the brain and the reflexes. Food adds weight to the two to four stone handicap I give away to the other drivers. For the hundred millionth time I thought I am too tall and too broad across the shoulders to be a racing driver. I should be a food writer and just once let fly with the tortellini, fettuccini, the gnocchi and fusili. More oil, waiter. More pepper, more formaggio, ancora tutto por favore. The lady was mopping up tiny ponds of sauce with a torn bread roll. "Did Guido's family always live here?" I asked her, the question bringing her mild moon face up from her plate.

"Oh heavens no." She said, wiping her chins with her linen napkin. "They moved in five years ago. It was a present for his bride, I think. There was quite a to-do about it at the time. Let me see . . . as I recall, Count Bigoni was here with his second wife, I forget her name. Cesare and Annalisa Dandini, Corrado and Veronica Gambarelli, you know him, he's the sculptor they're always featuring in *Vogue*. Dreadful beast of a man. And two Agnellis, I think. It was quite a do. They served wild boar.'' She bent back to her task, polishing her dish.

I didn't know Guido was married. Or had been married. I had to admit, I had never been curious about the man; he didn't inspire curiosity in me. But it struck me I knew next to nothing about him.

In the early days of Formula One, before the big-time sponsors and the personal jets took away our free time, the drivers were often friends, even best friends. They drank together, travelled together, went to each others' weddings, and looked after the widow and girlfriends when one of them died in a crash. Now there are almost no friendships among drivers at the top. We joke with each other on the rare occasions when someone lines us up for a group picture, but we talk to our crews during practice, and after a race we run like thieves from a bank after the alarm goes gong. We take the money and fly.

I had never met Guido before he arrived at our first practice session in Portugal in February that year. The car had a new body shape, the aerodynamicists had altered the wings, and Max had rung some changes on the suspension. Now the carbon-fibre pushrods were pumping a monoshock in the front where last year there had been two shock absorbers. And this year the uprights were spiderweb-thin titanium. So there was plenty of work to do, laps to run to see how the cars went with this change or that one or both changes or some other minor variation. It was also a chance to blow away the cobwebs of winter in the Estoril sunshine. I was looking forward to it like a junkie looking forward to his next score.

Don't let anybody fool you. Single-seater racing cars are seriously addictive. And a Formula One car is a concentrated capsule of the latest and the best high-tech hallucinogenic ingredients. A capsule that you crawl inside of and lie down in, inches off the ground with over seven hundred horses behind your neck, urging you on to the outer limits of physics and fortune . . . the high of all single-seater highs. A speed trip and a body buzz that lasts for hours.

Yes indeed, it is addictive.

Guido arrived at the track in Estoril with two delicious girls on his arm whom he didn't introduce. I told him I was glad to have another driver on the team. And that if there was anything I could do . . .

And he interrupted saying, "Yeah, cut the bullshit. You got any questions, I'll answer them." He had won the Formula Three Thousand Championship the year before, so it wasn't surprising that he was cocky. And I didn't really mind his rudeness. It doesn't mean much. I have seen the most arrogant men turn into pussycats out on the track and little mild unassuming pussycats turn into tigers with four wheels. Until they went out onto the track you never knew.

Out on the track Guido was ferocious. He would go deeper into a corner, charge harder over the kerbs and get on the loud pedal sooner than a driver with his limited experience in Formula One had any right to. So he was fast, very fast. But he wasn't consistent. That first day he spun the car four times.

"How the hell else am I going to find out where the limits are?" he said when Ken chided him. Which is more or less what the great Gilles Villeneuve said when he spun his Ferrari eight times in one early practice session at Silverstone back in 1977. The difference was that Silverstone gives you plenty of open space to spin, and Estoril does not. And I like to think that Gilles was laughing when he said it. Guido rarely laughed, especially when he had banged the car into the concrete for the third time.

Still, Guido could get down to a very fast time very quickly, sensing intuitively where to lift off, where to start getting on the brakes, turn in, clip the inside of a corner and get back on the throttle so the car was on its absolute limit of braking, cornering and power all the time. This sounds simple and it is. Much easier, really, than playing a concert piano. The difference is that the five hundred and forty kilos of racing car is covering nearly twenty-five yards a second, so placing a car precisely here, on this scuff mark, while making all of the transitions fluid and graceful, your head blasted by a 175 mile an hour breeze, the car skittering an inch over the surface of the earth in a maelstrom of grit, oil fog and shifty aerodynamics, the engine screaming 13,000 rpm gear-whine in tune with high octane explosions, the brake rotors glowing cherry red, your head and body dragged sideways by several tons of force, these little hair-trigger sensitivities are not easy to get exactly right down to the thousandths of a second it takes to separate the men from the boys.

But Guido could get down to a fast lap in a very short period of time, which is the mark of a great driver. It was almost as if he lost interest after that, and his times would come back up again, which is the mark of a bad driver. He always had excuses; this wasn't working right, or that was just a tiny bit out of adjustment. But the fact remained that he wasn't consistent. It was a quality he could learn, if he worked at it. And he would have to work at it to learn it. Great concentration over a period of time does not come automatically. Ask your local neighbourhood Zen master. But unless he learned to be consistent, he would be a talented driver but not a great one.

Worse, I thought he was dangerous. In the first race of the year at the American Grand Prix in Phoenix he had taken the pole position with the fastest lap in practice. Which was sensational. To take the pole from Senna, Prost and Mansell, from Ferrari and McLaren in your first Grand Prix was absolutely brilliant. Nobody expected it. Guido flung his car through those flat, bumpy streets like it was a go-kart, brushing the walls, sliding with the tail hung out. It is not the way to drive a Formula One car, several pundits said. But it was a fantastic sight, and again the comparison with Gilles Villeneuve came up. Here was a major new talent on the highwire of the Formula One Circus. I was eighth on the grid, which only served to show what an achievement it had been for a rookie to put virtually the same car on the pole in his first race.

But I have never cared about pole position. Except in the rain, where starting first means that once the race starts you are the only driver who can see because you are the only driver that doesn't have to drive through the spray from the other cars. But otherwise, doing a one-off, kamikaze lap doesn't interest me as much as getting the car set up right for the race.

Anyway, that was my excuse.

The way it went, Guido flubbed his start, spinning his wheels while Senna, Mansell and Prost went past him into the first corner. He was fifth when I came alongside him five laps later. I'd been following him for half a lap and I'd guessed that he'd overheated his tyres by braking and cornering too hard. Whatever the reason, he was ragged in the corners, seeming to get off-line on the turn in, running wide on the exit. I got alongside him on the Washington back straight, thinking I could outbrake him going into the right-hander into Adams.

Like most "moments" of most races it is an in-head video I can play any time. My head is bouncing like a rock singer but I am not conscious of it. My body vibrates with the buzz of 38,850 explosions a minute. There is a 160 mile an hour wind in my face which I expect and ignore. My feet move among the pedals of the machine and my hand turns the wheel with no more thought than an acrobat gives to his hands and feet in mid flight. My mind is two hundred yards ahead where I will be in a moment. When Guido claims my whole and undivided attention.

I gave him plenty of room, and he didn't look at me, he just jinked his car right at me. It's the sort of thing the kids do in Formula Three to intimidate each other. "Try to pass me, sucker, and I'll knock you into the next county."

I don't intimidate. But I didn't want to die either. Coming through the corner going into the straight, I had lain back a little to give myself some room to slingshot past him. With more grip and a cleaner exit, I had got on the power earlier, come right up behind Guido, using the vacuum behind his car to give me a tow (and a face full of grit), and flicked the wheel right and moved right, passing him. I was off the racing line, onto the grey area they call the marbles from the little balled up bits of rubber scuffed off the racing tyres scattered across the surface. On the straight, being off the beaten path doesn't matter much, but the car is skittish, and the unloving, unforgiving concrete wall on my right was just four feet away to remind me of the consequences of getting the car out of shape.

Given the choice between touching a concrete wall and another open-wheeled racing car at 160 miles an hour, I'll choose the concrete. Our big fat, sticky racing tyres, his and mine, nearly touch, rotating in opposite directions. The back of his front tyre is inches from the front of my back tyre, and if they touch, the effective speed is doubled as the tyres act like gears and the power of 160 mph is doubled to the force of 320. Which is more than enough to launch you high in the air and land who knows where. Or which side up.

Or which car. That was the insanity of Guido's move. You never know when you touch wheels who is going to go flying out of control. It isn't necessarily the other driver who goes off. It could be both of you. Or just you.

I gave a quick flick of the wrist right, and the car jerked towards the wall past the little cushion you get from the air squeezed between you and the wall, the car nervous and unpredictable on the dust and little rubber scrapings. The wall grew in size and I noticed the wall is not a solid wall of cast concrete. It's made up of concrete blocks set side by side, the air making a rapping sound as I passed the cracks between blocks. I kept my foot down hard on the power. A touch of my right rear wheel against the wall straightened me out and I came back at Guido. Hard.

My rear wheel was just clear of his front, and I pulled over sharply onto the racing line forcing him to brake hard to keep my back wheel from smashing his front wing. Goddamn him.

Apparently it made an impression on him because when I checked my mirrors I saw he almost lost it in the corner. He got his car all crossed up, holding it off the wall, but flat spotting his tyres.

Guido had to pit for new tyres, and later went out of the race with transmission trouble. He said. I finished fourth, not good enough to spray champagne from the podium, but good enough for three championship points. I didn't see Guido, he'd left early for the airport. And I hadn't seen much of Guido for the rest of the season. He was there, at the practice sessions and the races. But he was involved with his crew. And when the session or the race was over, he was gone.

There was a tapping on a wine glass from the head table. "My dear friends," said a stranger, speaking into a microphone. I slipped out.

That was another disadvantage of being at the back table. Nobody noticed me walking out on the "What-A Wonderful-Man-Guido-Is" speeches.

It was a fine Italian summer evening, soft and gold, as they say in Pianoro. I was standing in the front doorway of the old entrance hall, looking out over the countryside that must have once belonged to the house I was standing in. Bats made whirring sounds in the dying light, and in the distance, you could just make out the dark side of the valley. Further still the peaks of the mountains were tipped with gold of the sunset. Out across the valley there was a great sense of stillness and space, as if the world were at rest. Except, out there, somewhere, there was the buzz of a motor scooter and the random bells of a flock of sheep. Behind me there was an occasional round of applause. Then a feminine voice made me turn around. "Mi scusi please, Signor Mr. Evers," she said in English. "Can you please, give to me a lift?"

Chapter 5

I turned around and I was looking at the top of a head of very fine and silky black hair, pulled tight into a knot. She was looking down at her feet. Then she looked up and I was astonished. She had a small face. Or maybe her eyes just made her face seem small. Under her dark eyebrows there were the deepest, clearest blue eyes I had ever seen. They held me for a heartbeat and then she looked away. She was wearing a simple black dress and she was so shy I thought she was one of the maids. But her hands looked too delicate for hauling buckets and mops. And as we talked there was a finesse that suggested something else; the fine straight line of her nose, the slenderness of her ankles and wrists, the offhand grace of her gestures.

Most of the aristocrats I know range down towards the toad end of the beauty scale. And a title probably means that some ancestor had his hand in the treasury coffers but he didn't get caught. I don't have much time for "lineage," "heritage" and all the other empty luggage of privilege. If anyone cared, and they don't, I could trace my own ancestry back to Everard, Bishop of Norwich, AD 1155-74. But go back further, all the way to the beginning, and my ancestors and yours, old friend, were Mesopotamians. Deep down, we are all Mesopotamians.

Still, looking at her pale face framed by that fine glossy hair, I thought she was an aristocrat. She looked eighteen or nineteen and I thought she must have been the one who had grown up in a castle.

"Scusa me," she said into the long pause while I looked at her, "maybe I don't have the words right. Maybe first I should have the politeness, is that the word, 'politeness,' the, er, politeness to introduce myself." One of those astonishing blue eyes was just slightly off-centre, and it made her look vulnerable. As if she needed an Uncle Forrest to put his arm around her shoulder to protect her. Good old dirty Uncle Forrest.

"Your English is fine, but it's not really necessary," I said in Italian. "I speak a little Italian. Or at least I understand it well enough."

"Thank God," she said, crossing herself, and speaking Italian in her clear voice. "That makes everything so much easier. I am Rossella DiSanto. Guido's wife. Please, don't stand in the doorway, come here, over to the side," she said pulling my arm. "I'm afraid this is going to sound bizarre. Well OK, it is bizarre, doesn't matter. But I have to ask you, I mean I really don't have any choice. I want you to drive me to Rome. I mean subito, right now, please."

"Rome," I repeated, as if I was thinking about it. I didn't want to drive to Rome, but I did want to keep talking to this lovely woman. "Any special reason?" I thought if she wasn't joking, she might have a grudge against Guido. Or maybe she was just a bored and silly little rich girl.

"OK. I mean it's not going to help you, but if you want a story . . . " She held up her hand as if I were to wait for her story.

I nodded and started to walk out of the house, assuming she would follow me. Her hand reached out and held my sleeve. "No, no, please. I am not allowed out of the house tonight. If I go out someone will see me and there will be a big mess."

"Mrs. DiSanto, if you want me to drive you to Rome, you are going to have to leave the house."

"Sure. Yes, but that is escaping from here. That is not a walk in the garden. I don't want to come back. I can't come back. Please, can we go now? I have a map."

She was nervous and kept looking over her shoulder as if she was afraid that someone might see her. "If you want I'll get down on my knees and I'll beg you. But we have to leave now. We have to."

I believed her. And I didn't believe her. I didn't mind giving her a ride to Rome, it was only two or three hours away on the Autostrada. And the last thing I was worried about was insulting Guido. But stealing a man's wife is something else. Punishable by flogging or public castration in Italian law for all I knew. For all I knew she had just strangled the cat. Or she was miffed because Guido hadn't asked her to the party.

She saw me hesitating and she was nervous, looking over her shoulder, her face tense. She said, "I can't help it if it sounds crazy. It is crazy. There is too much to explain, and I can't explain. If you want I'll explain later, but it's nothing to do with you and the longer we wait the worse it will be for me. Look, he is saying he will kill me. He will do it. If not tonight, tomorrow, next week." She looked over her shoulder towards another distant round of applause.

"Please, Mr. Evers. You have to understand I cannot ask an Italian because I don't know if I can trust him. Guido controls everything around here. Everything and everybody. I can't drive, I don't know how." She started sinking to her knees. "But if you want, OK, I'll go down on my knees. Please, my parents live in Rome and if you could just take me there I know I will be safe."

She had started to cry, silently, and she was on her knees in front of me. It was an awkward gesture. Humiliating for her. Embarrassing for me. I pictured a group of Italian businessmen slipping out of the dining room for a breath of fresh air and finding Guido's wife kneeling on the floor in a dark corner in front of me and I thought I saw the risk she was taking. Or maybe it was some game she was playing. I couldn't tell. I couldn't tell if it was comedy or tragedy or just some silly girl playing games, but she was looking up at me and she really was pleading with those astonishing eyes staring out of her little face and I would have taken her to Afghanistan if that's where she wanted to go.

Forrest Evers, knight of the steering wheel, protector of women, spiriter of wives away in the dark, keys to the prancing black horse in his pocket. A romantic who is slow to learn that romance has done more damage to the world than Hitler. I reached out to help Rossella up but she pulled back and stood up out of reach. "Look, if you can't do it, don't worry about it. I understand, OK?" She gave a little half-laugh through her crying, "I mean maybe you don't have a car or something."

I smiled back at her, trying to be reassuring. Trying to ignore the feeling that I was about to drive off a cliff. "I have a car, and if you really want me to, I'll drive you to Rome. But give me a couple of minutes. I have to tell Ken I won't be flying back to London with him. Otherwise he'll be up all night beating the bushes." Which was true. But there was something else.

"Please hurry," she said. "Don't be long. We need as much head start as we can get. Which is your car?"

I pulled out the keys and looked at the registration number taped on the back of the fob. "It's the red Ferrari," I said. "British registration." I held it up close to read the tiny letters, "FOR2." Goddamn Jack. He'd given it a cutesy registration number to make it look like it really was my car. It wasn't enough that it was a rare and red Ferrari. It had to have my name on it too. Every soul from Pianoro to Brindisi who saw FOR 2 would remember it.

Back in the dining hall, Guido was finishing his speech. He was on the balls of his feet, leaning forward, holding a microphone like a pop singer, his whispering amplified to a breathy rasp. "And most of all . . . " he paused for effect, looking from face to face around the room, "I want to thank you for the support that you gave me and my family gives me, that is terrific and a major factor. Major. It's not just me out on the track out there, it is everyone who makes a contribution. I don't want to make any predictions because you never know what is going to happen, you know, God rolls the dice." More pause. "But if it's not tempting fate too much, I think we got a good shot at the World Championship, if not this year, maybe next. And if not with Team Arundel, maybe somebody else closer to home."

This last was a dig at Ken to remind him that if he wanted to renew Guido's contract next year, Guido was going to want a lot more money. Because now that Guido had won a Grand Prix, Guido was a popular man in Formula One. Already there were rumours that Guido was going to have lunch at Maranello (Ferrari's factory and test track, less than fifty miles away), maybe discuss a little contract. Formula One drivers are becoming like nations. They don't have friends, they have interests.

As the applause died down I walked up to the front table; and bent down between Ken and Guido to tell Ken I wouldn't be flying back to London with him.

"Well, you're a big boy now," Ken said laying his serving platter sized hand on mine. "I suppose I can put off your interview for the *Autosport* profile. They can do one on me," he said, "tell them all about my sexy lifestyle." He wheezed his awful wheezing laugh at his private joke. Years ago he had gone through a parade of women and wives. But since he had married Ruth he'd been the straightest of English arrows. Several people looked up at him, thinking he was ill.

I turned to Guido who was beaming into the applause and I said, "Your wife is very beautiful."

He didn't look at me, but kept smiling at the dying scatter of applause. "You think she's beautiful," he said through the public smile. "She looks like a cake of soap with hair. Where'd you see her?" still nodding and smiling.

"I saw her picture," I said.

"There are no pictures of her," he said, suddenly turning to me, his face set.

"Thanks for dinner, Guido," I said, walking away.

I wanted him to know.

Chapter 6

Fifteen acres of sailcloth ripping. Sixteen berserk elephants on motorcycles. RATCHETTARATCH RATCH SCREE-EECH VROOOM-VROOOM ROOARROAR AWHOMPAWHOMPA WHOMP WHOMP. Silence.

RATCHRATCHETA SCREEEECH.

A 4.4 litre, horizontally opposed twelve cylinder Ferrari starting up is not a subtle noise. It vibrates the bones and makes the teeth buzz. Rossella had sunk low down in her seat to hide. I couldn't see them, I was busy backing up somebody else's hundred and fifty thousand pound Ferrari in the dark, but I felt the faces at the castle windows, looking out at us as I reversed the car out into the gravel drive, graunched first gear and then second, the Ferrari barking, coughing and spitting its way down the long sweeping drive to the road. WHOMPITTA COUGH SPIT WHOMPITTA. The clutch needed adjusting and the car was going to take a while to warm up. It was not a discreet departure. "Left," she said.

"Right," I said. "We go right. Right back down to Bologna, get on the Autostrada, and zoom, a couple of hours later we'll turn off where the big green sign says 'Roma'."

"No, no, no. You don't understand, Forrest. No Autostrada. He will know where we go if we go on the Autostrada. Left. Up into the mountains. Left. It's OK. I have a map.'' She was working her way upright again peering left and right out of the windows. ''We go to Loiano up to the Passo di Raticosa, nine hundred and sixty-eight metres high and through the Passo di Futa, past Barbiero di Mugello and San Piero a Sieve and down into Florence. Left, left, go left.''

We had come to the gates and she was pointing impatiently. Masterful Forrest Evers taking charge of the runaway lady. I turned left.

''OK, but when we get to Florence, then we'll get on the Autostrada.''

''No. If we get on the Autostrada they will tell him. You don't know, you don't know anything, but they will tell him. After Florence we go down to the old Via Cassia, past Casciano, Castellina, past Siena, Buonconvento, Acquapendente, Lago Bolseno, Montefiascone, Viterbo, Vetrella, Sutri, all the way into Roma.''

''You make this trip often?''

''I know I am a joke to you, right? OK, I am a joke. You too. But it is not funny. When he locked me in the wing, for months there were no books, no television, no nothing. I didn't have anything to read except this map.'' She held up the faded crumpled document pointing straight ahead. ''So yes, I made this trip a million times. I memorize the names, the names of the villages and the mountains, the names of the lakes and the streams. For a long time now, I dreamed of making this trip.''

We were passing through the darkened village of Pianoro, a few shops on both sides of the road, a restaurant and a petrol station. The car was starting to warm up, running smoother. ''He locked you up?''

''For six months. Six months I couldn't go out,'' turning her head to see the village pass by. ''There are ten rooms in the wing and the food is OK, and there was a radio, but except for that and a couple of books somebody brought me later, the only entertainment was looking out the window. The only reason he let me out was a couple of months before I was going to have the baby I screamed so he couldn't sleep and he lets me out. But only with a bodyguard. Only at night." She was smiling happily, peering out at the darkness.

It was just a story. Modern wealthy Italian ladies are not locked up in castles. They have their own telephones and they carry them in their purses along with the gold and platinum credit cards. They fly to London, Paris and Manhattan to shop. They have friends they went to school with who they can telephone any time. Friends who run the country and who could blow little Guido away like a bit of stray fluff from their perfectly cut Giorgio Armani linen trousers.

She was beautiful though. The road straightened and I looked at her, her face lit from below by the lights of the speedometer and the gauges. She was relaxed and, looking back at me, looking as if there was a secret joke. No make-up, heavy dark eyebrows, a child's intensity, earnest, anxious to make me understand. There was a soft little point on the tip of her upper lip that gave her a tentative look, as if she were worried she might have said the wrong thing. But when she smiled, she grinned, wide and sunny, and it was hard to believe she had ever been worried about anything. "My parents," she said, closing her eyes for a moment, savouring the thought, "will be so glad to see me. We better hurry. I think we won't have more than an hour's start before Guido finds out I'm gone."

"He probably already knows. I told him I'd seen you."

Her eyes snapped open and she looked around inside the car as if she had to escape. Then she sank back down in her seat and let out a little puff of resignation. "He's already coming after us. You don't believe me do you? Forrest, for God's sake, we must go faster. We must go much faster or he will catch us. You think I'm kidding or something, but he will kill me. Maybe you too. Maybe then you'd believe me."

"Nobody wants to kill you."

"You don't know him at all do you? No, Forrest, he hasn't just told me, I am telling you he promises me." Rossella was looking forward, up where the road wound up into the hills, hugging her knees to her chest. "It's so strange. He used to love me once, you know, he really did. And I don't think I have ever done anything bad to him. But he swears on his mother he will kill me. Only now he can't because first he wants to find out where I have hidden our son. What he wants, what he really wants, Mr. Evers, even more than to kill me," she said slowly and deliberately, "is to kill my baby. That's what he really wants."

"Your baby?"

"Yes. Mine. Aldo. My new baby, just one week. His son. But my son is safe. The one thing I know I have done right is that my baby is safe. Guido will never find him. So now maybe it doesn't matter so much if he finds me. Aldo will be safe."

"You've hidden him?"

"Yes, of course I've hidden him. It is not a game. Just get me to my parents, my son will be safe and I will be safe and you can go, I don't know, wherever you want to go. I am sorry I have involved you, but really there was no choice for me, Forrest. For God's sake is this as fast as this thing will go?"

I slipped down into second, another graunch from the gears, second was going to be a problem, and coming out of the turn accelerated. "Ahhhhhh," Rossella was shouting, "wonderful!" I wondered if she was a manic depressive, suffering from delusions. Or just a hopeless romantic. When I looked at her, her face all blue eyes and wide smile,

I didn't care. She had that magical grace and presence that some women have that makes you feel privileged just to be in the same room with them. And besides, she wasn't my problem, was she? I was just doing what she had asked me to. I was just giving her a ride.

The Ferrari had 360 horsepower, about half the power of my Formula One car, and twice the weight. It took about five times the distance to stop and it had only a quarter of the cornering power. Compared to a Formula One car it was heavy, clumsy and slow. It also had a nasty habit of wanting to plough straight ahead and then the back end would suddenly and viciously kick out starting to spin and if you weren't quick you were a passenger as the Boxer went off on its own spinning trajectory. On the other hand, compared to the new generation of hot hatchbacks the Boxer was a ballistic missile. I drove it more like a rally car than a race car, sliding into corners, getting the car right up on the edge where it wanted to spin and keeping it there. In the wet, with its tall-section mid-seventies style tyres, the car was tail-happy, easy to hang out the rear end on a long slide with the accelerator. If we were racing, I would have wanted a big rear wing to nail down the rear end. On the other hand, the suspension soaked up most of the bumps like they weren't there and the power was always there. At any speed in any gear, just touch the throttle and whOOOOOm, away we went. In the rear-view mirror, in the far distance, there were no other headlights.

So I got down to the business of a long drive on a narrow twisting mountain road. At first, Rossella was delighted. The rush of corners out of the darkness, the sudden breaking loose of the back end as the car reached the limit and then went beyond. She was flung from side to side, pitched forward and back and she loved it.

Dynamically, the car was a pig. Its long flat-twelve engine sits over the transmission making its centre of gravity too high. And there were several times when I almost lost it, when the car lurched from understeer to oversteer and threatened to chuck us over the edge. But Rossella never knew that. And even if she had, she probably wouldn't have minded a bit. She loved the danger and the unknown. It was a dream she had before, but never with this intensity, this rush of landscape in a tunnel of light. We couldn't talk, there was too much noise. And even though I was leaving a margin for the unexpected, I was concentrating.

Once, coming over the crest of a rise, four wheels off the ground, we were headed straight for the weak, flickering headlamp of a scooter, and a farmer gripping the handlebars, amazed, transfixed by the fireball of noise and light aiming at his forehead. It was a little green three-wheeler with a flat-bed at the back and a tiny moped engine that makes a furious sound and very little forward motion, the Italian farmer's equivalent of a donkey and a cart. At our speed, as we approached him, sailing through the night air, he seemed as still as a statue.

Who knows what he was doing there in the middle of his road at one o'clock in the morning. Maybe he had been rumpling the sheets in his neighbour's bed with his neighbour's wife or drinking grappa at a cafe, or working his olive grove until the moon went down. Or all three. Whatever he had been doing, it was his road and we flew towards him with the force of a landing transcontinental jet, and the look on his face was frozen in mild surprise. Feathering the accelerator, keeping the car balanced, we landed twenty yards in front of him and I rolled on the power and eased the car left, the rear wheels spinning and cocking the car left, the left front wheel going over the little drainage ditch and just brushing the hillside, the side of the car grazing mud and grass, bouncing us back into the middle of the road and we were gone, over the next rise, leaving him a few inches forward of where he had been when we first saw him.

Then we came down from the mountains, past signs to Fiesole and into Florence. There were lights in some of the windows, and the storefronts, and the cafes were still open. Normal life still went on. Looking for the circular route around the city, we went through a red light and the wrong way through a small traffic circle, but the streets were nearly deserted and we boomed on, across the bridge towards Siena. Rossella's giddy excitement had worn off, but she still urged us on. Please, she said, whenever I slowed down to read a sign, don't slow down. We can't slow down.

The road to Siena winds in and out under the motorway. Overhead, Fiat Unos were making better time, placidly buzzing down the wide smooth highway, foot to the floor, flat out at 150 kph. Down below, like a berserk bee we screamed up and down the sonic scale, charging into corners hard on the brakes, charging out again hard on the loud pedal. Back and forth, back and forth. It was also hot as blazes, the heat rising up from the tunnel between us from the hot water pipes to the radiator in the front. Tired, hot and sweaty, we stopped for petrol just before Siena, Rossella sliding down into the foot well, afraid someone might see her. The Ferrari was getting around eleven miles to the gallon. It took on just over a hundred litres of fuel. Enough for a little hatchback to drive to Amsterdam. Enough for us to reach Rome.

After Siena, the Via Cassia flows through an open plain and the road opens out with long straights and fast, sweeping bends the Ferrari was designed for. From time to time we would pass a lonely car at triple their speed. On one long straight stretch, we passed a faded hand-painted sign, "Chiuso" in front of a restaurant that looked abandoned and I thought the sign meant the restaurant was closed. A few milliseconds later, signs with arrows on them rose out of the middle of the road indicating we should turn right-angle left, off the main road onto a little side road. Possibly in a Formula One car. Not in the 365 BB Ferrari. I got hard on the brakes, easing them on so as not to upset the car, but hard and we slowed from 170 miles an hour down to 130 to pass between two of the arrow signs. The surface of the road changed from smooth dry concrete road to the dirty rubble-strewn surface of an abandoned road. Fifty yards ahead, a blockade seemed to indicate that the road had washed away. On that surface, at that speed we were due to hit the barrier head-on at around 70 miles an hour. On the brakes, pumping them twenty times a second right up to the limit of adhesion until one wheel would break away, I put the car into a series of slides back and forth across the road, lengthening our path, scrubbing off speed, back and forth once, twice and the third time flipping the wheel so we slid backwards into the fence at around 20 miles an hour. An old Fangio trick. Although if the maestro had been driving we probably wouldn't have knocked the fence ten yards back and smashed both taillights. I got out to inspect the damage. Nothing that a few thousand pounds of careful hammering, a set of fresh, probably unobtainable Ferrari tail-lights and scarlet paint wouldn't fix. The registration plate was cracked and had a black smear across the middle. FOR 2 looked like it had been cancelled. In the still night, the moon slid behind a cloud and the river valley held that silence you hear after a crash. Rossella said, "Come, please, come back into the car, Forrest. We must hurry."

I was getting tired and we had been going too fast. What were we running away from anyway? The boredom of everyday life? A husband waving a meat cleaver? (I tried to work up a little fear of Guido, but I just couldn't do it.) Rossella was dozing as we took the detour, another irritating twisty little road that climbed all the way up to a hill village and back down again. Another half-hour of intense concentration, up and down and left and right while in the distance we could see the lights of the cars on the Autostrada on their glide path to Rome.

And on we went, Rossella alternately dozing and staring straight ahead, as if she were looking for signs of her parents' house in the distance. After Montefiascone she fell asleep again, and I felt I had had enough of twisty roads for one all-night drive. There was a sign for the Autostrada just before Viterbo and I took the turn. We were slowing down under the bright green fluorescent lights of the toll plaza when Rossella woke up with a start.

"What are you doing?"

"We're getting a ticket for the Autostrada."

She looked frightened and started to open the door. "You don't understand. We cannot go that way. Please. You will make me get out of the car." She was suddenly weeping again.

I could have argued with her. I should have simply told her to shut up, Uncle Forrest was in charge. But like all the men before me, I gave in to the girl's tears, turned around, headed back underneath the Autostrada and south. We were going slower now. I was tired. It was past three in the morning, the brakes were going soft and there was an expensive clicking sound from the engine. After the next village, Rossella said, "We have to stop."

"Next petrol station," I said.

"No, for the night. To rest. I can't go any further."

I told her she was crazy, we were only twenty miles from Rome. But no, I didn't understand. She really was too tired. She hadn't realized it would take this long. Maybe it wasn't such a good idea to wake up her parents at four in the morning. They wouldn't like it, they were too old. I could see she really was exhausted. She had given birth a week ago, and we'd had a bruising journey. The thought of lying down on cool fresh sheets had crept into my mind and I couldn't wait to stretch out and put my head down on a

pillow. When we came to a little village called Castelnuovo, a sign said there was a four-star hotel in the Castella
and I pulled off the main road, down into the town until
we came to the twelfth-century arch, drove across the cob-
blestones of a medieval courtyard to the old stone building
rising above us in the night. There was a light hanging
above the front door welcoming us.

Chapter 7

The hot steel bench was all mine. I also had a whole steel cage to myself. The cage and the bench had been bolted and welded together inside a grey oven with wheels disguised as a van. I might as well enjoy it, I thought. There wasn't much question of escape. Even if I could have got out of the cage, where does a man sporting shiny gold bikini knickers and his hands handcuffed behind his back run to in a foreign country?

The van had a leaking exhaust, its brakes pulled to the left and the shocks clanged to the beat of the bumps in the road, useless. The interior had been hosed out but there were still a few hardened lumps of vomit on the floor and the aroma lingered to mix with the exhaust fumes. Just above my head a honking two note siren blared on and on. Blee-blah, Blee-blah, Blee-blah.

I also had company. Sitting outside my cage with their backs against the back door, pointing Uzi machine-guns at me, two young, short, dark and overweight Carabinieri made faces like guard dogs for a while, as if they wanted to break my ankles. I named them Prunella and Priscilla.

After half an hour of the van's lurching from stop to go and back to stop again, they gave up playing vicious and ignored me. "Amelia don't wear no bra because with her tits she don't need no bra," said Pru.

"Ferrari was gonna kick ass next week at Monza," said Pris.

"And fuckin' Manzella was going to get his fuckin' ass kicked if he didn't get off my back and stop giving me bullshit duty like this one," said Pru. I tuned out. I had enough entertainment of my own.

I was sweating, nauseous and the pain in my side suggested some internal damage. My body was starred with other islands of pain that were beginning to shine as the fog retreated. A round bruise in my back hurt when I breathed in, a sharp headache radiated from behind my ear. A terrible ache from my palms flashed razor-sharp whenever my hands were forced against the cage by the bumps. I could breathe reasonably well, but it hurt. I wondered if it had been Rossella in the ambulance.

I remembered her walking in front of me into the Castelnuovo hotel towards the light at the check-in desk, the sound of her footsteps echoing in the darkness, her silhouette small and frail. I wanted to hold her and comfort her, but once we were out of the car, we were strangers again. The ride was over and she had a dignity I couldn't disturb.

We rang the bell several times until a heavy teenager with round spectacles, his hair tangled with sleep, emerged from the darkness, walked past us without looking and took up his position behind the desk. His eyes still hadn't quite focused when he asked us if we had a reservation. No, no reservation. Twin beds or double? Separate rooms. Separate rooms? He woke up and looked at us with a squint as if we had asked for something he had never heard of before. No doubt couples with no luggage did wake him up in the middle of the night from time to time. But not for separate rooms. He consulted his ledger. Yes, he had separate rooms. 104 and 315. Unfortunately he had nothing closer together. That was fine. Rossella, looking exhausted took 104 because it was nearer. I took 315 two floors away.

We rode up the lift together and I walked Rossella to her room. The hall was wide and buzzed with a timed light switch. The floor was polished stone with a wide thick Oriental carpet down the middle. When we got to her door, there was no little kiss on the cheek, no handshake. She kept her distance as if she were afraid she would break. She looked at me with those brilliant blue eyes, the left one just a little off to the side as if something else was about to catch her attention. She said, "I know it seems like a game to you. I am very grateful you have played it for me. Please, forgive me, I am so tired. Maybe in the morning we could have breakfast together and then a nice slow drive into the city. You could meet my parents if you like. If you don't want to, it's OK, I can call a taxi. It doesn't matter. I am safe now. I owe you everything, Forrest."

She gave me a brief radiant smile that brought back the playful schoolgirl she must have been, years ago. Then she turned, unlocked her door, nodded to me, went inside, shut the door and turned the key.

When I got to my room I took off my shirt and my trousers, my shoes and my socks, pulled back the yellow blanket, switched off the light, and fell asleep. And that was all.

That was all; but sitting in the van, in my cage, I felt waves of guilt. I told myself that a beating makes you feel guilty. It comes from the awful guilt of childhood: Bad Boy. Spank spank. Don't *ever* do *that* again!

I told myself that parading near-naked in public makes you feel guilty. We are all such puny creatures. I am in good, no, not just good, excellent physical shape. My diet is strictly controlled by a Swiss nutritional fanatic who sends me jars of what look like barn sweepings. And, except for an occasional night out when I pretend to be a normal human being, that is what I eat. If there are two ounces of extra fat on me you would have a hard time finding them. I work out for at least an hour a day seven days a week. I have to. You cannot balance 700 horsepower on the limits of physics for two hours at a time unless you are in peak physical condition. And the press call me "rug-

gedly handsome'' as if that were my christian name as in
"Ruggedly Handsome Evers.'' I think I look like a walking
crag. But I am not ashamed of the way I look and my
usually private, private parts are just fine, thank you. But
who can stand up to close public scrutiny? I have been out
with models, women so beautiful every single head spun
when they walked by. And almost every model I've known
was certain she had terrible flaws, a hand shielding a nose
she thought was crooked or mouth too wide or trotting out
a nervous laugh to cover the fear that maybe she was wearing the wrong thing when she could have worn a horse
blanket and still be the most beautiful woman for miles. It
didn't matter. The world could tell them they were beautiful, but they knew they weren't. They knew it was all
lighting, make-up, art direction and retouching. Nobody
feels beautiful in the mirror or in the harsh gaze of the
public.

Possibly the extra fillip of wearing those ridiculous gold
bikini underpants in front of a hostile crowd, a crowd that
hated me, my hands handcuffed behind my back, maybe
that was enough to fill my empty soul with guilt. But what,
I asked myself, did I have to feel guilty about? What had
I done? I was glad I gave Rossella a ride. And even if they
had thought I had stolen a man's wife, or even kidnapped
her, that couldn't have made them that angry, made them
shout and throw stones. Not on the eve of the twenty-first
century. Running off with Rossella couldn't have given the
police the excuse to treat a British or American citizen—I
wondered which passport I'd left at the hotel desk. My
British one. My American passport was still in my room.
Oh fuck, I thought, maybe they don't even know who I am.
Maybe they think I'm a rapist . . . .

No, running off with her can't have been the excuse for
them to treat me like a what, yes a rapist, a child kidnapper.
Maybe both. I told myself, "I am a famous racing driver.''
I have money, connections and the minor celebrity that
comes from being watched by some four billion fans over

sixteen races on five continents. I have nothing to worry about. Time and money would fix this nasty mistake. I knew I hadn't done anything. Didn't I. Guido couldn't have possibly found us. If he had followed us I know I would have seen him. Wouldn't I?

My mind kept circling, missing the point. I was exhausted and I remember thinking it's time to wake up.

From the squall of sirens up ahead, it sounded like we had a motorcycle escort, but it wasn't enough to dislodge the traffic. Stop, go, stop. Blee-blah, Blee-blah, Blee-blah. On and on.

The temperature crept up with the day to Hi-Bake, and I imagine we crawled along the outskirts of Rome, although all I had to go on was the car horns and the rage of the traffic outside and the complaints of the Carabinieri stuck inside with me. They had taken off their hats and jackets and were sweating steadily.

"Christ, I can't wait to get out of this shitbox. I ever tell you about the little peachfuzz works the Corso?" said Priscilla.

"I don't know why the fuck we gotta bring this asshole all the way into the middle. Yeah, you told me about her around ten times," said Prunella. "You're fulla shit. No girl's gonna do that. Not for an asshole like you."

I must have passed out because I woke up with a bump and the whirr and clank of gates as we moved forward. Then we stopped and the back doors of the van were opened. Pru and Pris backed out cautiously, holding their guns pointed at me while another lion tamer unlocked my cage.

Stumbling out into the bright sun, feeling naked, hands behind my back, it took my eyes a few moments to adjust to the brilliance of the light. We had come through a high, dirty yellow wall with barbed wire at the top angled out overhead. So even if you had a ladder . . . In front of us another blank, dirty yellow wall with a rusting steel door. One of the Carabinieri was ringing a bell. We stood in the sun, waiting. After a while the door opened with a quiet little click; we stepped inside to face another steel door. The guards smelled like five-day-old cheeseburgers. We waited for the door to shut and after it did the door in front of us opened onto a long wide hall painted light green and lit overhead by tubes of humming fluorescent lights. There were no doors along the hall and we walked twenty yards down to the end. More electronic double doors. But this time there was another Carabiniere waiting on the other side, clipboard in hand, backed by two armed guards. The man with the clipboard had the soft face and mild curiosity of an accountant. Looking at me, totting up the damage, he said, ''Jesus, Maria, what the hell did you guys do to him?''

''We didn't do nothin'. It was the Poliziotti made the initial arrest. Maybe they pushed him around a little. We just bring him here,'' said Priscilla.

''Doesn't he have any clothes?''

''I guess the Poliziotti didn't give him no time to pack,'' Prunella said. ''Gimme the sheet so we can sign it and get the hell out of here.''

The little man with the clipboard said, ''Take off his handcuffs, then you sign the sheet.''

Pris said, ''We ain't got the key. The Poliziotti cuffed him. Give them a ring, maybe they got the key.''

Pru said, ''They convict this asshole they can throw away the key.''

''I want to make a phone call,'' I said.

''I have you down here as an Article 17,'' the clipboard man said. ''You are going to get special treatment. As soon as we charge you, you can make your phone call.''

''What's the charge?'' I said, trying to sound important and angry.

''You have to be formally charged. As soon as the judge gets here. Don't worry. You're a very important case. Article 17. We'll take care of you.''

They found bolt cutters. When they saw the skin had peeled back off my palms like the skin of a ripe peach exposing the weeping flesh underneath, they found a man with dirty fingernails in a stained white smock to wrap some dry gauze around my hands. Then they led me to a small room with two wooden chairs and no window and shut the steel door leaving me alone. One of the chairs had cotton trousers and a shirt and some socks. The room smelt of sick men, drunks, and urine.

My hands were settling into a dull throb, and I was elaborately careful of them as I pulled on the socks, shirt and trousers. Naturally they were average Italian size, one size fits all. The shirt wouldn't button, the trousers ended halfway down my calves, I couldn't button the top button, and there were no shoes. But it was better than being naked. Much better. When they take away everything, the smallest favour is a gift.

I sat on one chair for a while. Then I sat on the other. Occasionally I heard footsteps approaching down the hall, passing then going away again. That happened several times. Time may have passed.

I was inspecting my palms, peering under the gauze bandages to look at the peeled skin that had curled up and dried as hard as toenails, and wondering if the oozing was infection or just simply the body cleansing the wound and if my hands would heal enough for Monza next week when the man with the clipboard unlocked my door and announced that he was sorry, but the judge that was going to charge me was in Reggio Calabria and wouldn't be back until tomorrow morning. Then he would formally charge me. Then I could call a lawyer. But right now, I was to follow him. Two more armed guards backed up his request with sub-machine-guns. Which almost made me laugh. I was sore, injured and looked like a clown in my tiny shirt and too-tight jeans. I was worried about Rossella, about Ken, about whether I could drive for Monza and how much longer I was going to have to endure this. I was many things. But I wasn't dangerous. I couldn't have given a bug a hard time. But evidently, they thought I was liable to explode at any moment.

We went up and down stairs, unlocking and locking doors. Then we went down three flights of stairs into the sub-basement where a series of doors led into a row of cells. In the corners of the low ceilings, TV cameras swivelled their glass eyes back and forth. The floor and the ceiling and the walls were white. When a high security cell door shuts these days, it doesn't clang, it makes a little whirr as the electronic servos slide the bolts home, then a little click as the servos shut off. More sensory deprivation for the serious offenders. No heavy "clink" as the steel bolt slides home. The "clink" that tells you, you are entirely alone with nothing on your side and the immense power of the state lining up their stone walls to flatten you.

I am so cushioned by money, I knew there would be lawyers in the afternoon working their way through the maze of intricate puzzles of the Italian legal system to get me out. Or in the morning at the latest. I knew that I had committed no crime.

Sure. Absolutely. No problem, just some terrible misunderstanding. I played those little reassurances on repeat for myself. But they all shrank and disappeared with the sound of that little "click." That little "click" just blew them away.

Believe me, an electronic "click" in the door of your prison cell sounds just as final as the "clink" that gave jails the name.

Chapter 8

Italian jails, if this one was anything to go by, don't have toilets, they have targets. A scratched and stained ceramic pan sunk in the floor with raised pads for the feet and a hole in the middle. Aim carefully. Step lively. But apart from that and the stink of sewage, it looked like the prison cell you see in bad dreams. Four walls painted gangrene green and scrawled with cocks, cunts and knives. One sink clogged with hair. One metal bunkbed. One wooden table painted grey, decorated with cigarette burns, names and phone numbers. One wooden chair probably painted grey. A TV hung from the ceiling out of reach. There was even a slot high up the wall to let in a shaft of light through the bars. Not a lot to look at.

There were brown blankets on the lower bunk. No sheets, no pillow case on the hard little bag of stained lumps that was the pillow. Perhaps I should complain to the management. Just a moment, darling, I'll ring the manager, I'm sure he'll sort it out. And have him send round a bowl of roses and a glass of chilled fresh-squeezed orange juice and a bottle of champagne, if you would be so kind. I'm terribly thirsty. I eased myself on the bunk. Nothing to do but wait.

I laid my head back, closed my eyes and heard screaming. "What the fuck you think you're doing, waking me up, you stupid asshole cocksucker. I'm going to chop your balls off and shove 'em down your throat. Tear your fuckin' windpipe out with my bare hands, wrap it around your neck. I'm gonna. . . ''

It was coming from the bunk above me. I got up to have a look. His back was to me and he was shouting into the wall. His size and basketball sneakers made him look about twelve.

"Was it something I said?" I said to his back.

"Don't you fucking condescend to me you dumb prick. I got a lotta connections. I know a lotta guys, made guys, not just wise-guys. You fuck around with me, you are in deep shit.'' He kept his face to the wall, his back curved with his knees drawn up.

"Looks to me like we're both in deep shit," I said.

"Yeah, what they get you for?"

"I don't know.''

That made him turn around. He looked at me with intense black eyes, black hair falling over a sharp little face that might have been as old as sixteen. But a second look and I saw he was only a frightened, skinny little boy and his red-rimmed eyes and the paths down his cheeks said that he had been crying like a child. "Don't gimme that bullshit,'' he said. "You got caught, they framed you, somebody set you up. You gotta know. At least you gotta have a theory. They don't throw you in here for pickin' pockets. Come on, what'd you do, kill somebody? You some kind of psycho?" He peered at me, interested.

"I don't know. I really don't know.''

"Hey, come on. You want to play stupid, you gotta be smarter than that. It's tougher than you think, playing stupid. You don't want to tell them anything because then they think you know something, know what I mean? Same time you don't want to tell them nothin' because that just pisses them off. And that's the one thing you don't want to do. Just don't piss them off. Listen, you need anything, smokes, coke, good food, bottle of wine, you let me know. I gotta lotta connections.''

"I'd appreciate a telephone.''

"Sure, no problem. There's a guard, comes in tomorrow, has a portable. It's expensive."

"You get me the phone, I'll get you the money. What's your name, kid?"

"Don't call me no fuckin' kid. I'm Vito. Vito Guzzetti."

"Pleased to meet you, Vito. What are you in for?"

His face lit up with pride. "Murder. Class A, section 17. Some fuckin' wise guy, you know, had it coming."

"You killed a man?"

"No, no. You really are fuckin' stupid, you know? Maybe with you it's not just an act. No, no, I didn't kill nobody. What they do, they kill a guy, there's a lot of witnesses, so they need somebody to stand up. So I stand up. I'm fourteen, they can't come down on me like I was an adult. They give me two, three years, I can do that easy." He blinked twice as if he was beginning to have his doubts. Then he shook his head, trying to bring back his childish imitation of the tough guy. As if he wasn't trapped. As if there was somebody somewhere who cared about him. He tried, but he was only fourteen and his voice was shaky. "I get out, I got respect, you know, connections. They owe me." He started to cry again.

"When I telephone tomorrow, do you want me to ring somebody for you? You want me to ring your mother and father?"

"What mother and father?"

"You don't have parents?"

"Of course I got parents. I just never see them." His eyes started to water and I changed the subject.

"Who's They then?"

"Yeah, they," he said, snuffling, pretending he wasn't crying. "You really are dumb. What's your name?"

"Forrest Evers," I said and his eyes went wide.

"Fuckin' hell," he said, brightening. "You're the guy."

"What guy?"

"On television this morning. Christ don't you fuck around do you?"

"No Vito, I don't fuck around," I said, impatient. "Now tell me what you saw this morning. What did I do?"

"Hey, don't get mad at me. I didn't do nothing. It was on television, on the news this morning. That goofy TV news reporter they got with the big boobs and the curly hair, you know the one, Caterina Calabrese, that's her name. She was in Castelnuovo and they showed pictures of you with a gold jockstrap. She said you stabbed this guy, your team-mate's wife. I mean she said you stabbed your team-mate's wife around forty times."

Chapter 9

"I'm flying back to London this evening and I assume you are going with me, Forrest. Or are you feeling too ill to fly? I must say you don't look your best." Ken was watching, bending over to watch the nurse scrub, his eyebrows arched in mild interest.

The pain was too much and I shouted, making the girl wince. She was only seventeen or eighteen and it seemed to hurt her more than me. She was scrubbing the raw flesh on my palms with a scrubbing brush, the kind you use for cleaning your nails. Without the protection of skin, the bristles felt like steel wires slicing a cross hatch about three inches deep.

"I'm sorry, Dottor Evers," she said, her little round face looking sad. She was cradling my hand gently in one hand and scrubbing with the other. "It's the only way we can get this grit out. It hurts now, but your hands will heal much quicker this way." Behind her, seated at a wide oak desk, the real Dottor was busy writing out his bill.

"How fast will they heal?" I asked her, trying to keep my voice sounding normal. Because they are usually in peak physical condition, racing drivers tend to heal much faster than average. I had less than a week to Monza, which is not the most demanding track on the hands, but you couldn't drive it if your palms were hamburger.

"You'll be able to play with yourself in around two, three weeks," the learned Dottor said, a little grin beneath his moustache.

"Probably how he scuffed his hands in the first place . . ."

"Ken," I said, interrupting, "you were there in Pianora after I left. What do you think?"

Ken lowered his vast, lengthy body in the doctor's worn red leather chair, his face as wrinkled and haggard as an old hound dog from a lack of sleep. "Think? There hasn't been time to think. You left like an elephant leaving a tea party. If you wanted to set Guido off you certainly did that. Like a rocket. That poor girl."

"Did he come after us?"

"No. Or at least not while I was there. Although to tell the truth I didn't stay long. But no, I doubt he came after you. Guido more or less ordered us out and I took Francesco, you remember Francesco Pagano, Pagano Computers, I took him up on his offer of a ride down to Rome. Guido had said he was sure that was the way you were headed. I heard him shouting on the phone just before we left."

"You're sure she has no chance."

"The poor thing has no chance. None at all, I'm afraid," said the doctor in slow and careful English from behind his desk, looking up from his writing. "They can't even close the wounds."

Then he brightened as if he had just thought of something cheerful. "You know she lived very near here, when she was a little girl. Her parents have, sorry, had, a palazzo on Bocca di Leone near the Spanish Steps, poor souls. Terrible what they did to her."

Ken had barged into the Carabinieri confine late in the afternoon with five lawyers waving writs demanding my release. It had taken all day for them to find out where I was, and by the time they finally found me, the Carabinieri were already telling me they were sorry, it was all a mistake on the part of the Poliziotti. I was quite free to go with their apologies. Here, look in the newspaper they said.

The newspaper had a photograph of the three-cornered knife that had stabbed Rossella. It had been found in Rome beside the bodies of her mother and father. They had both suffered the same multiple stab wounds as their daughter but the attack on Rossella's mother had been especially vicious. Along with all her other stab wounds she had been slashed several times in the face. They had been in bed, sleeping, in their "Palazzo." Even the Carabinieri had to admit that it was unlikely that I was the murderer since I was in their van when Rossella's parents were attacked.

Even though the Carabinieri were in the process of letting me out—"Wait here just a minute, we find you some trousers"—I was immensely glad to see Ken. His bulk was reassuring. And he had brought a shirt, shoes and a pair of trousers that didn't stink of prison.

Ken was wholly at ease in Italy, the way some Englishmen are who have spent a majority of their summers there. He had a pidgin Italian limited to the present tense and pronounced as if it were English badly spelled. He felt he was fluent and in a way he was. More important, he had a wide network of friends, including the doctor he insisted I see, Dr. Ammiratti, the one with an office just off the Piazza Navona.

I mistrusted Dottor Ammiratti. His office was an Italian impression of an English gentleman's study, with beams in the ceiling and oak panelling, a fireplace, a leather-top desk, pictures of hunting dogs. He wore those heavy oak-coloured wingtip shoes the Americans and the Italians think the English wear and a tweed jacket with patches at the elbows, a Tattersall shirt and a green woolly tie, a perfect miniature of a gamekeeper from the days when the sun never set.

But it wasn't his clothes that made me mistrust him. After all, Ken, the perfect English gentleman, was wearing black Italian loafers, a dark green Giorgio Armani shirt, and a double-breasted Cerutti blazer, an Englishman's version of what the well-dressed Italian gentleman wears. Those acres of dark silk made him look like an elderly bouncer. No, what put me off Dr. Ammiratti wasn't really his fault. No doubt he was just trying to be kind, but he had the elaborate friendliness and confidence of an insurance salesman. Rossella, they said, was dying. His grins and little jokes seemed like insults. When he checked me over, peering at my bruises and poking them with his finger he was "absolutely sure" I was "absolutely OK." "But please," he would have to "absolutely insist on some X-rays to be absolutely one hundred per cent sure." The pains in my side and my back had shrunk to a manageable size and I had stopped worrying about bleeding inside. All that left for him to treat were my hands. And while they hurt, they weren't any worse than what every schoolboy does when he falls off his push-bike. So there was no point in being harsh on the man. Especially since he knew the doctors at Rossella's hospital.

"I have to see her," I said.

"That's totally impossible," the doctor said, getting up from his chair to look over the nurse's shoulder at my now profusely bleeding palms. He seemed satisfied. "She's in intensive care, under sedation as well as under quite a siege from reporters. Are you familiar with our Italian press? Even if you could get past them she is still heavily sedated and she is dying, my good fellow. From what I understand from a friend of mine at the hospital, they are simply trying to make her as comfortable as possible. I don't think that would include you. It's a medieval weapon but I'm afraid with all our modern technology, there is nothing we can do."

"Forgive my being stupid," Ken said with the slow caution of a man who is used to being listened to, "but why should a medieval weapon cause you so much difficulty?"

"Well, apart from being triangular, which you probably know leaves a wound that is very difficult to close, the knife had another especially vicious feature. Little hooks folded against the edges when the knife went in and extended when the knife was withdrawn, making jagged tears in the flesh. Naturally the press exaggerate, there are not forty, just over a dozen traumatic invasions. But I am afraid they are far too much for the poor girl. Broadly speaking, apart from the punctures, she's suffering from multiple impacted fractures, myocardial infarction, myasthenia and systemic septicaemia. The septicaemia we can control but specifically . . . well, never mind, what's the point? It is a terrible, absolutely terrible weapon. It dates back to the fifteenth century, a professional assassin's knife. Quite valuable, they say. I would have thought the only place you could find one like it would be locked up in a museum. Monstrous weapon."

The nurse had finished scrubbing my schoolboy scrapes. I assumed the Poliziotti or the Carabinieri had pushed me and I had put out my hands to protect myself. Scratches compared to what they had done to poor Rossella. The nurse poured iodine over the open wounds. Scratches.

"The police could arrange it, seeing her," I said. "They owe me that."

"I dare say they do," Ken said. "I suppose I could ask my solicitors here, the gentlemen you met this morning, I could ask them to make inquiries."

"The lawyers here would take three weeks," Dr. Ammiratti said, reaching for his telephone. "The chief surgeon is a personal friend of mine." He started to dial, then paused, "Naturally. . . " he said, smiling his most ingratiating goldfish smile.

"Naturally," Ken said, reaching for his chequebook.

As Dr. Ammiratti spoke into the phone, loudly, so we could hear him emphasize his eminence and importance, I had one more favour to ask Ken. "There is one thing your Italian solicitors could do," I said. "There is a fourteen-year-old boy the Carabinieri are holding, Vito Guzzetti. The Mafia are framing him for a murder he didn't do."

"That's right," the doctor said into the phone for our benefit, "the naked Inglese. The one they arrested for stabbing her."

"You do make friends easily," Ken said.

Chapter 10

It was after seven in the evening and the heat of the day was fading with the light. Traffic, stalled as usual, hazed the night air with exhaust, horn honk, and the rasp of motor-scooters worming their way through. A stream of students and tourists, shoppers and office workers, heads down on their way home, crossed in front of the golden glow of the shop windows. We shouldered our way upstream, towards a parking lot near the Pantheon where Ken's driver was guarding a silver Alfa. Ken stopped suddenly, creating a major roadblock in the pedestrian traffic. A newspaper stand on the corner blared GRAND PRIX LOVE NEST SLASHED. DUCA, DUCHESSA E REGAZZA STABBED.

Several newspapers carried the story on the front page. A blurry, smiling girl smiled from a convent photo. Rossella at thirteen. The other photo of her was a close-up of her bruised and swollen face, eyes closed, mouth open, lolling on a stretcher. Her parents were photographed lying side by side in a church, their stab wounds cleaned but still gaping. There was also a picture of me, Mr. Bikini, with my hands handcuffed behind my back.

"Not exactly the sort of exposure our sponsors had in mind," Ken growled into my ear. "Shame about the boner."

I looked at the picture again, no erection. Ken's idea of

relieving the tension. Moving off before I could answer him, making the terrible wheezing sound that was his laugh, Ken was listing slightly to one side, like a tall ship under sail in a sea of heads that came up to his chest like waves.

Maybe I should try to laugh about it. Maybe that would make the nightmare go away. She really had been terrified of Guido. Terrified that he would follow her and kill her. Still, I knew Guido. And you can never picture anybody you know murdering a girl, stabbing her in the stomach. If Guido had done it, he would have had someone else do it for him.

When we were in the car, locked in the traffic, Ken was staring gloomily out his window at the street crowd. They were moving faster than we were, the girls in red, yellow and pink T-shirts and tube tops, their boyfriends' black hair slicked back, wearing black and drab, soldiers of the consumer revolution. "I don't want you to think it is just our sponsors who worry me," he said, turning around to face me.

I waited through a long pause. Ken coming to his point is like the QEII coming in to dock. He will not be hurried and you cannot deflect him. "And naturally I am terribly concerned for that poor girl although I have never met her."

"You would have liked her," I said, remembering Rossella's blue eyes darting back and forth when we had first met, as if she saw ghosts behind me.

"Yes. No doubt. But I'll tell you who I am quite worried about."

"Ken, if you are worried about me, don't. I'm fine."

"Worried about you," he said, his great black eyebrows rising high. "Why in God's name would I be worried about you? You've had a rough day, Evers, but you'll get over it. And I want you to take very good care of those hands. But it must be said, Forrest, one could be excused for thinking you had it coming. You stole another man's wife, from his house, when you were a guest at his party, and I don't imagine it bothers you a bit."

"That part of it, no. Not a bit."

"There are times, Evers, when I think you have the moral delicacy of a crocodile."

"Who then?"

"Guido, naturally. I mean this is almost over for you, but it is going to go on for him. He is losing his wife and in the most grotesque and shameful circumstances. He really is only a boy, you know."

He saw me grimace. "Yes, well. Guido may not be the most charming individual on earth. But he is terribly young."

"He is twenty-eight years old," I said.

"Should you ever reach the end of your sixties, Evers, I promise you, a twenty-eight-year-old man will look like a child to you."

"He's not that much younger than I am."

"Exactly."

Traffic was gridlocked going north out of the city and the next four hundred yards took twenty minutes before our driver found a clear back street to treat us to what an Italian chauffeur thinks is fast driving, lurching and screeching inches from pedestrians and parked cars, charging for open gaps in the traffic like a bull in a bullring seeing a red flag. Some people think that if they drive on the ragged edge of control, they are driving quickly when all they are doing is demonstrating that they are capable of smashing into a lamppost at very low speeds. I told the driver to relax and slow down. He glared back at me as if I'd asked the price of his mother, but he slowed down.

Twenty minutes later we drove up a hill just off Buozzi in the north of Rome. At the top the Ospedale Santa Maria della Croce rises out of the ruins of an old monastery. They have pasted some of the old monastery walls onto the front and it gave the steel and glass building a kinder face than the blank stare you usually get from a modern hospital. The driver circled around to the service entrance at the back where it was all business; delivery trucks, ambulances and rubbish bins. A male nurse in a white shirt, white trousers, red socks and black shoes was waiting for us in the parking lot and motioned for me to follow him. He had dark circles under his eyes and he looked us over quickly as if we had interrupted something much more important. We probably had. He led me past the loading dock where a drooling rubbish truck was swallowing steel bins full of needles and hospital effluvia. The nurse was in a hurry and I had a feeling that Rossella might die before we got there. Inside the building, we threaded our way through a crowded kitchen, through the steam and clash of dishes and the stale smell of boiled hospital dinner which followed us out to a small staff lift. Intensive Care was on fifth.

The three of us were almost too much for the lift which struggled up in a series of little jerks until it gave up and just stopped. Peering through the darkened window the nurse made out the number 5. He pulled back the door and we turned left down the hall, fluorescent lights overhead and scarred brown lino underfoot. The nurse unlocked an unmarked door with a key and we were in a tiled locker room. He gave me a pile of sterile green cotton and we dressed as acolytes in the temple of high medical tech: skullcaps down to our eyebrows, masks over our faces, green gowns, red plastic boots over our socks, and, for the bandages on my hands, large yellow rubber gloves. I looked at myself in the mirror. Bring on the clown.

Another door to unlock and we emerged in the intensive care room, a thousand square feet of concentrated suffering. On our right there was a six-foot long observation window. A glance told us that we really needn't have bothered with all the secrecy. Most of the reporters had left for the night and no one had cleaned up the piles of little foam espresso cups, the crumpled newspapers and cigarette butts they had left behind. A man and a woman still kept watch. He sat on a bench with his legs stuck straight out and his head thrown back, eyes shut. She bent forward over a newspaper.

In front of us, the room was a maze of lights, tubes dangling from the ceiling and video monitors. There was no centre that I could see, no single place that seemed to be in control. And no one came forward to question our presence. There were a dozen doctors and nurses in the same garb as we were, silently moving among the beds, eyes above the mask. There were fifteen or twenty beds. But they were not beds for rest or for love, they were battle stations. All the drugs, electronics, and mechanical gadgets of modern medicine were focused on each island of light where a human form lay close to death. Looking from bed to bed for Rossella, I could not always tell which bleached soul was a man or a woman . . . they were so swaddled in the tubes and wrappings of technology they could have been dummies, except for the erratic pulse in a tube or the tremble of a sheet. We were stopped by a tall man with a stripe of deep tan skin and black eyes behind the same anonymous medical mask that we wore. A heavy gold cross hung outside his green sterile garb.

"Good evening, Mr. Evers," he said. "I am Father Pancaldo. Rossella has told me that you would come."

He led us with the careful steps of an Indian in a rainforest, stepping over tubes and around electrical connections as if they were snakes and avoiding the sudden rush of a nurse charging from between the beds to meet a crisis head on. There was the vague whine of electrical machines permanently switched on.

Rossella was on her back with the top of her head wrapped in plastic. They had rigged an aluminium frame to hold the sheet away from her body, presumably so her wounds could drain easily. Underneath the tent she was naked except for a little cloth placed like a bikini bottom for modesty. She had deep purple circles under her eyes and purple and yellow bruises spread out from her wounds. The wounds on Rossella's legs and stomach and breasts and arms had been plugged with a greenish gel, but they still leaked fluid over her. Tubes ran into her body and tubes ran out. There was a vein in her neck that pulsed in time to a green monitor to let us know she was alive. And her breath came in short shallow little gasps. She looked as if some huge and terrible beast had chewed her, shaken her and then let her drop.

"Rossella," the priest said in the soft voice of the father to his child.

Her eyes flickered open and took a while to find me standing by the side of her raised bed. Cobalt, I thought, her eyes used to be cobalt blue.

"You are in terrible focus," she said. "And you have to stop weaving." She paused for breath from the effort of her joke. She tried to manage a smile and gave up. "I am so glad to see you. I was afraid they might hurt you too."

"Does it hurt?" I asked, thinking I wanted to help in some way. Knowing there was nothing I could do.

"There is no pain," she said with the trace of a smile coming back, "nothing."

"I'll wait here until you are ready to go home."

"You English," she said, "are such babies, always so afraid of the truth. I am dying, Forrest. Father Pancaldo has given me my last rites. And it is not difficult, dying. Anybody can do it." She closed her eyes for a moment and I took her hand. "My son is safe," she said with her eyes closed. "Aldo is safe now."

I started to say how sorry I was, but the priest stopped me with the slightest pressure on my arm. "Let her speak now," he said. "You and I will have plenty of time later."

"Please." She opened her eyes again. The whites were yellow, and the brilliance of the blue had gone filmy grey. I could not tell if she saw me or not. "Please Forrest. I have to ask you another thing. A favour. I have to ask you to make sure Aldo has his, his," there was a pause, "what is his. Keep him safe, you promise? For me?"

"I promise you," I said, not really sure what I was promising but willing to promise her anything at all. Her eyes had closed again and she was absolutely still. The vein in her neck continued to pulse and there was still the catch of breath at regular intervals but I have no way of knowing whether she heard me or not. There was another hand on my shoulder and a doctor was motioning me away. I didn't look back.

In the locker room, Father Pancaldo took off his mask and held the bridge of his nose and closed his eyes, as if he were lost in thought. He had deep grooves in his cheeks, he needed a shave and his broad forehead made him look tough, but his manner was gentle. "This must be a terrible shock for you," he said, after the male nurse left.

"It was my fault," I said.

"Well, fault," he said, putting his hands up in mock surrender. "We are all at 'fault'. Especially God, he can carry the lion's share of the 'fault'. He makes us play his game, but he never tells us all of the rules."

Father Pancaldo had slipped off his green hospital smock with an easy pull on a string, letting it drop to the floor. He was about my age, thirty, and he had the stillness of a man who is either extremely patient or exhausted. His face was narrow under his wide forehead and he had a small chin, dominated by a long nose. His eyes were deep set and he stood looking down at me as if there was something he expected me to do.

I sat on the bench, still struggling with the hospital smock. The bandages made it difficult to undo the ties, but I think that even if my hands had been fine, it would have been slow work. I was having trouble concentrating. And my eyesight was blurred. What do you do when you are alone with a priest? I made conversation. "You work here at the hospital?"

"No, no. I am from Pianoro. I have been Rossella's priest for years."

"So you know her sins," I said, pulling off a red boot.

"Yes, well, sins. I suppose you have been under some stress," he said looking for something in the ceiling. Then he turned back to me. "And I don't suppose you know her or you wouldn't have said such a thing. Let me tell you, Signor Evers, it would be difficult," he said pausing as he chose his words, "it would be difficult to imagine a more innocent child than Rossella. I don't mean that she was some damn goody-goody, she's not, poor child. But she has goodness in her. A rare quality these days, even, no especially, in the Church."

Whatever goodness is I didn't feel I had much of it. He continued to stare down at me as if there was something he expected me to say. I said "You knew her, then. You knew what she was going through. Why didn't you help her?"

"Why indeed? I did help her and God help me. When she first came to that place she was just fourteen. A child. A baby. She thought the world was as simple as her life had been inside a convent. My problem was that she was also Guido's wife before God. And I thought it was my duty to help her accept that. I am a foolish country priest, Mr. Evers. I thought it was my duty. And by the time I saw what Guido was, it was too late. She had accepted what I had told her. She believed it was her duty to obey him. I was taking her confessions when her husband had confined her in that terrible house. When he beat her. And I never heard her complain, let alone blame him."

Father Pancaldo put his hands on my shoulder, looking me in his eyes, letting me see the pain. "Oh, fault, Signor Evers. Blame me if you feel you have to blame somebody. She could have walked out of there. I offered to find her a ride. I gave her the money to pay for a taxi. I told her I would get the monastery's car to pick her up and she would not go. She would not go because I had convinced that poor child it was her duty as a wife before God to stay. And she believed me. Until last week when she had the child, and Guido threatened to kill the baby. Then she saw things differently.

"You said you feel guilty about her, Signor Evers. But

I think I am a long way ahead of you on that score if you want to keep score. Personally I don't like to make these judgements. But the one thing that is clear to me is that she is the innocent, possibly the only innocent person in this. Are you aware of what you have promised her?''

I thought for a moment. "I'm sorry. I don't mean to be rude. I think that I promised her—'' The words wouldn't come. "I don't know what I promised her," I said.

A weary smile, one for the stray lamb. "Her child is safe for the moment, in a hospital where the nuns are especially kind, although I can't tell you where. Not yet. She gave the child to me and I smuggled the infant out of the house. I expect God will forgive my kidnapping. But I'm sure you appreciate, we can't rely on the mercy of the Church to protect him for ever.''

"If it's a question of money," I said.

His hand waved the thought away. "It's not just a question of money. Or at least not your money. As I, er, understand it, the infant could be immensely wealthy; in fact it could be that little baby is right now one of the wealthiest individuals in Italy. That's not the point. The point is, I think, and correct me if you think I am mistaken, the point is you have agreed to see that the child receives his inheritance, his title from his mother and his money from his father.''

"I'm not sure there is much I can do about that.''

"Maybe not. And I'm sure no one could hold you to your promise. But I think that child really isn't very safe. I live in Pianoro, Mr. Evers. I have lived in the monastery there for several years. So I know some things that maybe you don't. And I really do think that however we hide that child, that child really is in danger. I believe, no, let me put it stronger than that, I have good reasons to believe that the child's father wants his son destroyed.''

"I'm sorry, I don't. . . ''

The priest raised his hands in his mock-surrender, I-don't-want-to-hear-it gesture. "My understanding is, and again, correct me if I am wrong, my understanding is you have agreed to ensure the safety of her child. She has asked you to protect her child and look after his future, Mr. Evers. She has asked me too. And I will do what I can. I don't think there is much you can do. The only thing I am saying, if there is something you could do, maybe Guido would let you adopt the child, something. I don't know. Anyway I would be grateful if you could keep in touch with me.''

When I got back in the car I answered Ken's questions. Yes, she was alive. No, she was dying. No, there was no hope. And then I told him that I was going to be a kind of father. Not the kind who changes nappies and holds the smiling baby boy. But I had promised. I was going to be the one who tries to do what fathers have always tried to do, to make the world safe for the boy.

Ken gave me a hard look. ''Do you mean to tell me,'' his great bushy eyebrows lowered over his eyes, ''that you are going to take his child from him as well?''

Chapter 11

I rolled over, holding the pillow over my head.

Evers' Law: The noise of an Italian engine is in inverse proportion to its size. Evers' Thought for the Day: Rome wakes with the same quiet ease as a hornets' nest poked with a stick. The Judgement of Evers: The inventor of the steel roller blind that covers every shopfront in Rome and sounds like the Gatling guns of World War One, shall be rolled up in his invention at dawn.

I looked at my watch. Not quite seven. My hands ached but they were more flexible. I felt sick, sore, lame and disabled, as the lawyers say. But I could move, and none of the pains was as sharp as it was the day before. I reached over and pulled back the dusty curtain that covered the window. No change, still total darkness. So I swung my legs out of bed and opened the layers of ancient wooden louvres, doors and shutters. The sun was hot and the courtyard rattled to the tune of several million Italian fossil-fuel engines chewing on the city. Their breath had eaten away the faces of the monuments and their appetite was increasing. Time to get up, it was going to be a full day.

I'd ridden with Ken out to the airport from the hospital. The transporter would be in Vallelunga the day after tomorrow for practice, but there were a number of things he needed to do back in London. But if I didn't mind terribly, he said with his elephantine sarcasm, possibly I could attend the session at Vallelunga even if my hands made driving "unwise." And possibly he might arrange a truce between my good self and young Guido. One to which I would adhere if I wanted him to take on this Vito, this Italian street urchin (I didn't know anybody still said "street urchin").

I would make every effort, he told me, to at the very least be civil to a man who has just suffered the loss of his young wife. He also said his lawyers were having less trouble getting Vito out of jail than they were getting the Carabinieri to part with the Ferrari. Apparently it was registered in the name of some woman in Dorking who would not answer the phone. Goddamn Jack Boyce.

After I'd left Ken at the airport, I'd planned to check in the hotel and walk down the Bocca di Leone to take a look at Rossella's parents' house. But when I'd got to the Hotel d'Inghilterra, I was barely able to stand. I told myself I'd just splash some cold water on my face and when I'd got to my room I thought I'd just lie down for a moment and the last sound I'd heard was the creak of bedsprings as I hit the mattress face down. The next instant I was waking to those ol' Roman early morning favourites, the Chainsaw Chorus and The Rattling of the Steel Roller Shop Fronts.

I rang the hospital. Rossella was not conscious was all they would say. As if that answered my questions.

Rossella's parents' address was just down the street from the d'Inghilterra, on the Bocca di Leone. Turn left two blocks and you couldn't miss the small crowd gossiping and gaping, held back by a striped plastic police tape.

I started to duck under the tape and a middle-aged Poliziotto stopped me. His face looked like boiled polenta and he had a way of holding his head back as if he was looking down at me. "Excuse me, Signor, but you don't see the signs? You think the tape is for somebody else?"

"I am Forrest Evers, a friend of the family."

"Forrest Evers," he said slowly as if he was savouring the name, "the racing driver. The team-mate of Guido

DiSanto. Very good," he said. "Back behind the tape."

"I am here for Rossella, their daughter. She asked me to come."

He glared at me. "What are you, a fuckin' ghoul? You want to see the bodies, go to the church, Santa Caterina. They got the Signor and Signora Fanesi there. Up on the altar, side by side. You go look at them there, see what innocent dead people look like. Get back behind the fuckin' tape or I arrest you." He started to poke at me with his finger and I was thinking how pleasant and how stupid it would be to point his finger back at him when there was a feminine voice and a delicious scent of earthy perfume, like cinnamon and almonds.

"Just a moment, Luigi. Who are you?" she said to me, looking at me with suspicion. She was impeccably tailored and thin and wearing black, with hair that ranged from pale gold to bright copper down to her shoulders, dark green eyes and skin the colour of cinnamon. There was something steely about her, not stiff but tough. The effect made the gentleman of the police and myself forget what we were talking about. Her eyes were too far apart, and her wide, thick, Mick Jagger mouth was too big for her little face. She was young, not much more than twenty, but she had the look and the confidence of several billion carefully invested Italian lire.

She looked away, at the house, then back at me, giving herself time. "I'm sorry, maybe I am mistaken but I think I have seen you this morning on television," she said. Her voice was low and clear with a northern accent that could have been Milan. She looked at me, up and down, with her wonderful wide mouth almost breaking into a smile before she caught herself. "But of course you weren't quite so nicely dressed."

She stood looking beyond me at the crowd for a moment, as if deciding, then she tossed her head. "What do you want?" Her mouth turned down, stern, forbidding.

"If it's not too much trouble, I'd like to have a look at the house."

"What for? It's not a good time. You call tomorrow, maybe the next day. Make an appointment."

"I'd like to see the house for Rossella. I was bringing her here."

"Rossella?" She rolled her eyes up in disbelief. "Rossella is dying."

"Rossella is dying," I said.

She looked at me again for a long moment and then shrugged, as if she could bear this little bit more. "It is all right, Luigi," she said to the Poliziotto. Then she turned and walked back through the door into the courtyard of the house, assuming I would follow. Which I did.

Her clothes were black, but there was a real swish when she walked. Despite the monstrosity of what happened, life for her would certainly go on. But then, Italy deals with tragedy differently than do we of the pallid north. Or maybe they just have more of it so it is not so crushing or so strange.

The contrast, as I followed her, between her slim, elegant, expensively dressed figure and the house she was leading me to couldn't have been greater.

Outside, in the Bocca di Leone, there had been an immense, polished oak door and engraved bronze plaques. Through the smaller open door in the archway you could glimpse a tree, a garden and a fountain. But inside the courtyard what had once been one large Renaissance palazzo had been cut up into several houses. The woman I was following went into the one that had dirty windows, a broken window pane on the top floor flying a tattered, blackened nylon curtain for a flag. Outside the door a rusted sign said "rooms," and the dark and peeling stain of time took the place of paint. The house was huge, as if it had been built for Roman Renaissance princes. But the sheer size made its decay all the more depressing. When I walked in the front door into the entrance hall with the high beams and a dusty glass chandelier, there was the unmistakable smell of mould, of forgotten rooms that were no longer used or swept.

"Excuse me," she said, burying her face in her hands for a moment. "I am not a very good hostess." She looked up again, and started running her hand along the wall in the gloom. "This thing, what has happened, I am very upset. And on top of that I have to confess, it has been years since I was here so I forget where things are." She fumbled for a while before she found the light switch and the chandelier went on in a blaze of two fifteen-watt bulbs. "But if you like, I can show you around. Show you where they . . . where it happened if you can stand it. And maybe you can tell me what really happened to my little sister."

Her name was Anna. And as she led me from room to dusty, dark and faded room, the sunlight coming in thin shafts between the drawn curtains, we put together a picture of two old people living alone. There was a path that had worn the carpet down to bare threads and left a shuffling trail through the dust of the once-polished floor. We followed it from the kitchen to the room with the TV where the drapes were forever closed. To the sunken, soiled and depressed cushions on the couch where old Carmella, the Duchess, sat on the sofa. To the worn green leather chair facing the old television with a wooden cabinet, the leather cushions and the arms cracked and dotted with cigarette burns. This was the throne where old Giovanni, the Duke, took his meals as he watched the pretty girls strip on *Colpo Grosso*, an atoll of cigarette butts, crusts and fruit peels at the sides. From high on the walls, dark portraits of forgotten ancestors glared down from their gilt frames, down on the empty bookshelves, on mouse droppings, and on the filthy floor. A thick film of dust on the stairs told us the old couple had not gone up and down the stairs for at least a year. They slept in the back, in what must have once been a servants' room by the kitchen. The police had marked the place where the bodies had lain on the browning, blood-soaked sheets. But the deep depressions from the years of lying side by side could have told them just as well. The rooms, for all their high ceilings and wide floors, were stuffy and claustrophobic and I felt trapped.

"No, please, stay here for a little while with me, Mr. Evers. If it is not too much trouble for you. It is very depressing for me and I am glad you are here. Perhaps I can make you some coffee. Maybe we'll be lucky and find some milk in the refrigerator and I can make us a cup of cappuccino. Please?" Her wide mouth spread into a smile for an instant. She found a bag of coffee open on the kitchen counter and she boiled water in a dented aluminium saucepan.

We stared at each other for a moment, across a cluttered kitchen table, her head cocked to one side as if she was trying to remember something about me.

"I am sorry," I said.

"You know my sister well?"

"I never met her before yesterday."

"Do you often pick up other men's wives?" she said. "I'm sorry, that's a terrible thing to say. I don't mean to be rude."

"It's all right," I said, "it must be a terrible shock."

She looked at me, suddenly angry. "Maybe you should go see them, lying in the church. Take a good look. Giovanni and Carmella. Il Signor Duca and La Signora Duchessa. Look at her with all those stabs in her face. And then you tell me what you see. It means something, you know, stabs in the face. It means revenge. In Rome, in the old days, when somebody steals your pride, steals your reputation, you stab them in the face to get back your respect."

Anna leaned back, looking at me. "I'll tell you something. I think the old cow, she had it coming."

I started to object but she went on. "No, wait. Maybe you don't know. Maybe you don't know Rossella is not her daughter." Her head went back, her eyes challenging me, as if I should know the rest of the story.

"You see, you meddle in these things and you don't know anything." Then she leaned forward, her face softening, her green eyes kind again. "I'm sorry, it is not your fault you don't know. I will tell you." This last with a wry smile for the hopelessly uninformed. "You see, Carmella adopted Rossella when Rossella was a little baby. And you know why? She only adopted Rossella so she could sell her off for the money. You know, you know about this? How she adopted the child and taught her good manners so she can pass her off to some rich fool who thinks a title is something worth having. That's what she did. She sold Rossella to Guido."

"You mean like a slave," I said, leading her on so she could see the absurdity of it, thinking that what she was saying was a mild form of hysteria, an hysterical reaction to the murder of her family.

"No, no, not so crude. They get a lawyer to draw up their will so Rossella inherits the title. She inherits the title so Guido can say, my wife, the Duchess, when Carmella dies. It's worth nothing, but Guido wants that. He wants the respect. He sets up a trust fund for the old man and for the old lady, enough to pay their taxes, and their bills. Twenty years they owe, their food, their bills. They say, how kind, we consent you marry our daughter. You want, Signor Evers, we can go upstairs and I can show you the ball gowns Carmella bought for herself, disgusting stupid dresses like nobody wears any more except maybe in some magazine. All the best labels. She doesn't have to walk far. Valentino, Missoni, Givenchy, they are all a few blocks from here and they are happy to sell last year's fashions to an old lady who never goes anywhere and doesn't know the difference. Maybe she tries them on when she gets home, looks at herself in the mirror. Maybe she never wears any of them, I don't know. There is an empty room upstairs with mirrors and clothes racks full of them, thirty, forty, maybe sixty ugly gowns, I don't know, I don't count them. It is the same thing."

Anna pushed back her chair and stood up, looking down at me. Then she leaned forward, her hands on the table, her face inches from mine. "Rossella was only fourteen, in the convent, when they tell her she has to leave because she is going to be married in two weeks to this Guido who she never heard of. They sold her, Signor Evers. They sold Rossella for money so Carmella could wear those stupid ball gowns. They deserved what they got."

Chapter 12

Out on the street, as I went back through the police cordon, the policeman gave me a servile little smile showing teeth the same grainy yellow as his skin. My old friend.

Bocca di Leone and the streets around the Spanish Steps are reasonably untroubled by traffic. Traditionally, thugs, murderers and thieves hung around the Spanish Steps because an ancient privilege protected them from arrest, as long as they didn't stray from the steps. Now cars and trucks are outlaws in the district during the day, and the street stones are polished by wall to wall pedestrians. Over there, poking through the fabric of a wall, a stained and pockmarked marble doric column, carved when Britain was a muddy peasant colony in the North-western Frontier. And over there, the remains of a statue of a boy, carved long before Christ and neglected ever since. Rome has so much history, so much time has passed here, that I felt as if I were suspended on the surface over a bottomless depth of time. One stone thrown from behind a wall would break the surface tension and I would sink without a trace.

I should have stopped in the d'Inghilterra and rung Rossella's hospital from the sanctity of its cool white marble floors and polished mahogany panelling. But I didn't. I didn't want to hear that she was closer to death or that she had died. Anna's story raised more questions than it answered. Not the least of which was this: what excuse did I have for using Rossella in my petty, egotistical little war with Guido. Rossella was dying and there was no excuse. I didn't even have the ball gowns hanging like accusations in an empty room. I would ring the hospital later.

It was eleven and the heat of the day was already making me sweat. I looked down for the first time at the clothes Ken had given me, brought the morning before from an expensive men's store. Italy's largest sizes, too small for me. A plain white shirt that was tight around the shoulders but wasn't too bad as long as I didn't try to button the collar and kept the sleeves rolled up. And expensive grey wool trousers that were only a little too short. I would have to get some new clothes, I thought, looking in the designer shop windows. After I got Vito out. That, at least, I could do.

The lawyers had arranged to have him moved to a holding cell prior to release. A much better grade of cell, they said.

An Italian police station is like an Italian airport. They never expected so many people to show up today. But they had shown up with their lawyers and their wives and husbands, mistresses and lovers, friends and relations, witnesses and victims. They were all screaming at the men behind the counter, at each other and at the ceiling and the walls.

In the doorway of the station, with two armed Carabinieri standing guard outside in the street, and fifty people shouting inside, the lawyer told me the situation. He kept putting his hand on my arm and on my shoulder when he talked, a gesture I think he meant as ''shut up and let me do the talking, I know my way around here and you are from another planet. But it's OK, there's no problem. I've got the whole thing under control.'' But of course I was just guessing. No doubt somewhere there is the official fifty-three-volume abbreviated guide to Italian gestures, but I haven't got around to reading it yet. What he said was, ''It's fine. He's here, we'll have him out soon. But there are just one or two complications."

"What complications?"

The lawyer was an earnest bald man, the size and shape of a twelve-year-old boy and with the eyes of a bloodhound looking into his own grave.

"It's expensive," he said with the gloom that Italians have when they tell you that someone has to be bribed. "There's a lotta documents have to be signed. In Italy, I don't know if you know, but you can die waiting for somebody to sign a paper for free. We have to pay."

"What's the other complication?"

"He don't want to come out."

Vito was waiting for me in what the Carabinieri who led me down the hall called an "interview room." Maybe an Italian psychiatrist had done a study that showed that criminals were more likely to confess in the presence of violent colour. Maybe some cop wanted a pretty loo at home and got the station to order ten gallons of the stuff.

"Monkey dick pink," Vito said gesturing at the glossy freshly painted wall when I walked in the room. "Will you look at this shit? Where the fuck you been?" he said. "And what the fuck you doin'? I've been here six hours and I have to tell you, this place sucks. I mean it really sucks."

Under the garish light, he looked smaller and frail, a fourteen-year-old kid trying to act hard. His hair was greasy and hung over his thin face. And he was nervous, he kept looking over my shoulder as if he saw somebody sneaking up on me. "I thought the cells here were supposed to be better than that one we were in," I said.

"Are you kidding? You know what they got here? They got no television. How the fuck can you do time with no television? They got me in a cell here twenty minutes and I'm goin' nuts. I don't have the mental equipment." He was wearing the same grey T-shirt and cotton trousers and he smelled like old tennis shoes. "What the fuck you trying to do to me anyway?"

"I am trying to get you out of here. The lawyer says he should have you out of here by tomorrow morning."

"Who asked you? Who the fuck asked you to do me a favour? You get me out of here, you know what you're doing to me? I'm finished. I'm outcast. They kill me slow, you know? Take maybe ten, fifteen years, doesn't matter, they don't give a shit. But I can't get no work, I can't get no jobs, I got no place on the street. I can't even beg. Where am I gonna go? What am I gonna do? I can't even get a job washing cars. I got a contract here. I break my contract, I'm finished. Get the fuck out of here. Leave me alone. At least I had a television."

"I got you a job. But listen, Vito, you want to stay here, fine. If this is where you want to be for the next four or five years, be my guest."

"What do you mean a job. Some kind of blowjob bullshit. I ain't suckin' no cocks."

"Relax, Vito, it's nothing like that. It's work. You know what that is, work?"

"What do you mean? Sweeping up?"

"Partly. But you'll get an Arundel Formula One uniform, bed and board and £125 a week."

"Working on a Formula One Team?"

"You'll be in our custody until the trial. If you fuck up, we ship you back in here."

"You mean if you fuck up, I go back in here."

"That too."

"I'll think about it."

"You'll let me know." I pushed back my chair and got up to go.

"No, hey. Wait, man. I was just joking. Are you kidding? I'll take it. What took you so long?"

"It may take a little while. It could be longer than tomorrow morning. The lawyer says the paperwork could take some time."

"So come on. Where you been? You can't bullshit me. Something is on your mind."

I looked up at the glossy pink ceiling and around the glossy pink walls. I wondered if wombs were this claustrophobic. He was just a kid, but he had real spirit. Underneath that tough exterior there was a tough kid. And he probably knew more about Guido and Rossella than I did. Everybody seemed to know more than I did.

"I went to Rossella's parents' house on Bocca di Leone this morning. Her sister said Rossella was adopted."

"Yeah, sure, of course she was. Christ, Evers, you really don't know a damn thing, do you? What are you talking, 'sister'? Rossella don't have no sister."

"I just talked to her. She has red hair and a mouth like Mick Jagger."

"I don't know who you talked to, but I'm tellin' you, Rossella don't have no sister. The whole reason her parents adopted her was that they couldn't have no kids."

"How the hell do you know all this?"

"TV news, man. Don't you ever watch no TV?"

"You're sure."

"How do I know? Maybe Rai 1, Rai 5, the biggest TV network in Italy got it wrong. But that's what they say. They do a whole story about them and about Guido. I mean all the cops think he must have done it, except he never leaves his house until the next day. Pick up a newspaper, man, it's a big story. They're probably still running it."

"What else they say about Guido?"

Vito smiled for the first time since I'd met him. A lot of crooked teeth. "What are you?" he said. "Some kind of detective? You got to interview me to see what I saw on TV?"

"You know something about Guido?"

"You know what I can tell you about Guido? Nothing. He's a good driver. Comes from Sicily. End of story."

"You do know something."

"And you, listen I don't mean no disrespect, but you really know fuck all. What, you think somebody's gonna just tell you? Nobody's going to tell you. Nobody who knows anything is going to tell you nothing. No, wait a minute. One thing I can tell you. You go looking for the Mafia and they are going to see you a long time before you see them.''

Chapter 13

After I saw Vito, I didn't ring the hospital, I went there. The surgeon in charge wouldn't let me in the intensive care room, not without a special dispensation from the director of the hospital or the doctor in charge of Rossella's case.

They were right. I would have been out of place and in their way. She was unconscious and there was nothing I could have done, apart from hold her hand. And I wasn't at all sure she would have wanted that.

So I peered at Rossella through the window in the dim corridor. She was a distant figure several beds away in that harsh green light, naked under her domed sheet except for a single towel and the obscene plastic tubes. From what I could see of a monitor over her bed her breathing was slow and regular. I stood at the window for an hour, feeling useless, helpless, and guilty. I had no doubt that it had been Guido who had done this to her, or had it done, it didn't matter. But I had played my selfish part.

She didn't move.

When I came back in the evening she was in the same condition and in the same position, eyes closed, breathing slowly. There was nothing I could do and that is what I did, nothing, standing at the window for another hour or it could easily have been two, I couldn't tell you the time.

However long it was there was plenty of time to imagine how it must have been done. Guido making his phone calls, alerting the network. Maybe the desk clerk at the hotel, or someone in the village hearing the Ferrari, phoned someone who phoned Guido. It wouldn't have been difficult to guess that we had headed for Rome. Guido must have heard us driving off up into the mountains. And where else would she have gone?

Then there would have been two men, or who knows in these days of equal opportunity, women, walking slowly and quietly up the stairs and down the hall to her door, opening her door with a key or a plastic card slid in the lock, walking across the room while Rossella was sleeping, one of them clamping his hand over her eyes and her mouth in the dark and the other pulling down the sheet and stabbing her and stabbing her until she was too weak to scream. Would they have washed themselves before leaving, or was there a trail of bloody hands on the walls as they felt their way back down the stairs? They would have washed in Rossella's bathroom because they had to drive down to Rome to stab Rossella's parents, stab the old woman in the face. They would be gone now, in another country, in New York City having a hamburger, in a movie theatre in Puerto Vallarta in Mexico, somewhere beyond the reach of any law.

In the morning, when I came back at seven, she was gone. I rapped on the window and got the attention of a nurse. She came out into the corridor, leaving her green cap and face mask on. "Mrs. DiSanto died early this morning," she said from behind the mask.

"Where is she now?"

"I'm sorry, I don't know," she said, a touch of impatience in her voice. Her job was inside. Patients who were still alive needed her. There could easily be a crisis with any of the patients at any moment. "I'm sorry," she said, moving away.

"Is there anybody who does know? Who could tell me?"

"The ward superintendent should have a record."

"Where's he? Or she," I said to her as she hurried away.

"He should be back in half an hour, I'll tell him," she said as she went through the door, back inside to her battered and feverish flock.

There was a clock in the corridor, and no place to sit. Someone had taken or stolen the chairs. Doctors and nurses went by, preoccupied, faces down. An elderly man in dirty yellow pyjamas hobbled past, holding a jar of clear liquid high on a wooden pole, a tube running from the jar to his nose.

Time is flexible in Italy. The clocks in the train stations read fifteen minutes fast giving everybody plenty of time to get on the train. On the train the clocks are set a few minutes slow, giving the passengers the illusion their train is on time, or at least, not so late. The clock in the hospital corridor seemed to take around four or five minutes for the second hand to crawl around the dots and the numbers to complete one lap. I would watch the intensive care room for as long as I could stand it and look back at the clock and see that ten seconds had passed.

After an hour and a half, a portly man in his fifties in a pinstriped suit and a solemn striped tie told me he was Dottor Benito Guadagni, the head of public affairs for the hospital and could he possibly be of any assistance.

I told him I was looking for a Mrs. Rossella DiSanto who had died some time that morning.

"Yes," he said, "I am very sorry. I am afraid there was really nothing the hospital was able to do. I understand she passed away quite peacefully in her sleep."

"Can you tell me where the body is now?"

"Again, I am very sorry but the family has requested complete privacy."

"Her family is dead."

"The DiSanto family. They have requested the hospital to please respect their privacy. Under the circumstances . . ." His voice trailed off, and after a few moments, the look of deep concern on his face faded, as his mind went on to other problems and he turned and walked away. I watched him wait for the lift at the end of the corridor. After a while, the doors opened, and without looking in my direction he got on, and the doors slid shut behind him. Leaving the corridor empty.

I don't know why we need to mourn, but we do. We need to hear the words spoken, if not in a church or temple or beside the grave, at least somewhere, by someone, in public. We need to hold the hand of someone who knew her when she was a child and scraped her knees, to share that look of loss from the eyes of someone who had held her and had loved her. We need to look inside our own souls and see the terrifying speed we are travelling through these few moments of time. We need to mourn before we can feel free to live again. It is what the dead teach us, the love of life.

If they had killed her so savagely, how would they bury her?

Part 2

Part 2

Chapter 14

Outside my taxi window, in the street, smog bronzed the sky and the air, turning the cars and the people picking their way through the stalled traffic the sepia of old photographs, as if they were already memories in a box, in the back of a drawer, in grandfather's desk.

The Boxer Ferrari was, I was told by Ken's lawyers on the phone, in a police pound on the south-eastern outskirts of Rome. I could go pick it up any time. No, it would be no trouble. Getting out of Rome during the morning rush hour is like trying to fight your way out of a toasted marshmallow. Every way you turn, you're stuck.

Once we were clear of the centre, we were lost. It's just behind the airport, the lawyer said, you can't miss it. Believe me, you can. After six wrong turns the taxi driver drove down a dirt cart-track on the no-man's land between Ciampino airport and the railway tracks and found a ten-foot high chainlink fence topped with barbed wire. On the other side of the fence there were row upon row of dust-covered refugee cars. I paid the taxi and banged on the locked gate. After a while a penguin with a dirty yellow sweater and baggy blue pants and a baggy blue face shuffled out of the little wooden hut at the gate.

"You gotta ticket?"

I pushed the ticket through the fence. He took it back into his hut, head bowed over his treasure. Five minutes later he came out again, holding the other half of my yellow ticket. He looked at the two halves suspiciously as if one of them might have been a fake. Then he looked up at me, pouches above and below his eyes. "Five hundred thousand lire," he said through the fence.

That translated into two hundred and fifty pounds. "The police didn't say anything about a fee."

"It is five hundred thousand lire."

"I heard you. It has only been here three days."

"It's a Ferrari." He held his hands up and shrugged his shoulders as if to say of course a Ferrari driver pays ten times what anybody else pays. It's a law of nature. Nothing to do with him. I gave him the slight tilt back of the head which in Italian sign language means, you will have to do better than that and I am not a patient man.

He said, "Insurance. You don't want to pay, go talk to the police."

I felt my sore hands. I had talked to the police. They must have talked to poor Rossella. What could she have told them? Poor Rossella had disappeared as if she had never existed. She had died, she had been murdered, and I was an accomplice. My selfish ego, my childish revenge on Guido. My little prank. Forrest Evers, Mr. Bigtime Macho Racing Driver. Mess with him and he'll make your wife disappear in a cloud of wheelspin and Ferrari smoke. But of course that was only part of it. I wasn't just getting back at Guido. There was no point in fooling myself.

She was a sexy and lovely woman and I had the thought there might be something else. Beneath the shining armour the knight was anything but squeaky clean. I could say I had been trying to save her, that she had asked for my help. And you might believe me. But in a dark corner of my mind when I was debating with myself whether I should drive her to Rome, or not, I had seen the thought come and go and asked it back again. "What the hell, maybe she just wants to screw." And a part of me had answered, "And why not? Take off her black and lacy panties slowly, a little

at a time because she would be shy.'' The old brainless
ding-dong urge of the cock, swinging like a compass, pointing this way, that way, this one, that one. Still believing in
the ancient elusive myth of every cock, in the carefree, no
obligation, no cost fuck.

I felt sad and dirty and small. She had died, they had
taken her away and there was nothing I could do about it.
There was no family to mourn her. And even if there were,
apart from her infant son, I would still be the uninvited
guest at the grave, the pornographer at the funeral. I hadn't
really killed her, I had just made it possible. And the joke
was, the hilarious joke was that Mother Nature had pointed
the random cock where she always points the carefree, random cock, to Daddyhood. I was a father, or at least I had
been given the part of father protector. Without any of the
intervening romance, love, sex, pain or worry. I had an
infant to protect and his mother and I hadn't even kissed.
I was supposed to protect him from his father. Something
else Guido was going to thank me for.

Signor Pinguino looked at me expectantly, waiting for
an answer. The world went on. I looked at my watch, re-
alizing I was over an hour late for practice. I didn't want
to argue with the man holding the two halves of the yellow
ticket. But when you are in Rome. . . I said, ''I'll talk to
somebody but it won't be the police. Twenty thousand.''

He looked outraged. Then his face relaxed into a grin of
small yellow teeth. ''Two hundred thousand.''

''Forty thousand.'' I made a mental note to start writing
down expenses for Jack Boyce.

''OK. Fifty thousand.'' He took the money through the
fence, stuffed it in his pocket, and fished around in his other
pocket until he found the keys for the gate. There were two
padlocks and I stood in the hot sun while he sorted out
which key fitted into which lock. Evidently it wasn't easy.
When he got the gate open he handed me the keys to the
Ferrari. ''It's over there,'' he said, pointing. ''In the back.''

I walked through the rows of abandoned cars. The car companies should dig graveyards for their dead so they can be buried in dignity. With gravestones that say "Fiat 128. Born, July 1977, died September 1985. Humble and sometimes faithful taxi of Giuseppi Schiavarelli. Rust in peace."

We leave them to decay above ground, their glass shattered, drooling their fluids, cancerous with rust, their once comfortable upholstery splitting with mould, reminders that the expensive new cars glittering with promise in the dealer showrooms have a shorter life expectancy than a parakeet.

The Ferrari was surrounded by mundane Fiats and Fords, all of them smashed or broken in some way, victims of thieves, crashes and time. The Ferrari looked right at home. The back end was a mess of broken tail-lights and bent hand-formed aluminium showing bare metal where the paint had flaked off. There was a long crease and scratches down the side. Its scarlet skin was dulled and streaked with dirt. Mementos from my drive down from Pianoro with Rossella. There was also a fresh dent in the nose, courtesy, no doubt, of the Poliziotti tow truck.

It was as hot as a pizza oven inside from sitting in the sun. But it started on the third try and I was on the Autostrada heading north in less than five minutes, accelerating hard.

Vallelunga is only twenty-five kilometres north of the outskirts of Rome, but it is another world, hidden in the hills and vineyards. The air is clear and blue and you can see the sun when it shines. Turn off on a little side road off another minor road and it feels as if Rome were five hundred miles away.

The track has had its moments. In 1963 they held the Grand Prix of Rome on a little short oval track at Vallelunga and an American won in a Lola. But time has passed it by and weeds grow in the old concrete grandstand across from the pits.

Ken's theory was that if we moved the barriers away from the back straight, cut out the switchbacks where the track twists back and forth across the infield and just used the outer section of the track, it would be helpful in setting the cars up for Monza. Which was a smokescreen.

No track is like any other track. The surface, the radius and the camber of the corners, the length of the straights are never the same. Even the same track changes from hour to hour with the heat, humidity and light changing the adhesion of the surface. And the set-ups we would make for Vallelunga wouldn't be right for Monza. But still, there were things to test, there were always things to test. I just didn't like the track. Without the switchbacks it would have some of the speed of Monza, but none of the subtlety. Monza is 3.6 miles around and Vallelunga even with the switchbacks is just over a mile and a half long. They are both like a long paperclip slightly bent in the middle. The difference is that Vallelunga is narrow and uneven and a Mickey Mouse track. I could go on but I recognize the symptoms of PRT, Pre-Race Tension. I get irritable, moody and bad mannered before getting on a race track. Reporters who come up to me before a race, people whom I count as friends, get bitten. But this was just a routine exercise and there was no point whingeing. Look on the bright side, Evers. It was near Rome and it was good PR for our Italian sponsors who could invite their clients along to watch ''their'' Formula One team on a private test day. PR we do six days a week. Racing, only on Sunday.

I drove through the parking lot that slopes down to the track entrance and a guard waved me through the tunnel that runs under the track and comes out in the infield and the pits. There were the two blue and white Team Arundel transporters and the tech truck which lugs around enough electronic gear to bring the Pentagon to its knees. There were several other vans and cars from local caterers, reporters, photographers, friends of friends and their friends. The three Arundels (mine, Guido's and the backup) were under a big, open-sided tent to keep the sun off, surrounded by extra nose and wing sections, tyres, banks of big computers in rolling aluminium packing cases, mechanics and the usual crowd of tyre, computer, electronic, engine and aerodynamic technicians, reporters and spectators. And the pretty girls, pit poppies who would smile hopefully at every man in a Nomex driving suit. In the days of AIDS and rubber sex they were still there, the ones dim enough to think that racing drivers are sexy.

Off to the side, in the shade of the timing tower, there was a large dark blue motorhome. Guido was standing on the steps, talking to Ken. Guido had his driving suit on, open at the neck. His driving boots were flame red and came half-way up his calves, a touch of the dandy. He stood on the third step so he could look Ken in the eye. They both turned and watched me park.

I locked the Ferrari and walked across the dry grass to them. The sun was straight overhead and it was hot. "I'm very sorry about Rossella," I said, photographers gathering at my back.

Guido looked at me and then looked off into the sky. "Let me tell you something," he said quietly as if he were reading the words written in the distance. "You mind your own fucking business. You understand?"

"Where's the funeral?"

"I'm not going to tell you again," he said and went down the steps and walked across the grass and disappeared into a camper, slamming the door.

"You have to understand," Ken said, "Guido's wife died early this morning and he is very upset."

"Of course he's upset, he killed her."

At six foot seven, Ken towers over me, his face gathered in folds around a large nose. "I am not familiar with the laws of slander and libel in this country, Evers. But I will say that the police have established that Guido is not a suspect in that horrendous crime. And I consider it to be the worst possible taste to make an accusation like that when a man is mourning the loss of his wife."

"She told me he was going to."

"I'm sure she told you a great many things. Now I would appreciate it if you would suit up and put in some laps so this day is not a complete waste of my and our sponsors' money. I've brought two motorhomes. Because my hero drivers are too childish to share one. So each of my number one drivers has one. Identical. Exactly the same. Although I wouldn't be surprised if you found Guido's had more tread on the tyres than yours. Yours is next door. You are very much welcome."

"I thought you were going to patch things up between us."

"For God's sake just get in your car and drive, Evers."

What the junkie feels when he is about to take a hit. Sliding down into the cockpit, feeling the back of my seat grip with the absolutely perfect mould of my shape down to little indentations and bumps for my lumpy spine. The thin pads they have taped to the sides of the cockpit to soften the bruising, remind my shins, my shoulders, and my forearms of bone bruises I'd forgotten.

My feet are too big for the footwell, my toes catch on the top of the footbox and I cannot stretch my legs out and for the thousandth time I think how ridiculous it is to be so Goddamned cramped, forced to drive in a kind of crouch. They invest several million pounds in the car, plus a couple more to pay me to drive it, and they still can't find room for me to fit in it. It's like giving a Maradona shoes two sizes too small and then telling him to go out there and win the World Cup.

Like all the other components of a racing car they are shrinking the drivers for better aerodynamics and less weight. These days if a team is considering two drivers, they'll pick the smaller one every time. In the future the ideal Formula One driver will be six inches tall and weigh less than a boiled egg. Don't worry about pushing the pedals, or turning the wheel, they'd work it out. He could push buttons on a computer. He wouldn't even have to get in the car. He could sit in Tokyo or Detroit and do it by satellite.

The cockpit looks unfinished, like a half-scale model of a jet fighter waiting for the final cosmetic touches. But there will be no cosmetic touches. The cockpit is formed out of hardened black waffle-cloth, carbon fibre. There are no dials, just one display unit where you would expect to find the rev counter, a steering wheel with three buttons and several switches marked on the dash "ign," "pump," "light" and "display" with Dymo tape, and idiot lights for oil pressure and water temperature. Black plastic tape lines the footwell, and a big red bomb of a fire extinguisher is strapped to the floor just under my knees.

I pull on my gloves, push the pedals, reset the rev counter display to zero. Touch the small wooden knob on the gearshift, wood for good luck; it's the only natural material in this lightweight child of aerospace. It is also a vestigial organ. It is there because I want it there. Buttons marked forward and reverse would do as well. For the genius of Max's automatic transmission is that it is truly automatic. Ferrari has electromagnetic servos to shift conventional gears and pop the clutch faster than you or I could. When it is working right. But Max's automatic is closer to the CVT or constant velocity transmission you find on little Fiats and Fords these days. The engine runs at peak revs virtually all the time and the only shift I do is to slip the lever forward and backward for reverse. So I can keep both hands on the wheel and, more important, the car isn't unsettled by the power coming on and off while you shift down and back up again under braking and acceleration.

The lower lip of the dashboard has a deep arch on each side of the steering wheel for my legs. The car is shrink-wrapped around me and there is no extra space for anything, anywhere. No passengers and no prisoners. I settled back, hands around the tiny suede-covered wheel. This is what I do and I stop moaning about the past and I stop worrying about the future and I forget about my aches and my bruises. This is now and my whole body is wired to put my foot down and go. This is the most expensive and sophisticated racing machine on earth and I am going to make it scream.

Chapter 15

There was a short straight coming off the banked hairpin that ran past the pits and grandstand and lasted for nearly three seconds. Three seconds is a long time at 170 miles an hour. In those three seconds I cover nearly a fifth of a mile. There is plenty of time to relax, go back to the quiet place in my mind, stretch, check the buzzing little mirrors for traffic behind, check the pits for signals, scan the idiot lights and the display. Time for the computer in the car to talk to Big Brother in the pits and flash the news of the zillion events that have taken place inside the engine, drive train and suspension on the last lap. A silent blip as we cross the start-finish line—and several thousand coded numbers scroll across the videos in the electronics van, and the technicians strain to find the news. My display, a bright red arc across a scale, reads 13.250, maximum revs, close to 180 miles an hour with the low ratios for this dinky track.

Time, as I approached the shallow left-hand bend after the grandstands, to worry about safety. Not my safety, Guido's.

Vallelunga doesn't have the usual "300," "200," "100," and "50" signs to mark off the distance in metres going into a corner, signs that help you find your braking point and turning in point on the track. But Vallelunga does have hundreds of patches on the tarmac where the surface changes colour. And as I come into the first bend I see the dark grey rectangle where I start to just touch the brakes, to settle the car, half-lifting, easing off the pressure as the engine starts to overrun as I let up on the accelerator and when the grey strip runs out I start to turn in at the dark black of an old oil stain twenty yards later, coming off the brake and starting to feed the throttle. If you were watching me you would have seen a blur of foot lifting off the accelerator, tapping the brake and smashing back down on the accelerator. But if you could see it in slow motion you'd see my foot in a dancer's arc, accelerate up to the peak, slow down as it begins to touch the brake pedal, apply just the gentlest pressure, lift and accelerate back up to the peak of the arc and then decelerate to get back on the throttle smoothly. A simple gesture at 180 miles an hour, done with the speed of a hummingbird's wing while the car covers thirty yards and several tons of force begins to turn.

Two black smudges on the track. Guido hadn't lifted. There were short black streaks on the track where he had cocked the car with a twist of the wrist, foot flat to the floor, flat out at 180, scrubbing off a little speed with the skid, treating several million pounds of advanced aerospace technology like a go-kart.

That is not the way to drive a Formula One car. It's too dangerous. Abuse the tyres and they overheat, and their grip goes away. Get the car a little sideways and you lose downforce, the aerodynamics stop working so you can lose your adhesion all at once. Flick the car in the face of the gods like that and they will use the excuse of a micro-miscalculation or a tiny, almost invisible spot of oil on the surface of the track to lubricate a tyre fighting for grip and hurl you face first into the armco.

His marks were all over the track. Locking up a wheel coming into the right-hander at the end of the straight, getting the car out of shape in the long hairpin leading into the grandstand straight, black streaks told he had gone over the limit time after time. And brought it back.

So it didn't matter what I did. He might break the car. He might crash. His driving was rough and it was crude, and it was dangerous. But it was fast. I could tell by the marks that he had braked later than I had and that he had gone through the corner at the end of the pit straight faster than I had. He was faster around the whole track than I was. Faster than I could be. And that was all that mattered. You can talk about theory and technique all day. But there is only one reason to be a racing driver. To go faster than anybody else. If you can't do that, or if at the very least you don't believe that one day, given the right equipment and the chance, you could be the fastest man on the track, if you can't do that you might as well hang up your helmet and watch the race on television.

I did three more laps and came in.

There is a kind of flywheel effect that keeps your mind spinning at speed while the car is slowing down. The car slows down and you still see a pinprick of clarity at the end of the tunnel of blurs as you come down off the mountain of speed. Easing the car right, onto the pit lane entrance road, and through the chicane, it was like looking through the wrong end of a telescope . . . a hundred yards away, Ken was looking towards me, his tall form stooped more than I had realized, he was growing older. Max, the fat man, a giant jelly of anxiety, his little pig eyes squinting with suspicion in my direction, worried I'd done some terrible damage to ''his'' darling little sweetheart, ''his'' car. Phil, my engineer, and his three assistants, Ed, Steve and Richard, mechanics who were the neurosurgeons of their profession. Behind them, a clump of technicians, the aerodynamicists, physicists and mathematicians who have given up their jobs in aerospace to make this surface projectile defy the laws of physics and, off to one side, standing next to Vito, with her hand on his shoulder, a small blaze of colour, a redhead, a woman I did not immediately recognize.

I went through the chicane, slowing down to the slow crawl of 75 miles an hour and the blurred tunnel began to open up, my eyes shifting to wide angle to take in the whole circus, the race-vans, cars, fans, friends and moneymen, tents and caravans behind the pits on my right and the concrete grandstands across the track on my left with, I was surprised to see, over a hundred spectators sitting in the hot sun watching a blue and white racing car slow down and come into the pits.

I flicked off the switch and all the noise and vibration stopped, bringing, in their place, heat and pain where my shins and thighs banged the car on the bumps and corners. Max was putting the little video screen in front of me, before I could get my helmet off and Phil was down on one knee beside the cockpit waiting for the news.

"Max, I thought you were going to swap the EE-PROM," I shouted up at him. EEPROM is the little chip that controls the engine. Like the seat you can contour it to the driver's whims. If a driver wants a sharper throttle response or more torque coming out of corners, just change the little chip. It just takes a few seconds to alter the brain of a Formula One car.

"And the front end is soft, we need more wing. The whole car feels sloppy." As I said this, I was reading the numbers on the screen. My laps were over a second slower than Guido's, a huge space of time on a short track like this where you make up a hundredth of a second here and there. And, when you are really lucky, you might make up as much as a whole tenth of a second when you find a place where you can ease onto the throttle a microsecond quicker than before. Nobody said anything about it, they didn't have to. There was time to get it right. I knew that with a few adjustments and learning the track I would be faster. But I also knew that I would still not be as fast as Guido. I was stalling. He was taking risks that I was not going to take. "What tyres was Guido on?"

"Bs," Phil said, unbuckling my harness. "Same as yours."

Ken loomed behind him, his shadow falling across the car. "Let me see your hands," he said.

I didn't know what he was talking about.

"Take off your gloves, Evers. Let me see your hands."

As I pulled off my gloves, sharp little prickles of pain from my palms reminded me. Inside my driving gloves there was another layer of white Nomex gloves, and the palms were wet with fluid and blood.

"Out of the car, Forrest. I don't want you doing any more laps today. Get the doctor to look at them before you leave. I want him to tell me if you are going to be fit for Monza or if we are going to have to get another driver."

At first the water was cold, coming out of the showerhead in a high-pressure needle stream. When I'd washed away the blaze of heat my body had soaked up from the car and the day, I nudged the control lever with my elbow up to *calde* to open up the pores and holding my hands up over my head, keeping them dry, I turned in the tiny cubicle of the camper's shower feeling the luxury of a warm shower in cool, air-conditioned air.

"You look like a rain dancer," she said.

Chapter 16

I turned around, arms over my head like a hostage. On the other side of the glass door there was a mottled face topped with a splash of orange. It moved closer, peering in.

"Usually people knock," I shouted over the shower.

"I'm sorry. I did. I went 'knock knock knock'. No answer." The mottled face was backing away. "I saw you go in, so I knew you were inside and when nobody answered, I opened the door and I heard water running. I thought I should check, you know? Look, if you want me to leave, no problem. I didn't mean to intrude." She was outside the bathroom, a pink and blue blur. Leaving behind a faint trace of a scent, cinnamon and almonds.

"I'll be out in a minute."

"It's OK if I have a soda or something?"

"Look in the fridge."

"I know where it is."

Pulling on jeans and a Team Arundel T-shirt (dark blue, discreet white letters just above the left breast, £32.50, £29.00 profit included, from Team Arundel, Buckingham, Bucks.) I came out of the shower room, padding barefoot on the deep carpet. She was huddled on a corner of the sofa, knees drawn up, head down, her pale gold and copper hair tied back in a pony tail down to her shoulders, green eyes looking up as if she were expecting to be punished. She was younger and more uncertain than the expensively tailored woman I remembered. "What colour is it really?" I said.

She made a clown's face with the corners of her wide mouth turned down and looked away. "A lot of Italians have red hair," she said to the window.

"They're famous for it," I said.

"OK, maybe not a lot. Some. My mother was a redhead. Testa Rossa like the Ferrari."

"You sure? The last time I saw you, your name was Anna and you told me your mother was dead. You also told me that you were Rossella's sister."

"My name is Anna, but Rossella is not my sister. My mother is dead but she died a long time ago."

"You lied."

"I lied. She isn't, I'm sorry, Rossella wasn't my sister. But I loved her. I didn't lie about that. She was a very good friend of mine, my best friend. I used to talk to her almost every day."

"And you know where the Aranciata is in the fridge."

"Third shelf in the back just like Guido's. Look, I don't blame you, I'd be angry too." She had her head buried between her knees and she was talking very softly. "I mean I am very sorry I lied." Then she looked up at me, her eyes looking as if she was about to cry. "I want to apologize to you. You want to grill me, is that what you say in England, you 'grill' somebody? You want to ask me questions, Forrest, it's OK. Or I don't know, maybe you want me to just go away. I understand, I know today is a bad day for you. It is bad for me too, but if you want, I'll go away."

I looked around the motorhome. It looked like an executive suite whittled down to quarter scale by budget cuts. High gloss walnut panelling, soft green curtains, dark green walls, and a soft, cappuccino leather sofa that doubled as a bed. Pleasant, dull, middle management Italian luxury, perfect for sleeping. I felt drained, empty of any emotion unless exhaustion counts as an emotion. I had no idea what she was up to or even who she was. I was too tired to care. But she was right, there were questions. I had the thought, not for the first time, that if only I had been born just a wee bit dimmer my life wouldn't have been complicated by so many questions. Or a good deal smarter and I would have known the answers. I looked at her eyes for a moment, clear and green and full of life, her wide fish mouth hovering between a frown and a grin. I had plenty of questions.

"Just like Guido's," I repeated. "You know Guido?"

"He is my brother. Half-brother. I know him a little, not too well."

As she talked her hands formed the words. "Half," "a little," "not too well," were each finely shaped in the air, and dismissed at the same time.

"So it's not important he's your brother."

"What do you mean?" She stood up, angry, her face close enough to see the fine gold hairs above her lip. "Of course, it is very important. I am very proud of him. In Italy he is a big man, like a movie star almost. I think maybe he is going to be The World Champion, OK? He is my brother. I just don't know him so well, that's all." She got up, turned away and went to the fridge, taking out another Aranciata. "OK if I have another one of these?" she said holding up the little round bottle.

She moved quickly and easily and I thought I could see the resemblance. The same impatience, a certain flat ironic smile. Guido was short and tough, muscle and bone. Anna was probably two inches taller than Guido, but more finely formed. She had long delicate fingers, delicate wrists and ankles. And under her plain white cotton tank-top shirt, long and slender breasts pointed this way and that way. She was full of motion and life and I had the feeling that she wasn't going to stay feeling sorry about anything for very long.

"You want something like a beer maybe? There's a lotta cold beer in here." Her voice was muffled as she bent inside the fridge, again, moving cans and bottles around. Not a woman to do things half-way.

"Bottle of water," I said, "no gas." A leather patch on the back of her stonewashed jeans spelled out Valentino. Just like any ol' cowgirl would wear if she owned a few oil wells down in Dallas. I wondered what she did to keep in shape. And where her money came from. But then, designer labels don't mean much in modern Italy, unless you have the courage not to wear them. The whole country had turned itself into walking point-of-sale merchandising units with the retailers' labels displayed like the battle flags of conformity. Not that different, I suppose, than my racing driver suit which is paved with the gaudy logos of the corporations who pay half a million pounds a square inch to have their name sewn on my suit. In my darkest moods I think I am just another highly paid corporate clown. Keep 'em laughing down at the Colosseum, Forrest. Then I think, well, if those clowns are dumb enough to pay me when I'd do it for free, who am I to complain? Pedal to the metal, balls to the wall, if you haven't got paid a million a race you haven't got paid at all.

Anna settled herself on the leather sofa that doubled as a bed, knees drawn up to her chin, like before. I stretched out on the pillows at the other end, and raised my water bottle in a mock toast. "Nice to see you again, Anna," I said. "How come?"

She shook her head in puzzlement.

"It's an American expression. It means why. How come you were there? How come I get the pleasure of seeing you again?"

"I'm sorry. I thought I apologized for that."

"Sure you did. But you didn't tell me why you were there."

"OK, back on the grill. I don't mind." She gave me a quick little smile, like an actress on a talk show. "I was checking it out for my brother. As a favour, you know? I mean he asked me to see if there was any of Rossella's stuff maybe he might want to keep, like a photograph or a school book or something like a keepsake.''

"Did he mention anything specific, anything special you were supposed to find for him?''

"No, not really. I think mostly he wants to know how is the house, like is the roof leaking and needs to be fixed right away. And I was supposed to make sure the place is locked so the thieves and the reporters don't go in and trash the place. You know, just make sure everything is OK. There were still a lot of reporters around. He can't go himself without raising a big fuss.''

Outside the window, in the distance, Guido was accelerating back on to the track for another run, the noise of his car almost drowned in the buzz of the air-conditioning. "I still don't understand why you lied to me. Why didn't you just tell me the truth?''

"You scared me, you know? You still scare me a little. Could you stop looking at me like that? Please? It was not easy coming here and I don't mean to be impolite but you are not making it easier. I mean maybe you could lighten up, say hello or something. Never mind,'' she said, waving her hand to dismiss the thought. "I recognized you. You were in the newspapers and on television. First they said you killed Rossella. Then they said that you were the bastard who told the police that Guido killed Rossella and her parents. And I wasn't sure at first, I thought maybe you did stab Rossella. It was possible, I didn't know. Anyway I didn't want to say I was Guido's sister. You scared me.''

"Well, you are a good liar, Anna. Usually I know when somebody is lying to me. And you didn't look scared. You didn't look a bit scared.''

"Of course not. I would never let you see that. I am a professional. A reporter.''

I raised my eyebrows at this.

"Well, not a reporter really, not for salary because I'm not on the staff of a magazine but I would like to be. On top of that I loved Rossella and I really don't know what happened and I wanted to know. After you came into the house I thought maybe if you didn't know I was Guido's sister I could learn from you what really happened, as long as you don't think, you know, that I am on Guido's side. I am sorry Forrest, it was so horrible there in that gloomy place. You saw the place, you know, these murders and that house were so depressing. I wasn't thinking. But now I feel even worse because I think you are OK and I screwed everything up. I know it was a shitty thing to do. I'm sorry."

"I'm sorry too," I said. I wanted to believe her. She looked small and vulnerable. But that wasn't really the reason. Reason had nothing to do with it. As she talked, she used her hands the way Italians do, making the air between us agree with and emphasize what she was saying. And as she moved her hands, her breasts moved in a wobbling dance to the music of her language, a lovely and unpredictable dance (first this one then that one, now both), that held me foolishly, making me nod my head and smile, yes, yes. O wise and mourning Forrest Evers, show him a bit of the ancient dance of the boobs and you will have him nodding like a puppet on a string, dangling like a fish on a hook.

The thought of Rossella in the hospital under the green light brought me back with a jolt. "You're telling me that you don't think Guido killed his wife?" I said, looking away. There was another note to the scent of cinnamon and almonds, but I couldn't quite place it. Musk maybe.

"Let me explain to you about Guido. I mean I don't really know him all that well. I only met him for the first time three years ago. And he has helped me. He paid for my university and he has always been generous to me. But he is away all the time these days and I don't see him that much any more." She took a long sip, draining the bottle, and put it down carefully on the deep brown velvet carpet.

"My mother died five years ago and she never told me who my father was. But she gave off a lot of hints. That he was handsome, and that he was very rich. And I always thought it was a lot of romantic rubbish, you know what single mothers tell their children so they don't feel like a bastard? Like they are really some prince or princess.

"A year after she died I was really broke at university. I was studying journalism and I was doing OK, better than OK, but I couldn't stay without some more money so I start doing some research. The first thing I found was that on my birth certificate, the father, I mean my father, is listed as Sig. DiSanto. No Christian name, just Sig. DiSanto. And that is all. But in the christening book, you know the guest list everybody signs, there is a G. DiSanto among the guests, but nothing else. Nothing that says he is my father. Nothing to say who he is or what he does or where he lives. And when I saw that, I begin to wonder if he is still alive. And I think what it would be like to meet him. So I start looking in telephone books, which is crazy, I know. I mean there are six G. DiSantos in Rome and eight in Palermo. But who's to say, he could live in a little village in Calabria or maybe up in the Alps or maybe he's moved to Australia and doesn't have a phone, I don't know.

"And it was hard calling them up, Forrest. I mean what do you say? 'Excuse me but do you have a daughter who is a redhead you forgot about?' I didn't know what to say. I didn't call anybody. Then I saw in the papers, Guido DiSanto, racing driver wins, I forget, some race. I mean of course, Guido is G. DiSanto and I know he's not my father, he's only a couple of years older than me, but I thought maybe he knows something so I rang him up."

"Just like that."

"It's not that difficult. I rang up the reporter from the newspaper and I asked her to tell Guido to ring his sister and I leave my number. And a couple of days later the reporter rings back and asks me if I have a picture. In colour. So I sent him one." She turned her head to look out of the dim glass of the smoked window, remembering. "He rang me the next week and he was very nice on the phone.

I told him a couple of things and he said it was possible. His father told him he had a brother and a couple of sisters he didn't know about.''

"You mean there are a lot of little Annas and Guidos running around Italy looking for their brothers and sisters?''

She laughed, touching the tip of her pink tongue to her lip. "OK, it's funny but it's not a joke. Not for me. Guido has been very good to me. You know when I asked him about my father, what he was like, what he looked like and what he did, Guido said my father was dead. Forget about it. But I don't think he is telling me the truth. He won't tell me anything about my father, nothing my mother hadn't already told me. You know, the same old fairy tale, that he was rich, he was nice, he was handsome. More smoke screen. I know when people are lying to me. It is crazy, I know, but I feel he is still alive. I think maybe some day I will run into him and I will know who he is.''

She turned back toward me and I said, "Are you all right, do you want a tissue?''

"I am not crying. OK, maybe a little. I'm sorry. This is a terrible day. I keep thinking of Rossella.'' I got up and brought her a handful of Kleenex from the loo. She took them and motioned for me to sit down again. There was more to tell.

"You don't understand," she said. "Guido arranged for us to meet in this fancy restaurant in Rome. And I am sitting alone in the restaurant and it is very crowded, very noisy, lots of people. And after a little while I feel conspicuous, I wasn't used to a nice restaurant, especially not on my own. And I thought I looked wrong, you know I was just a scruffy student. And I thought I can't leave, I'll have to pay them something and it's probably really expensive and I don't think I have enough money so I am stuck.

"So finally I say to hell with it and I am reaching down to pick up my purse and before I see him I can feel him. He is standing behind me and I know I'm just imagining this, but I stop hearing all the noise, maybe two hundred people talking loud to make themselves heard over lunch. For me the restaurant goes quiet and I turn around. We looked at each other and he smiles and he is like a missing part of me. We understand, we know we are brother and sister. I don't know why, I can't explain it to you, but we know. And I feel like crying now because Guido has been almost like my father and I don't want to think he could do something like this. Like a monster. He is my brother. But you know Rossella was like my sister, too. And he treated her very badly. He treated her like a dog. Worse than a dog. What was that?'' she said springing up and looking out the window.

"Do you see anything?"

"I thought I heard something. I get jumpy sometimes."

"You think maybe he did kill Rossella."

Anna turned back from the window and sat down, taking her time, being careful. "No, I can't think that. I don't know. But you have to understand he was very angry, I mean really he was in a rage."

"You mean because of what you told me before, that Rossella was adopted, that she wasn't really an aristocrat."

"No, you don't understand, Forrest. It's worse than that. You know Guido has a lot of pride. He is a very proud man. But underneath that he is afraid. He is very short and a very short man is always in danger of being a joke. So his dignity is important to him. Maybe that's why he does this stupid thing of marrying some girl he doesn't know for her title. Some title nobody gives a shit about. But he liked the idea, like a family crest. Like he could be Count Guido, the racing driver, and then he could get much better sponsorship. It was what, five years ago, I don't know. But he told me when he first saw Rossella, she was very shy and very beautiful. But her parents said, 'Sure, she is the perfect girl for you. But she is only fourteen, you have to wait two or three years, at least.' And Guido cannot wait. He wants her, he wants the title, maybe one or the other, maybe both right away. He is a very impatient man. So the parents say, 'OK, we'll give our consent on one condition,' because they say they have to look after the family name. Their honour, you know. And they get him to sign this document their lawyers had drawn up saying that their grandson, Guido's first son, if he and Rossella have a son, would inherit his money and his property.

"When Old Carmella and Giovanni hear that their daughter Rossella is pregnant, they take the train from Rome for the first time since Rossella was married and they go visit her. They think their rich son-in-law is going to treat them like royalty. And he is not nice to them. They are expecting to be treated like royalty and he doesn't like having them in his house. In fact Guido hates having the Old Duke and Duchess in his house because they remind him how much he paid for Rossella and he feels cheated because he knows now she is not really their daughter."

"How did he find out?"

"Somebody in the street, maybe, knew her mother, told somebody. Guido has a lot of connections, you know? A lot of people tell him things. I don't know exactly how he knows but he knows she is adopted. So he tells the maids not to clean Rossella's parents' room. And he refuses to give them lunch or supper. He says they should go out to the local restaurants. And there is no heat in their room. So they get very angry and they tell Guido that yes, his wife is adopted, that Rossella is not their daughter. And Guido gets angry and he says something nasty to Carmella. I don't know what but I know the Old Duke was screaming at Guido. It was Rossella who told me. She said she was upstairs and she heard them. And Carmella is in a rage that she is treated like this, she thinks she should be treated like a cousin to the Queen of England or something. And she tells Guido that when she adopted Rossella, she adopted her from a prostitute."

"She must have been furious," I said. "She must have been in a rage to say that. I mean Guido wouldn't believe that, would he? I met Rossella and I thought Rossella was, you know . . . ''

"Yeah, an aristocrat. Everybody thought that. But it's true, what the old woman says. And she tells Guido something so he knows it's true.

"It is late at night and he throws them out of the house. I mean he really throws them out and locks the door. And the old man and the old woman have to walk down to the village and knock on doors to wake somebody up so they can call a taxi and they go down to Bologna to the station without their luggage. And later, when Guido checks the records in Rome, he finds out for sure that it is true, that Rossella's real mother was a prostitute. So the child, the little boy Rossella just had not only reminds him that he married the bastard of a prostitute, but that son of a bastard of a prostitute is going to get all his money.

"He hates that. I'm not so sure he could kill Rossella, but you know I think maybe he could kill that baby. He told me sometimes he can't sleep at night because he wants to know who the grandfather, you know, Rossella's real father is and if he was still alive so he could kill him.''

"And that's why you came here, Anna, to tell me this?''

"I came here because I made a fool of both of us. I owe you something and I want you to know the truth. I loved Rossella, I really did, Forrest. She was always lovely to me and I don't know what I can do but I hope maybe I can do something. Something for her. I feel so bad for her.''

Chapter 17

Footsteps pounded up the stairs outside the door.

The door banged open and Vito, his hair slick with gel, was looking at me, at Anna, and back to me, his black eyes snapping back and forth. Then he stopped at me, staring, his eyes blazing.

"So what the fuck, you don't say hello or nothin' to your old cellmate?" Eyes back to Anna. "We were in prison together, maybe he didn't tell you that?" He stuck out his hand. "Vito Guzzetti. Glad to meet you."

A half-beat pause to hold up his hand to signify to Anna that a handshake wasn't necessary and eyes back to me. "So what do you got, a thing goin' with her? You talk to her, you don't talk to me—you too busy or what?" Then he took a half-step back for us admire his Team Arundel blue and white coveralls. "What do you think?"

"You look like a somebody, Vito. You want a soda?" He was already moving towards the fridge.

"Couple of beers would be good. What are you up to?"

"Put the beer back, Vito. You're only fourteen."

He came back with a beer in his hand, grinning at Anna. "You know what I was up for? Murder," he took a swig out of the bottle from the side of his mouth, looking at Anna.

Anna gave him the sort of smile you'd give a wet Dobermann you found standing on your bed just after you shut the bedroom door. "Why'd they let you out?" she said.

"Him," he said pointing the beer bottle towards me. "He got some smartass lawyers to get me out on bail. And Ken."

"You let him loose?" Anna said, not taking her eyes off him. "How do you know he's not a killer or a pimp or a dope dealer, Forrest?"

"He's just a fourteen-year-old kid, Anna. He doesn't know where his parents are. And he doesn't know if he is going to have to spend the next four years in jail. He doesn't know anything."

"What the fuck you mean I don't know nothing? I know more shit than you'll ever know."

"Do you know how to read?"

"Shit," he said waving his hand like it was beneath his dignity.

"Shit, Vito, is not going to take you very far. You know how to read?"

"Yeah, sure. I read a lot of stuff."

"Read this." I tossed him a copy of *Oggi* that had been lying on the leather couch.

"All of it?"

"Just a few sentences."

He shook his head, saying, "I gotta go," as if he had more important things on his mind.

"Try it."

He opened the magazine and held it out at arm's length, coughing twice for effect. "The question is, does she or doesn't she?" Vito had switched to falsetto. "She may only be a baby Gorilla but Princess Di has her keepers guessing." He closed the magazine quietly. "OK, smartass?" he added in his normal voice.

"It'd be more convincing if you moved your eyes."

"Whatta you mean, move my eyes?"

"When people read, their eyes move."

"You mean he made it up?" Anna said. "Forrest, he couldn't."

"He's a very bright, bright lad, but he can't read. Tell the nice lady, Vito."

"What the fuck I need to read for? It's all a lotta garbage what they print anyway. Why don't you teach me something useful like how to drive a racing car. I could be world champion."

"You learn to read a sentence, Vito, and I'll teach you to drive a racing car."

"Sure, you'll teach me," he said, moving up and down the narrow space in the motorhome as if he was looking for something to smash. "That's the way it always works isn't it? I gotta do something for you before you'll do something for me. But let me make a prediction here. You're not gonna teach me. You're not gonna do nothing for me. You're gonna be gone. You fly in for a race, the race is over, you fly out again. Fuckin' seagull, make a lot of noise, crap all over everything, flap your wings and bye, bye until next year, race fans. Yeah this is great, the uniform, the job, getting out of the fucking cell. But it's going to last ten minutes. What are you going to do, take me to London? Make me your pet? Maybe you give me a bowl on the floor in the kitchen I can eat out of. Says 'Vito' on the side so I can learn to read."

"Vito, I can promise you, nobody is going to try to make you their pet."

"Yeah, who wants a dogface like me around? Let's face it, Forrest, what's gonna happen is you're gonna take off, the team is gonna take off, maybe you leave me the uniform for a memento, then the wiseguys come around, and they say, 'Hey, Vito, I thought we had a deal. Hey Vito, you were supposed to stand up for us.' Then I am truly fucked."

"You're right, Vito," I said, "there's not a lot that I can do for you or anybody can do for you. If you want to make something happen you are going to have to do it yourself."

"Hey, man, I'm only fuckin' fourteen."

"And," I continued like the worst arrogant and ignorant schoolmaster, "if you don't know how to read, forget being a racing driver, Vito. If you can't read, you can't even get a driving licence. No driving licence, no racing licence. If you can't read, Vito, you walk.''

Vito gave me his tough-guy cynical smile. ''Don't let him jerk you around, lady. He's a bullshit artist. All this learn to read shit means is he doesn't want to take the trouble to give me a driving lesson. He wants to lie back in his fancy camper, talk to the pretty lady.''

''Vito,'' Anna said quietly, ''Rossella died this morning. Mr. Evers has injured his hands. It's not a good time.''

The tough-guy tension faded from Vito's face and he was a boy again. ''Hey look, I'm sorry. I'm sorry, Forrest. I didn't know she died. I'm sorry Mr. Evers. You liked her, didn't you?''

''She wasn't much older than you, Vito. And yes, I liked her. Listen,'' I said, ''get a helmet. See if Ken's got a spare one that'll fit you. I'll take you around for a couple of laps in the Ferrari.'' He was out of the door, down the steps and running across the grass towards the pits before I finished the sentence. ''We'll have a burn up,'' I said.

''Forrest, why are you doing this? You can't drive with your hands like that.'' Anna had come up behind me in the door.

''You want to come?''

''You won't go too fast?'' she said, touching her lips with the tip of her tongue like she did.

There is a kind of peace, wailing along on an empty track. The corners loom ahead, the laws of physics make their absolute demands and you throw your mind a half-second ahead into the future, half-way around the next turn, willing the car to follow. For a while you can almost believe that it is your hand that rolls the dice.

Anna and Vito were strapped in the passenger seat alongside, hanging on, thrown together. I was telling Vito about the driving, saying, ''You see how I get onto the brake and off the brake, easily, gradually, keeping the car settled, not upsetting the car's balance. And as I am getting off the brake with the car still loaded up on its front wheels, see how I am just turning into the corner here, with my fingertips, lightly, making the transition gradual as I ease back onto the throttle, letting the car do the work. I don't even have to touch the wheel with my palms.''

It was a standard litany, and I had done it many times for journalists and friends. Driving a car that had twice the weight and less than half the power of my Formula One car at nine-tenths of its capability not only let me drive it with my fingertips, it left me plenty of time for my mind to wander back to Rossella, who had been the last person I had seen in the passenger seat. And I remembered her face lit from the glow of the instruments of the dashboard, as delighted as a child about to blow out the candles on her birthday cake. And I thought of Rossella bruised and dying, naked on the bed in the hospital. Father Pancaldo was right. Of all the people involved in this, she was the only innocent. Her real mother had abandoned her. Worse, had sold her. And her real father . . . who knew what or who her real father was apart from a patron of prostitutes. Her foster parents had sold her. Guido had bought her and probably killed her. And my motives for playing the brave and rescuing knight were small and shabby things. We all had something to answer for. Except Rossella. At least, I thought, I could keep my promise to her. Whatever it took.

Anna, I thought, really could help if she wanted to. Her Italian was much better than mine, and she could go places that I could not. If she wanted to help was one question. What Guido's sister really wanted was another.

While I was thinking that and talking Vito through the corners, saying; ''Watch how I'm keeping the steering wheel pointing almost straight ahead, Vito, steering on the throttle, turning the car by feeding more power, making the car oversteer, straightening it out by letting up just a bit on the throttle, and now as the car straightens out coming back on the power again,'' another almost subconscious part of my mind was listening to the rise and fall of the big, flat twelve-cylinder engine, one of the strongest Ferrari ever made.

The design goes back to a little 1.5 Formula One Grand Prix car in the 1960s. Mauro Forghieri revived the layout for the 3-litre Formula One Ferrari that won three World Championships in the 1970s. It was a beautiful, almost unbreakable engine and a close cousin to this one in the Boxer, the first mid-engine road car to carry the Ferrari name. As well as the grandfather of the flat 12 in today's Testa Rossa. Its pistons and con rods were from the car it replaced, the Ferrari Daytona, a car that sells for around a million pounds now. But the Boxer was lower, wider, faster, smoother and if you didn't mind the sudden vicious snap from understeer . . .

"Ohmigod," Anna said.

" . . . although, as you see there is a sudden transition from understeer to oversteer." We sailed into the first of the two turns that reminded me of Lesmo One and Two at Monza. Anna was turned towards me, her green eyes darting back and forth between me and the race track. She had tied her copper and gold hair back with a green scarf and it gave her face a taut, stretched look, her cinnamon skin tight around her high cheekbones.

"Your hands, Forrest. What about your hands!" Anna shouted over the din. "You shouldn't be driving. You'll hurt yourself. You'll kill us."

"I'm only using my fingertips. See?" I twirled the wheel back and forth as we came out of the hairpin sending the car into a series of slides back and forth.

"It's hard to tell," Anna shouted, "whether you are childish or just stupid," starting to smile in spite of herself.

"Probably both," I said. Vito was grinning, showing gaps between his teeth. He was wedged between us and I put his hand under mine on the gearshift, so he could feel the moves from gear to gear and feel the transmission of power rise and fall.

We were going anti-clockwise around the Vallelunga track because the two turns at the far end were more like Lesmo One and Lesmo Two at Monza that way. The Vallelunga curves didn't have Monza's bone-breaking kerbs and they didn't have the slight banking in Lesmo One and they weren't as fast, but there were similarities. They were two nearly ninety-degree turns in quick succession with the first tighter than the second and a short straight between. Like Lesmo One, coming into the first turn you are accelerating so hard in fourth it is difficult to judge your entry speed. And like Lesmo Two, coming into the second turn, you are going so fast it is difficult to get your turn-in point exactly right. A couple of feet one way or the other and you are going to run wide or hit the apex too soon. Unlike Lesmo One and Two at Monza though, there is plenty of room at Vallelunga if you get it wrong.

We exited out of the second turn, throttle to the floor, the Ferrari flat out. Not bad, I thought, patting myself on the back, to have so much mental capacity left over when you are only going nine-tenths.

But that wasn't it at all, that wasn't even a half-truth. The truth is that last tenth takes as much effort as the first nine put together. And the last hundredth, that is where the serious driving begins to separate the men from the boys, and where you cross over into the border country, where the building blocks of time you play with are down to a thousandth of a second.

A wailing in the distance reminded me of another Evers' law: patting yourself on the back means you've only got one hand on the wheel. In one instant he was in my mirrors and in another he was past, a flash of blue and white disappearing down the straight. Guido was warming up his car and it was time to pull in.

I stopped the car just outside the paddock entrance. "OK, Vito, you drive us into the parking lot. I'll show you how to shift into first."

Vito was out of his side of the car, running around the front and holding my door open for me. When I took Anna's place in the passenger seat, Vito was already sliding his seat forward, blipping the throttle, getting the feel of the car. I said, "The first thing you do is push down the clutch. That's the pedal on the left."

"I know all that shit," he said, snapping out the clutch and spinning the rear wheels. "I stole plenty of cars."

Chapter 18

"What was Rossella like?"

"She was like a dancer. You know how a dancer moves? Very serious, you know, solemn sometimes, with her feet sticking out. You know how a child, when the child is trying to do something adult, like pour a pot of hot tea, is very serious? Like that, sometimes. I think she got that from the nuns, I don't know. But probably she was just sad from being locked up for so long. Sometimes she could be really goofy. You know, funny. She was just a girl."

"You said you loved her."

"Oh, love." Anna dismissed the word with a toss of her head. "I don't know about love, Forrest. I mean I say that I loved her but we fought too, like sisters. Like tigers sometimes. I mean she wasn't so serious all the time. Once she put a frog in Guido's salad. That was before either of them knew she was adopted. And he hit her. I think he hit her a lot. But there were afternoons, when I was visiting Guido, a few months ago, and he would let me in to see her. The sunlight was coming in the window in the library and Rossella and I told stories like we were girls. Rossella loved to make up stories but they were cornball, you know, kings and queens and knights on white horses rescuing princesses. Kid stuff."

"Guido really locked her up?"

"He was furious when he found out her real mother was

a whore. I don't know what he was thinking. Maybe he thought if nobody sees Rossella he can forget about her. I don't know, but nobody could talk to him about it. Nobody could do anything about it.''

"But you were allowed to visit her.''

"Sure. After he found out she was pregnant. When she was pregnant, that's when I got to know her. I brought her some books, she liked books. But it was hard to find the right ones because she was, she was, I don't know the word I want, naïve. A kid. She was always really glad to see me. You know I lied when I said she was my sister, but it was like that, like she was my sister.''

"Stop crying now, it doesn't help.''

"OK. You tell me what helps. Tell me what helps Rossella. I am not crying just because of Rossella.''

"Why then?''

"You don't know anything.''

Later she said, "Can you move over a little? No, no, not that much. I can't kiss you,'' she said.

"Would you like. . . ''

"No, no. Just the way you are. That's perfect.''

"You sure?''

"Sure. I'll let you know if I change my mind.''

Outside the window above us the sun was low on the horizon, filling the camper with a soft and golden light.

"Wait. Talk to me first, Mr. Racing Driver. I feel so sad, talk to me about something I know nothing about, something unimportant. Something nothing to do with her.''

"Like racing drivers.''

"Oh yes, that is very good. You know Forrest, you're not so bad for a racing driver.''

"What's wrong with racing drivers?''

"Oh, I don't know. I mean I never . . . It's just that I imagine they are always looking for short cuts, ways to get to the finish line quicker. You know, faster, faster. Always the big rush. I haven't met so many, but don't you agree? Most of them are such wankers. And they have these big thick calluses.''

"From wanking?"

"No. I mean maybe that too, I don't know. But I was thinking about that when I was watching you and Guido out on the track before.''

"About calluses?"

"Oh shut up. I was thinking that a driver who is any good, in some way has to grow a thick skin over his heart, because if he fears too much what could happen to him, he cannot go so fast.''

"Maybe. But I need fear, I need to feel it. Fear is the border between life and death. If I stay inside my limits, never stray into that margin of fear I know I'll be plenty safe. I'll never crash, I'll never win a race and I might as well watch it on television. If I want to be at all quick, I have to go faster than I think I can. I have to know what my limits are and then I have to push them out as much as I can and more. And that's when I start creeping into that border zone.'' I moved over to the edge of the couch. "But if I ignore it, you know, pretend I don't have any fear, I can go over the far eeeaaaeeedge.''

"Hey, come back here."

I pulled her down with me onto the soft carpet. "The difference between the good drivers and the slow ones is how wide that border is. You try to get your fear down to a thin bright stripe, like the edge of a knife, and you try to keep your balance there.''

"You see, you are a wanker too. You make everything so big-time dramatic when all you are really doing is operating some stupid machine. Stop for a minute, it's OK.'' She propped herself up on her elbows. "What I was thinking was different, not so much life and death stuff. I think because a racing driver doesn't care so much for himself, he doesn't care about anybody else either. He doesn't grow calluses over just one emotion like fear. He grows these

calluses over his whole heart and then he doesn't give a
damn about anybody.''

"Like your brother.''

"Yes, like that, only do it slowly. No, no, let me show
you. I mean yes, maybe like you, I don't know if you give
a damn about anybody. I'm not so sure about my brother.
Yes, I guess Guido has a hard heart. Maybe he has to be
so tough to be the world champion. Maybe that's why he
makes so much money.'' She lay back down again.

"You think rich men are lousy lovers too.''

"Probably. Could be. I don't know. What's that got to
do with anything? I'm only twenty-three, Forrest, I'm not
an expert. I don't really know anything. And I don't like
to think of my brother in bed, it puts me off.''

"What about his money?''

"What do you mean, 'what about his money?' ''

"I mean where does his money come from? How did he
get to be so rich?''

"I would like to know. Maybe I could be rich too. I
think he works very hard. But he is generous to me.''

"He doesn't tell you?''

"Forrest, it is rude to talk about money. Especially now.
Didn't your mother ever tell you? You should be talking
about love.''

"My mother always talked about money. It was her favourite subject.''

"I think maybe his, my, our father was very, very rich.
I don't know. Yes I would. Like to know. Where Guido.
Yes. But not so hard. Forrest, you are rocking the motorhome. Everybody will see. Everybody will know. Everybody will see. Everybody will know. . . ''

So we began, conventionally enough, the way foolish men
and foolish women do, ignoring the terrible risks and all
the compelling reasons not to. Ignoring the big red stop
signs the conscience and convention post along the way.
You would not believe me if I said we were mourning

Rossella. You would say we were selfish and obscene. And we were.

But listen.

Listen for a moment. You and I may mourn in our own and different ways. But there is a common sound, as regular as a heartbeat. In every mourning, there is an undercurrent, faint at first and then embarrassing as it grows. Embarrassing or not, it grows. In the sadness and the loss, the heart begins its little tin drum tap tap and grows deeper and stronger until it booms. What begins as the slow toll of the bells becomes a ding-dong celebration of life like a New Orleans Jazz Parade on the way to the mausoleum.

"How would you feel about going to Sicily for a couple of days?" I said into her ear.

"I'm not going anywhere," she said, her voice warm and lazy. "Sicily?"

"I had an uncle who went there. Everard, Bishop of Norwich. It's an old family story."

"Your uncle is a bishop?"

"In the twelfth century. The Normans invaded Sicily six years before the battle of Hastings. . . "

"When was that?"

"Anna, that's the most famous date in English history. Every English schoolboy knows that."

"I am not an English schoolboy."

I looked at her lying on the soft leather. Soft copper and gold hair for ornament here and there, cinnamon skin, green eyes alive with imagination and intelligence, nipples so pale they were almost translucent, and that astonishing wide and sensual mouth, a mouth made for exaggeration. "Not an English schoolboy" was the understatement of the year.

"Time for your English schoolboy lesson," I said, running my hand down her long, knobbly spine.

"The Normans invaded Sicily in 1060 and England in 1066. So there was plenty of contact between England and Sicily. Especially around a hundred years later when England was divided over Thomas à Becket on the one hand, and King Henry II on the other. Becket, who was the Archbishop of Canterbury and head of the Church in England, wanted to keep the Church separate and Catholic. Henry wanted his own Church. Both camps, church and state, sent envoys, emissaries, ambassadors, whatever you call them down to Sicily to see if they could make an alliance with Normans in Sicily who controlled the Mediterranean. It was early power politics.

"Then, as every English schoolboy knows, Becket was assassinated and the Church made him a saint. There are statues and shrines to him all over Sicily. Henry did penance and claimed he was innocent, nothing to do with Becket's assassination. And eventually Henry managed to get his ten-year-old daughter Joanna engaged to William the Good, King of Sicily. King Henry sent my ancestor, Everard, Bishop of Norfolk, down to Sicily to make the arrangements for the wedding."

"He have a nice trip?" Anna's voice was slurred and sleepy.

"Well, his diary said, 'the mountains vomit flame, the land devours its inhabitants, and the stench from the rowers in the ship makes me sick.' So I don't think it was a day at the beach. But he must have done all right. King William of Sicily sent twenty-five ships to meet this little ten-year-old princess at the mouth of the Rhone. When they arrived in Palermo, it was at night, and William met her at the city gates. He put her on his finest horse and escorted her to the palace, with the city lit by torches. One of William's courtiers wrote that 'the stars in the heavens could scarcely be seen for the lights.' Joanna married William the Good on the eve of St Valentine's Day and when she grew up she was the Queen of Sicily."

"I don't understand. You want to go to Sicily because of some family fairy story?"

"I am going to Sicily because I think that is where Guido's money comes from."

"And if it came from God you would go fly in the sky to chase the clouds. Forrest, why are you so hard on my brother? Guido hasn't hurt you. The only thing he has done to you is to go faster than you. You can fix that. At Monza you go faster, end of problem. And if you don't, so what, the world will go on."

"This doesn't have anything to do with that."

"Tell me."

"I promised Rossella I would look after her child. I told her I would see that he gets his inheritance. The other part of it is that she told me the same thing that you did. She said Guido would kill the baby if he could. I can't ignore that."

"He is Guido's son, not yours. Do you even know what his name is or where he is?"

"Sure I know his name. But it doesn't matter. I promised Rossella."

"Rossella is dead. You see, it is just like I said. A real fairy story. No, no it is worse than that, it is bigger, more spectacular, more stupid. It is opera."

"I don't have any choice," I said.

"Forrest," she said, kissing my forehead as if I were a bad boy being forgiven, "I will come with you if you like. Wherever you want to go. For a couple of days anyway. But don't expect me to take you seriously."

Chapter 19

Palermo looks good from the air, ochre and cream with patches of green for the parks. From a distance it dances in the heat waves alongside an aquamarine sea. Down on the ground, standing in a frying pan would have had more charm. Palermo Raisi airport was an unfinished construction site and the air conditioning had shut down, exhausted.

There was a long queue quietly pushing and shoving to get past the two policemen who were too hot and too bored to care about a British-American racing driver carrying a British passport. But they roused out of their doze and put a half a thousand people on hold to question Anna.

You couldn't really blame them. Anna wasn't pretty enough to be on the cover of a magazine, but there was a freshness about her face, a kind of innocent scrubbed look that, combined with the sorrowful look in her eyes, and that sad clown mouth, made her look vulnerable, as if she needed protection. Well, she had her vulnerable sides. She worried about flying, worried about the weather. "What if it rains Forrest? I don't like the rain." She worried that nobody liked her and that she had forgotten her passport. She worried that her clothes were wrong and that she looked too tarty.

She looked like a backup singer in a pop group and when she was by herself she looked lost. Men were constantly offering her a seat, their coat, advice, a newspaper, anything they could lay their hands on as an excuse to talk to her. She wore a lime-green cotton top that stopped short of her navel, a short white skirt with the leather American deck shoes that everybody in Italy under the age of thirty-five was wearing that year and nothing else. In the land of the long black sack dress and the black scarf knotted under the chin, where mourning seems to start at birth, she stood out like a poppy in a corn-field. Where was she staying and how long, and was there a phone number, the policemen wanted to know. She smiled sweetly and made up answers.

Only one carousel was working and all the luggage from all the flights, including a holiday charter jumbo from Frankfurt, was heaped on it. I tried to push through the crowd of hot, impatient passengers struggling for their luggage, and Anna said, ''Relax, Forrest. Why are you in such a rush? Sicily has been invaded non-stop since God dropped it in the sea. Phoenicians, Greeks, Romans, Vandals, Ostrogoths, Arabs, Saracens. And your stupid Normans. And then there were Turks, Germans, Americans and even Italians. There is always room for one more.''

I doubted it. The far side of customs was another sea wall of stalled humanity. Past their heads the traffic had stopped in front of the terminal. Buses, trucks, taxis and a swarm of tiny Fiats blew their horns in frustration. I couldn't see what was holding them up, but I imagined it was more buses, trucks, taxis and wall to wall etc. The air smelt of diesel fumes, sea and pine trees with a garland of garbage.

There was nobody at the Hertz counter. The man at the Europcar counter next door said the Hertz man would be back ''probably in a little while.'' I looked at Anna and incredibly she was smiling happily. ''It's very good we have come here. I feel at home here.''

''Fine, let's pitch a tent.''

''Don't be such an old dogface. I was a little girl here, you know and it is almost like home to me. I can feel it in my blood. In a little while, we'll be by the sea. Then you will be cooler and the sun will cheer you up."

We waited probably a little while, gave up and rented a Fiat Uno from Europcar. Anonymity, I thought, counts. And you can't get more anonymous in Italy than a blue-grey Fiat Uno.

By the time we had our luggage in the car and were headed out of the parking lot, the traffic had built up enough pressure to force whatever had been blocking it out of the way. Palermo's airport juts out into the Mediterranean with just one road running along a causeway carrying all the traffic in and out. So we could see the sea on our left, blue and sparkling and refreshing, tantalizingly out of reach as we staggered along with the halting, crippled, stop and go gait of modern traffic.

At least, with the windows down there was a breeze. We told ourselves we were just two tourists, down for some sun and holiday. Reflected upside-down in a pair of binoculars or telescope. Or, more likely, in the eyes of some anonymous man or woman in black at the airport. They will see us, Anna said, long before we see them. Vito had said the same thing and I assumed it was true.

Anna said.

Anna said she had studied journalism at the University of Bologna, but two years after graduation she was still freelancing. She had a few credits for articles in the Milanese newspaper magazines; an Italian vice squad from the point of view of the hookers and an interview with the Central Social opposition minister for education which gained half a page in a Milano daily. She said.

But she had never taken the time to hound the editors with ideas for stories. Because newspaper editors don't assign feature stories these days, she said, they accept them. Or, more often, reject them. Which made her think of going into PR, since most of the feature stories in the newspapers were written by PR agents anyway. And they were better paid. So this trip to Sicily was just, she said, what she needed to keep from "sinking into Public Relations."

She had contacts. It had taken her less than two hours, using the phone in the motorhome, to find two assignments for Sicily. One was an Italian tourist's eye view of the Sicilian wine country for a small glossy Italian food magazine published in Rome. And another was background for a major story on the Mafia planned by Milan's leading paper. Not big assignments, and they wouldn't pay her expenses. But it was a start, she said. A "kick start," she said. "Maybe get my career going again. Maybe meet Him."

"Him" was her father and he kept making special guest appearances in her conversation. "It's like when you are missing an arm or a leg," she said. "When it is gone they say you can still feel it, like the nerves are still there. OK, I know I don't have a father but I can feel him as if he really was out there. Don't worry, Forrest," she said, putting her hand on my knee. "He's my ghost. He won't hurt you."

As we turned onto the motorway to Palermo, picking up speed, Anna sat poring over the map on her lap, pursing her big lips, tracing her finger along the red and blue lines of the roads.

"The Autostrada stops when we get to the city," she said, "but there is a peripheral road around it. Maybe we can avoid the traffic."

And maybe it will snow in Palermo in July. The motorway was fine while it lasted. The peripheral road was not. Some freak flood of two-, three-, four- and ten-wheel machinery, a tidal wave of rubber and steel had dumped all the vehicles of the western world into Palermo, blocking the drains. We couldn't go forward, we couldn't go back, all we could do was wait and inhale the fumes. Occasionally twenty yards of clear road opened up.

"What are you doing? You'll get us killed," she said.

"I was stopping for a red light."

"What, you never drive in Italy before? In the south of Italy red lights are optional. You almost got us rammed from behind. Let's get off this terrible road, turn right.''

''That's a one-way street.''

''Sure, but it's only for one block. Nobody's coming. I thought you were a racing driver.''

''Yeah, but there's a cop standing over there.''

''That's a Vigile Urbano and he doesn't give a shit. Come on, I'll teach you to drive Italian. 'Forte con i deboli, debole con i forti,' '' she said. Strong with the timid, timid with the strong.

We dived into the dark maze of Palermo slums, blocks of flats towering overhead, the light coming down in shafts, the noise of the traffic and the shouts of people echoing above us like a dim and ruined underground cathedral. We zig-zagged down the crowded streets, trying to make our way parallel to the peripheral road, squeezing past buses, going up on the kerb and the wrong way down one-way streets. After ten minutes of a lot of effort and not much progress we turned the wrong way down a one-way bus lane towards an oncoming bus. ''Time to be timid,'' I said and drove into a dead end alley. The bus stopped at the mouth of the alley and the driver was kind enough to lean out his window to give me a lecture on advanced Italian driving techniques.

So we returned to the relative peace and quiet of the peripheral road, inching our way around the city.

''Maybe it's not so bad, going slowly. I have to tell you, Forrest, I'm worried.''

''Not about the traffic?''

''Don't be stupid. No, I just have a bad feeling. Creepy, you know? Probably it's just being in Sicily.'' She paused for a moment, looking out at the wall of tenements. ''No, it's not that. It's going to see these Mafia, these Vini Cristalli people. It's not good.''

''What makes you think these people will be Mafia?'' I said.

''I don't know. It's a possibility. Everybody in Italy is Mafia a little. We love our family. We have contempt for outsiders, and everybody is an outsider,'' she said, giving me a hard look. ''The law is an obstacle, you know, something to get around, never obey if you can help it. But this is playing, this is cose all'italiana. In Sicily it's different. In Sicily there is the real Mafia. Not the guys in striped suits carrying violin cases, but very, very rich international businessmen. Let me tell you.''

She shifted in her seat, her hand resting lightly on my arm. ''The article I am working on is about the link between the Mafia and the Medelin. They think maybe there is a deal where the Mafia distribute cocaine for the Medelin in Europe and the Medelin buys heroin from the Mafia to distribute in their markets in America. Heroin sells for $70,000 a kilo in Italy and for $300,000 in New York. With cocaine it is the other way around. Cocaine sells for $15,000 a kilo in New York and $65,000 in Italy. So they make a lot of money just moving it back and forth. They estimate Europe consumed almost twenty tons of heroin last year.'' Anna kept turning to look at the bleak tenements lining the road and looking back to me so I could see her anger and her frustration.

''You don't have to deal with them,'' I said.

''It's not a question of that. You don't have a choice.'' Her voice was angry, rising. ''What the Mafia says is that they are only supplying a need, you know, giving people what they want. But what they do is the pusher says to a kid on the street, 'Here, I'll give you a nice hit for nothing. You don't like it don't worry about it.' They do that to children. The children don't know you don't get something for nothing. Except addicted. They say that fifty per cent of children who try crack are addicted on their first dose.

''And the bastards shit in their own backyard. We have almost half a million heroin addicts in Italy now. That's around three times as many as there are for the population in America. Oh, and Naples, poor Naples. You want the figures? I have them here. Naples has over fifty thousand heroin addicts now. You walk down the main shopping street and you have to be careful you don't step on a used needle. So don't have any illusions about the Mafia being romantic or Robin Hood. They are bastards and they ruin the reputation of my country. They are killing my country's children.''

"I didn't know you felt so strongly about it." We were finally moving, the road opening up again after a half a mile of bumping along in the dirt through a massive construction project. I couldn't tell if they were rebuilding the road or just digging it up.

"Yeah, well, you don't have so much to be smug about. There are a quarter of a million heroin addicts in Britain and that number is increasing by twenty-five per cent a year. Here, you read these, you see what I mean,'' she said, pulling out a sheaf of notes from her handbag, thrusting it at me.

"I'm driving," I said.

"No you're not, you're parking. Look, there's a gap there. A bus could drive through it." As she spoke a scooter snaked through a closing gap between two cement trucks.

"And you haven't answered my question," I said, slipping the car into neutral for the several thousandth time.

"What question?"

"Vini Cristalli?"

"Oh. Yeah. I don't know. A feeling. Maybe I'm just being crazy, maybe they are just businessmen. You start looking for Mafia and you think everybody you see is 'a man of respect,' you know? But these Vini Cristalli people, they have so much money. They were Guido's sponsor from the beginning, from way before I knew him. But I don't think they are going to be glad to see us."

"Come on, Anna. They'll be delighted. You are a reporter doing a story on wine for a fashionable Roman magazine. That's good PR. I am a famous racing driver. Guido's teammate. They can brag about my visiting their factory to their shippers."

"In Sicily, nobody answers questions. And only the fools ask them."

"Is that another one of your Italian sayings?"

"No, it's not funny. It is just the way it is. Omertà, you know omertà, the code of silence? It means to be a man and it comes from being invaded so many times, I think. Sicilians are suspicious of outsiders. Everybody is suspicious of outsiders but in Sicily it is an art and a religion. And it doesn't help you if they know you. They are suspicious of their neighbours. I mean if you had been raped for two thousand years what would you say to the nice man who asked you the way to the beach?"

Chapter 20

Once out of Palermo, past the gypsy camps, past the dark men by the side of the road selling used and stolen car parts and the rows of desolate tenements landscaped with dirt and trash built by the Mafia with the first flushes of their drug money, the Autostrada skims along the sea towards Cefalù and Messina and the countryside softens and the hills are covered with orchards and vineyards. We turned off at Artale and looped back underneath the motorway and drove up into the hills towards Chiavelli. Chiavelli, as on the labels, ''Vini Cristalli, Chiavelli, Sicilia.''

The hills were green and soft under the bright blue sky. The air was fresh and we drove on a narrow, winding, concrete road through vineyards and orchards. Occasionally we would come up behind a little motor scooter with a flat-bed on the back heaped with dirt, tools and bags of fertilizer. But except for those wobbling and screaming little farm carts, there was no traffic. Here and there a little road coiled off leading to a cluster of farmhouses. The land felt green and peaceful after the fury of the stalled traffic in Palermo. Anna and I had two days, three at the most if I flew from Palermo to Milan on Thursday morning and hired a helicopter to the track at Monza.

My thought had been to look for the source of Guido's money. Or at least a source. One that might be a little less well guarded and could lead to other sources. Find one

stream and maybe I could find the source of the river for
Aldo, Guido's son. My responsibility. A hopelessly long
shot, a "hairy brained idea," as Anna said. But it seemed
more promising than doing nothing.

Anna walked the hairy brained idea another step. "OK,
suppose we go to the headquarters of Guido's largest personal sponsor, Vini Cristalli. Maybe they have a young
marketing manager and if I talk to him for my article,
maybe I can get him to tell me something about how they
promote Guido . . . who his contacts are, what they paid
him and what he does for their money. Nobody ever asks
marketing managers what they do," she said. "So maybe
he might tell us something. You never know."

As it turned out, Vini Cristalli was not heavily into pro-
motion, as they say in PR.

We couldn't even find it. I thought there would be signs
saying "Visit Our Caves" or "Fattoria Cristalli, Visitors
Welcome." Something to encourage the fools to rush in.
But there were no signs and we could not find it.

Sicily is so heavily populated that what look like little
villages on the map turn out to be gloomy concentrations
of tall blocks of flats and one-way streets. We wasted more
time circling in and out of Chiavelli until I parked the car
and found a couple of men having "corectos" (coffee cor-
rected with a shot of Italian brandy or digestivo), who knew
where it was. It was "that way," one of them said with a
slight nod of his head. I asked how far and he nodded his
head back and said something like "tut." Evidently he had
already said more than he meant to. A real Sicilian
blabbermouth.

So it wasn't easy, but at least we had a direction and
eventually, six kilometres outside Chiavelli, we found a
large concrete building set back from the road surrounded
by vineyards and guarded by a high barbed wire fence.
There were no signs saying Vini Cristalli, but there were
several tall, green vertical holding tanks and several large
tanker trucks. Evidently the harvest had not come in yet

because the place looked deserted even though the gate was open.

We drove in and pulled into one of fifty empty parking places and as I turned off the key there was the sound of a door shutting. I rolled my window up and was about to get out of the car when there was a rap on the window. I rolled my window back down and a man with dark curly hair and a white Armani T-shirt and pleated chino trousers and a new oxblood belt said, "Yeah?"

Anna leaned across me and stared up into the man's face. "I'm doing an article for *Vini Vici*," she said, "and I wondered if I could have a look around the fattoria, possibly talk to your PR officer?"

"No."

"We'd just like a look around," I said. "Maybe talk to somebody about your wines."

"You can walk around, but there's nothing to see. Park outside the gate."

"Can't we talk to anybody. Like the manager?"

"You got an appointment?"

"Sure," Anna lied, "my magazine rang up. Here's my card. I'm supposed to interview the manager. I talked to somebody in PR. She said she'd arrange it."

He was twenty-eight or thirty. Short with thick curly hair, long in the back. His eyes were deep set and there were creases around his eyes that relaxed. The expression of mild irritation drained from his face as he listened to Anna who was giving him her most vulnerable, worried smile. He looked bored, but there was something else. "You're fulla shit," he said.

I started to open the door and Anna stayed my hand. His face was perfectly still but his eyes were moving, taking inventory. "I must have the date wrong," she said. "I'll ring up my office to check." In a whisper she said, "For Christ's sake, Forrest, get us out of here."

The car started on the first turn of the key, I backed up to head out of the gate. He was standing where our car had been, his eyes glittering in the sun. I gave him a friendly wave.

On the way out, a hundred yards from the fattoria and just before the main road, a little Piaggio farm scooter, heaped with pruning from the vines, blocked the road. The road was raised on a dirt viaduct above the vineyard so there was no getting around the Piaggio.

I stopped and we both got out. Anna gave a worried look back to the factory but our new friend was out of sight behind a screen of bushes. The scooter's handlebars were rusted and grimy and the black horn button was polished with years of use. It made a sound like a strangled buzzard. I pressed it again and a head of grey hair, a neck of cords and creases, stooped shoulders, emerged from the vines, holding more leafy green twigs. The old man scrambled up the bank, dumped the cuttings in the Piaggio and said, "I saw you go in."

He was almost as tall as I am, his dry skin hanging loosely from his bones. His face was heavily grooved and as dark as if it were carved from a beam over an old fireplace.

"So you blocked the road," I said.

"You noticed," he said.

I waited. "A rentacar from Palermo," he said, looking at the licence plate. His voice had a heavy rasp. There was a pause while he looked across the vineyards to the factory. He had dignity and he was not going to be rushed. Which was fine with us. We still had three days and nowhere else to go except back to the airport. We waited.

"You work here?" I said.

"I just come here in the winter for my health." Then he produced a big wide grin. His favourite joke. We smiled with him. "What are you looking for?"

"We wanted to talk to the owners. I'm doing an article about Sicilian wine for a magazine in Rome," Anna said, pushing her sunglasses up to the top of her head.

"The owners," he said, and spat on the ground. He fished around in a pocket of his black trousers and pulled out a rumpled packet of Nazionali and offered them to us. No, thanks very much. His fingers, groping for a cigarette squashed inside the pack, were wide and blunt, black lines of dirt mapping the cracks in his calluses, his nails split and chipped. He pulled a cigarette out of the packet with delicacy, holding it between his thumb and forefinger. Then he found a match, lit his cigarette, inhaled, and studied our faces, savouring the blue smoke, letting it out slowly.

"If you want to know about Sicilian wine," he said, "you don't want to talk to the owners. They'd sell horse-piss if they thought they could get money for it. Anyway, they're not here, they never come here now. When the harvest comes they send out a couple of assholes from Palermo. In the spring they send out some Dottore di Vinicultura, some young man who knows more about insecticides than he knows about wine." He took another drag and a long appreciative look at Anna.

"They only press the juice here now, and truck it into Palermo. They got some factory there . . . Uditore, Altorello . . . one of those places. Somewhere. I don't want to know. But wherever they do it, they don't know about wine. If you want to talk about wine you should talk to Ambrogio Pagano. He built this factory. He knows about wine,"

"Ambrogio Pagano?" I said, making it a question.

The man reached under the seat of the Piaggio and brought out a grimy wine bottle half-full of red wine with a cork stuck in it. He pulled out the cork with his teeth and held the flask out to us, displaying long, yellow and wine-black teeth in invitation. We took a sip to be polite and it was thick and sweet and had enough alcohol and acid to dissolve your vocal cords in a single swallow. It was a wonder he could talk at all. We told him it was good wine. And he agreed and then he put the cork back in. It was precious stuff, no point wasting it. "Ambrogio Pagano," he said, "he knows."

• • •

Ambrogio Pagano knows how to handle a shot-gun.

His house was fifteen kilometres away on the winding roads. It wasn't numbered, and there was no name outside, none of the houses have names or numbers. But the rusting steel gates, painted a faded blue, padlocked with a chain, and the long white drive leading up to a simple concrete house with a vineyard in front were just as the old man described them. We drove up to the gates, got out of the car and called out "Signor," to a man in dirty brown shorts and a torn T-shirt bent over his vines, half-way up the hill. The man scooped up a double-barrelled shot-gun that had been lying on a blanket next to him and pointed it at us. He was fifty-five yards away so it probably wouldn't have done much damage if it was, like most Italian shot-guns, loaded with birdshot. On the other hand, if he had loaded it with rifled slugs he could get lucky and blow a hole the size of a birdcage through each of us. We smiled brightly as he walked towards us. "Buongiorno," Anna said. "Ambrogio Pagano," I said. The two of us were smiling like toothpaste ads.

"Who the fuck are you?" he said. He stopped ten yards away with the barrels pointing up just slightly, around chest high.

"I'm doing a story on wine," Anna said. The gun stayed pointed at us and he came closer. From a distance of five yards the barrels of a twelve-gauge shot-gun aimed at your chest look big enough to crawl into.

There was a pause.

"An old man, Odoardo, said you might talk to us," I said.

"He said you used to own the Fattoria Cristalli."

The man lowered the shot-gun so it was only pointing at our knees. He looked puzzled for a moment, then he smiled. "Odoardo? How is Odoardo?"

"He makes terrible wine. And he sends his greetings to Ambrogio Pagano."

He shifted the shot-gun to his left hand and let it droop, barrels pointing down to the ground, and he shook his head as if there was something he hadn't expected, something he didn't quite believe.

He was about fifty with a wide paunch, the legs of a mountain climber and a face that looked as tough as an olive stone. He wiped his forehead with the back of a thick, sweating wrist leaving a streak of dirt. Then he reached into the pockets of his shorts, found his keys and unlocked the padlock. "I'm sorry," he said. "It's been a while since I've had visitors. I've lost the knack of hospitality." He swung open the gate. "Ambrogio Pagano. Padrone of the vast Pagano estate," he said, sweeping his arm to indicate the half-hectare in front of his house, and smiling to make sure we appreciated the irony. "Come up to the house and I will pour you a glass of wine you will remember." We walked up the steep drive of white crushed rock, blinding in the hot sun, and entered the lower half of the house into the dark cool shade and spilled-wine smell of a wine cave. There were crates of empty bottles neatly stacked, two large stainless steel vats, a press and a stainless steel centrifuge. The walls and floors were whitewashed and spotlessly clean. Ambrogio Pagano walked past them without looking at them and led us up the stairs and into his house.

"Alessandra," he said softly as we emerged in a light and spacious room. Light blue tiles echoed the sea on the floors. The room had a sparse and rustic feeling, a few ancient pieces of leather and darkened oak furniture, and floor to ceiling windows overlooking the valley and the hills beyond. At the same time there was the feeling that each item had been chosen with care by some member of the family several generations ago. There was a porch outside the windows that served to keep the sun from pouring in.

A pretty, slender woman, who could have been in her thirties but might have been more, wearing an aqua-blue woven silk blouse and lime green trousers, sandals and silver bracelets came out of a doorway and her hand flew up to her throat at the sight of us, making the bracelets jangle in the still room.

"It is all right," he said to her, "they are all right. Odoardo told them I know something about wine."

She recovered in an instant and reflected his warm smile. "I am sorry," she said to us. "I do not have the honour to know your names."

Chapter 21

Ambrogio went off to shower and change as Alessandra led Anna to the front window to point out a cluster of towers on a distant hill. "You see—" Alessandra pointed—"that tower on the near corner, the one on the right. I can just see it if I squint, but maybe your eyesight is better than mine. I used to climb up there to the top when I was a girl and pretend the hills were full of handsome princes, slaying dragons. And that one of them would come up and rescue me from the dreary pile of rocks and take me away someplace wonderful like New York City. I was a pretty dopey kid. But now, from this distance, I look out at it and I like to think of it as a Fairy Tale Castle."

"I had a friend who used to dream of living in a Fairy Tale Castle," Anna said.

"Well I can tell you living in a real castle is no fairy tale. Not that one, anyway. It is a terrible old place to live. It was built by the Normans to keep an eye on the peasants below and I don't think the Normans cared very much about things like heat and plumbing. It was cold in the winter, and terrible to keep up. My father was always saying my mother and I would have to go out and pick grapes so he could get the roof fixed. So maybe I should be glad we don't have to do that any more, to keep up that old pretentious pile." She looked down at her sleeve, finding some stray fluff, whisking it away.

Then she saw me and rolled out a long hand towards a chair. "Please sit down, I'd like to think you feel at home. May I call you Forrest? It's not a name I have heard a man called before in English. Forrest is an English name, isn't it?"

"I think it was my mother's idea of an English name. She was American. But you're right, it sounds a bit wooden in English."

"Well, you English had your Twiggy, didn't you. 'Forrest' opens up a whole new possibility for English names. How about a butler called 'Hemlock'? No, he'd poison the sherry. Or yes, I have it. How about 'Walnut'? Fetch the tea, Walnut," she said with a little laugh.

Anna said, "What about 'Spruce'? Don't you think a little boy called 'Spruce' would be adorable?"

I smiled, woodenly.

Then Alessandra turned back towards the window, looking out at the distance as she must have done every day for as long as she had lived in the house. When she spoke the humour was gone.

"Of course we didn't build our castle, we took it. We took it a long time ago. The Normans built it and my ancestors moved into it one night and cut the bastards' throats in their sleep. So I suppose if you want to be picky you could say we didn't own it. Never paid for it, we just lived in it for centuries. But I cannot tell you how much I hate the thought of those ignorant bastards living there now, showing their pornographic movies. They took everything. And then they had the gall to sell our things to antique dealers. I was supposed to be grateful for the few sticks they let us keep," she said indicating the furniture behind her.

She went over to a sideboard and made a show of opening a bottle of "Ambrogio's little stiffener," pouring the wine into tall hand-blown crystal glasses and calling out to Ambrogio to hurry up before we drank all his wine. She took Anna by the hand and said, "No one comes here now and I have to say I am very glad to have your company. It is very good for my Ambrogio. He gets so depressed.''

"You never go back there?'' Anna asked. Alessandra let go of Anna's hand and looked back across the valley at the castle.

Alessandra shook her head, no. "Although you never know,'' she said, her face brightening, "maybe one night we'll sharpen our knives and sneak in the back door.''

Ambrogio appeared, drops of water on his forehead and his hair slicked back from the shower. He poured himself a large glass and went over to the window, holding his glass up to the light. He was transformed, in white linen trousers, a voluminous white shirt that billowed out like the sails of a galleon, Gucci loafers that had seen hard service but still took a shine, and no socks. He looked like the captain of his own ship on a holiday cruise, a little faded and a little out of date, but still the captain. His glass, like ours, was shaped like a tall old-fashioned balloon, infinitely fragile and with a bottom wide enough to hold a quarter of a bottle of wine. The wine was a deep and clear ruby against the blue sky outside, catching the light and sending a few faint rays of red sunlight into the room.

"You see how this comes naturally to me, entertaining visitors over a glass of wine, making pleasant conversation while we look over the countryside and consider the pleasure of being alive. Forgive me if I ramble on like an old man. Well, I am an old man. But I am also in your debt for giving me the opportunity to do this again, just for a moment to pretend it is like the old days.''

Ambrogio took a deep sip of his wine and I joined him in a toast to our good health. Just a sip, I told my conscience.

Ah, there are sips and then there are sips. Ambrogio hadn't exaggerated, it was a wine to remember. A wine for celebrations. A big, rich, powerful, and infinitely smoother aristocratic cousin of Odoardo's tooth dissolver, loaded with clean black cherry flavours that filled the mouth with fruit, as they say in *Vini Vici*. Followed by a light and pleasant finish that disappeared without a trace, making you wish for more. I wished for more. But I put my glass firmly down cursing the limitations of my profession. It's not enough to train as hard as any professional athlete. You have to practise denial every waking moment. And the pundits say that speed gives you a heightened sense of being alive. The pundits don't know a goddamn thing.

Ambrogio put his wine glass down on the white marble window ledge, looked out over the countryside and continued. "Odoardo was my Capo di Produzione. He was a farmer, but you should have seen his farm. I swear the goats lined up in rows and saluted you when you went past, he kept it so well. So I asked him to come work for me and he did. And like we do in Sicily he liked to feel he had a little extra, a little something to make it worth his while. And I told him, 'Odoardo if you are going to steal my grapes, steal the best ones. Steal the dark ones, the Nebbiolo.'

"Odoardo steals the best grapes, the Nebbiolo, but he won't age his wine. He is too impatient. He says he is too old to wait." He took another sip. "I brought the Nebbiolo grapes here, I planted them. They said the Nebbiolo is fine for Barolo in the Piedmonte in the north on the mainland, but the sun is too hot in Sicily. And I said, 'If you know how to irrigate and to shade the vines . . . ' "

"Ambrogio, I think our guests are more curious about the new owners."

"Forgive me. I sell a little wine now to a couple of restaurants in Lyon. The French appreciate a good wine and these Frenchmen are not 'friends of the friends' so I don't have to deal with the bastards, the 'men of honour' scum. I suppose I shouldn't complain. They kept their part of the bargain, so far. Although I think the reason they let me live was that I am just too damn much trouble to kill."

"Who do you mean 'they'?" I said.

"The men of respect. The men of honour. The parasites they call Mafia. It's an old term, Mr. Evers, 'Mafia'. Everybody will tell you where it comes from but nobody knows for sure. There are many theories; Freemasons in a Sicilian fishing village at the end of the eighteenth century, the bandits who fought back against the Moors . . . there are many, many stories. My favourite is a witch in the Inquisition they called 'Catarina la Licatisa nomatta ancor Maffia'. Which maybe you could roughly translate as one with audacity, power, madness and arrogance. That's the way the bastards like to think of themselves."

Another sip to drain his glass. "But it's all just folklore, PR that adds a shine to these shit-eating bastards."

"Ambrogio, please."

"Forgive my French. I think the term Mafia comes from Garibaldi's red shirts, the young men who hid in caves called maha in Arabic. The locals called them squadra della Mafia. But it's all folklore. Folklore," he said looking out the window. "I will tell you the reality."

He went over to the sideboard to open another bottle. The handle of his corkscrew was made from an old twisted vine and his powerful forearm pulled the cork with the ease of an accountant lifting a pen from his suit pocket.

Anna held up her glass as he poured, looking at him. He was breathing hard and there were dark circles under his eyes. He poured himself another glass, tasted it thoughtfully and went back to the window to sip his wine and look out over his vineyard down to the road and his eyes went to the deep valley on the other side and the green hills in the distance.

"When Alessandra and I married we combined our families' estates. This was not a great deal of land, not all of what you see, but a good deal of it. Most of the vineyards you see out there are small individual holdings. But our estate, Alessandra's and mine, was large enough for us to decide, as the largest grower in the area, to decide to take the big step and start our own label. A big decision, but we took it.

"My idea, and I will forgive you if you laugh, was to compete with the great estates of the Piedmonte. What the hell, if you are going to aim, aim high. We organized the local farmers, helped them with their viniculture, showed them how to grow the right grapes and we built the fattoria. We had to borrow heavily to do it, to buy the equipment and the trucks. But we had some success.

"That was our mistake, success. We were written up in a Naples paper. And we got a steady contract with a few restaurants in Rome, Naples and Milan, as well as Palermo, Messina and Catania. So we started to make a little money and I spent it on new machinery and a fleet of new trucks. And one day I got a phone call saying that somebody important was interested in buying my business. Would I care to name a price? I said no, I had no interest in selling. Which was true. As far as I was concerned I was just beginning. I planned opening several factories, producing a whole line of fine wines. I knew we could do it. Then one day, a worker tells me one of the big fermenting vats has gone bad.

"Wine is a living thing. It can get sick, but very often, if you know what you are doing the sickness can be cured. What we found was that there were over a hundred rats drowned in the wine. So I not only lose a third of my production that year, I lose my reputation. If you hear a man has dead rats in his wine, how do you wash that away? It doesn't matter that you steam clean the vat. It doesn't matter what you do, once the story gets out, your wine is spoiled. To everyone who has heard the story, your wine never tastes good again.

"This is harassment. This is terrible harassment. I think this is the worst and if I can get through it I can get through anything. So at the time it felt like a catastrophe, but it is not enough to make me sell. When a man comes around a week after and tells me he is sorry I am having trouble, maybe if I took a partner, an 'adviser' he called it, I would find business easier. I tell him not to come back. The next autumn, when the harvest begins, they stop playing pranks.

"I was in my office at the time and my phone rang from one of the farmers and he says that one of my trucks has come off the road and is in his field and it doesn't look good. It was Tonino, his vineyard was not far, about five kilometres away. So I jump in my car and two other men come with me; Giulio, who was a young scientist, an oenologist down from Milano to do his doctorate on fermentation and we put him to work. And Odoardo.

"He, this Giulio and Odoardo are with me in the front seat. And we drive, I drive, not in a big hurry because I think we are going to have a pig of a time getting the truck back on the road and worse we are probably going to have to offload all the grapes and load them back on again. And when we get there, and I see the truck with its nose in the dirt I know it is worse than that. I know it is bad. It doesn't look bad, the truck is upright and it hasn't spilled any grapes but I know it is bad. I walk first and Odoardo is behind me. The field is very quiet and there is no sound. Nothing. When I walk to the front of the truck I see the windscreen has been blasted away. I look through the windscreen and I see a bloody mess. I climb up on the front bumper to see better, but I cannot recognize the man. His face has been blown away and what I can see is the bones of the neck, the bones of the neck and there is no face, just a mess of blood and bone. Odoardo opens the door and from the clothes he recognizes that the driver was his son, Massimo.

"That was five years ago and today is the first time I have heard a word from Odoardo. The first time he has spoken to me since that day. All right, he didn't speak to me directly, but he sent me his greetings and I am very moved by that. That is why I opened my gate to you." He paused for a moment staring into his nearly empty glass then continued.

"After that day, no driver will deliver grapes to me. I don't blame the drivers. You can't ask a man to get shotgunned in the face just so you can make wine.

"When the bastards call me on the phone, they say they would be willing to pay a little for my factory but not much because now it is no longer a working factory. I still tell them no. I still imagine I can fight them. And for a year, my factory is abandoned. Nothing. And the farmers come to me and ask me why am I being such a bastard? They are starving. They cannot sell their grapes. Nobody will truck them. And even if they deliver the grapes nobody will buy them.

"The bastards call me again and they say they are tired of being polite. My two little girls are at school and they name the school and they say the school is not safe. They say there are savage dogs nearby, Rottweilers, that are badly treated and not well fed. They say that my wife will suffer a cosmetic accident. That was the word they used, 'cosmetic.' They say if that doesn't work then they will blow my head off. They are not subtle. And none of this is a new story. They have taken over hundreds, maybe thousands of businesses this way.

"If I go to the police the Mafia will set the dogs on my children. And there is no point in going to the police anyway because there are Mafia in the police. I used to believe that I was a strong man, Signor Evers. That I could make my own life. Maybe I was strong before. But it doesn't matter whether you are strong or weak in the end . . . you sign the papers for the factory, for the land, for the rights, for everything. And they say, 'Good, fine, for that we will let you live.'

"What would you do, Mr. Evers? Don't worry, don't pull a face like that. It's not a question you have to answer because it doesn't matter what you do. It doesn't make any difference what you do because the result is the same. They walk you down the line step by step and the more you resist them the more they use you as an example to keep everybody else in line. This is my country Signor Evers. We have been making wine here for three thousand years. My family has had an estate here since the records began and probably before. Eleventh century at least. And I am ashamed to tell you there is nothing I can do about it.''

He paused for a moment. ''Are you sure you wouldn't like another glass of wine?''

Signor Pagano walked us down the long drive to his gate, the late afternoon sun throwing our shadows across the rows of grapevines. He unlocked the chain to let us out and locked it again. ''What was the name of the man you talked to, the one who offered to 'buy' your business?''

Ambrogio looked around him as if he were checking to see if anybody was listening. ''He never said his name. I never asked.''

''But you must know a name, the name of the man who was behind it.''

''There are a lot of names. It's a big organization and they come and go. And sometimes the same man uses several different names. But I remember one, I think the name of the Capo dei Capi was DiSanto; Giambatista DiSanto.''

Holding the bars of his gate, he watched us get into our car and gave us a smile and a wave as we drove off.

''Come back soon,'' he said.

Chapter 22

It was the time in the Sicilian autumn afternoon when the air smells of sage and hawks circle in the sky and the only sound in the hot fields is the buzzing of the cicadas and the bells of a herd somewhere miles away, grazing.

We were driving slowly, through the vineyards, taking our time on another twisting single lane concrete road, heading back towards the Autostrada.

"I think we should revert to Plan B," Anna said.

I pulled over to the side of the road and stopped. We got out of the car and Anna leaned against it. The valley fell away and spread out for miles beneath us with the mountains rising up in the distance. It looked as orderly and as peaceful as a children's book and it was hard to believe that it was crawling with snakes. I reached across and pulled Anna to me for a long salty kiss. A man could get lost in that mouth.

"Plan B," I said eventually, "was only if we didn't find anything."

"Plan B," she said, "was always the real point of this trip as far as I am concerned. To get away. To rest and relax and forget before Monza. Swim in the sea. Find the good restaurants. Lie on the beach. We might even get to like each other." She looked away, across the valley. At the nape of her neck, where her hair was pulled up, there were little beads of moisture from the heat. I leaned forward and kissed the back of her neck.

"We know now," I said into her ear. "We know that there is a connection between Guido and the Mafia. And we know the connection is G. DiSanto."

"Christ," she said turning to me, furious. "You don't know a goddamn thing do you? Vito is right, you really don't. You think the Mafia are some local gangsters who bully local farmers. They are not some little local gang. What we are looking at here is just the tip of one claw, Forrest. They are the largest business in Europe, bigger than Ford, bigger than Fiat. You find that hard to believe—let me give you a couple of figures. And I don't have to look at my notes, ask anybody, they'll tell you something similar. Just the Sicilian Mafia, forget 'Ndrangheta' in Calabria, and forget the Camorra in Naples . . . you know what the editor of my paper told me for my article? He told me the Sicilian Mafia took in thirty billion dollars in drugs last year. Thirty billion *dollars*, not lire. Six thousand dollars for every single person in Sicily. They can buy anything they want, Forrest. Anybody they want. And the only answer they have for people who come sniffing at their door is to kill them. Kill them, maim them, ruin their lives. What are you going to do? Who are you going to tell?" she said, her voice rising out over the valley.

I put my hand on her shoulder to calm her and it had the opposite effect. "You big dumb stupid idiot. You give me a little lesson every English schoolboy knows. Some stupid fairy tale that ends up some little English Princess gets to be the Queen of Sicily. Let me give you a lesson every Italian schoolboy knows. You think maybe there is something glamorous, something honourable about the Mafia. They are called men of honour because they have the honour to have killed somebody. You are not accepted until you kill somebody. Think about that. The more you kill, the more respect you get. And they don't kill neat, they make a big mess.

"Most of the people the Mafia kill just disappear. They call it the white death. The ones they want to make an example of they kill on the street in front of everybody. They blow you up so they find your foot in the middle of the street and a piece of your face on a window ledge three blocks away. They can blow up anybody, they don't give a shit. You know about Dalla Chiesa?"

"What Dalla Chiesa? Look Anna, I can't just walk away from this," I said, but Anna went on as if she hadn't heard me.

"You don't know about Dalla Chiesa? OK, listen then, I will tell you this lesson, what every Italian schoolboy knows. This was a few years ago, 1982. There is a Mafia war in Palermo. They are fighting for who is going to control the international heroin and cocaine and there are killings almost every day, sometimes several a day in Palermo. The killers roamed the streets on big motorcycles. They left corpses with no heads in cars at the railroad station, bodies were dumped in front of police stations, burned in the streets. And Andreotti, the Prime Minister, says it has got to stop. And he appoints a very distinguished General, General Dalla Chiesa of the Carabinieri to be his special Prefect of Palermo, to sort out the Mafia in Sicily. He grants Dalla Chiesa special broad powers. Special broad powers that are never made into law; they never arrive these special broad powers, but that is another story.

"Dalla Chiesa is an honourable man, he is a national figure. He is the head of the Carabinieri in Palermo with the special backing of the Prime Minister.

"The Mafia don't give a shit. Dalla Chiesa has a beautiful young wife who comes to pick him up at the Prefectura one evening. And two big motorcycles follow them from the Carabinieri headquarters. In the old city where they are going to dinner, Dalla Chiesa and his beautiful wife are ambushed by eight men with Kalashnikov machine-guns in the Via Carini which is narrow and they can't turn around, they can't get away. The men empty their guns into his wife first. Then they shoot Dalla Chiesa rapid fire with enough bullets to kill twenty men. Then they stand there and shoot more bullets into the car just to be sure. Nobody comes to help him. Nobody does anything. Then the eight men get in their car and they get on their motorcycles and they drive away.''

She was shaking, breathing hard. I held her by the shoulders and said, ''It's all right, Anna. Relax. I'm not doing anything more than what you are doing researching an article. I may be taking some risks, but so are you.''

''Sure,'' she said walking around to the other side of the car. She leaned her chin on the roof of the car, looking at me, green eyes against the green vineyards behind her. ''Some risks because it is a worse risk to do nothing. But let me tell you, if you want to knock down a hornets' nest you do it with a long stick. You don't go sticking your face in the nest. Forrest, please, let's stick to our Plan B. Let's go to a nice hotel, have a nice dinner. Tomorrow go to the beach, maybe visit a couple of wine growers. We'll have a nice holiday, I'll do a little research with the Guardia for my articles and then you can go back to Monza and play with your racing cars. Or do you want to go back to that Cristalli Fattoria and see if they have something else to tell you? I mean think it through, Forrest. Where would you begin?'' She got back in the car as if there was no answer to that.

''You are afraid,'' I said to the top of the car, ''of finding your father.''

Five minutes of silence later, Anna was leaning her head on her arm out the window with her face in the breeze as we headed back for Palermo. The name DiSanto was bound to be a coincidence, but if this DiSanto was Guido's father, then he probably would sponsor his son through the corporations he controlled.

Father, son. Father, daughter. Guido told Rossella that he would kill his son if he could find him. He told Anna her father was dead. Anna didn't believe him, she was still looking for her father. And I was playing surrogate father to a child I wouldn't recognize if he fell in my lap. It made me think of my first memory of my father, reading his paper in his green leather chair by the fire, the flames making our shadows dance on the high walls in that old and cold stone house in Norfolk, his trouser leg warm in my hand, the cold draught on the back of my legs.

"Whose little boy are you?" he said peering down from the side of his newspaper. His face was a landscape of crags and he had bushy eyebrows above gold-rimmed glasses and he terrified me. "Not bloody mine," he said, drawing the paper back across his face. My mother scolded him for that at dinner, but he said what did she expect after taking so long to "bring me around" for him to see. "Bring me around" meant crossing the Atlantic Ocean from New York in freezing, seasick December.

I was thinking of that cold Christmas in Norfolk and I was half-watching the hawks circle overhead and half-watching the road when, coming around a sharp turn, I had to brake hard and spin the wheel and skid to keep from hitting a little grey Fiat Panda that had overturned in the middle of the road. We stopped about five feet from it. It was lying on its side, showing us the black tangle of pipes and wires on its underside. One of its rear wheels was still spinning.

I bounded out of the car to see if anybody was hurt; if anybody was injured inside. Two heads rose up from behind the car, one curly, one sleek. I stopped and they walked around from the back of their car, one of the men reaching out casually to stop the spinning wheel. They looked relaxed, in no hurry and one of them had an Uzi pointed at me. They stopped.

"It's nothing to worry about," one of them said, "but we'd like you to come with us." They were both dark, well dressed in casual summery pinks and blues, wearing polished American loafers and in their early twenties, about five foot seven or eight.

One of them had a long sharp nose and deep set eyes in a delicate face and his black hair was combed straight back. He said, "You mind getting out of the car, miss? I'd like you out here in front where I can see you." The other one had a softer face, round cheeks with a full, mamma's boy mouth and big soft brown eyes with long lashes, and a full crown of black curly hair. He carried the Uzi and he never took his eyes off me.

Long Nose said, "Don't fuck around. Don't fuck around and you'll be just fine, OK? No problem. First, help me roll the car back on its feet." The one with the soft and gentle eyes held his gun level, pointed at me, while I walked over to the car, put my hands on the roof of the Panda and pushed. It didn't take much, the car rolled back on its tyres with a little bounce, as if it had done its little trick of playing dead many times.

Long Nose motioned me back alongside Anna and opened the door of the Panda and pulled out a mobile phone. This was the second time in one day we had a gun pointed at us and I can report that you do not become more relaxed with practice. The black hole of a barrel of a gun pointed in your direction saps your dignity, your strength and your will. It makes strong men anxious to please. No wonder diplomats love them. Saves all the bickering.

Long Nose spoke a dialect I did not understand into the phone, although one phrase was clear enough. "Depends on the traffic," he said.

Chapter 23

Palermo is a fine old corpse of a city. Here and there, there are traces of the rich, lush and beautiful tropical lady she once was; vast abandoned villas surrounded by palm gardens and guard dogs, dark cathedrals glittering inside with the gold mosaics of the Saracens and the Normans. A spume of green palm fronds behind a high wall. But the fallen body of Dame Palermo is beyond mouth to mouth resuscitation. The façades of the grandiose public buildings (built in the days when Palermo controlled an empire rather than vice versa) are cracked and split, exposing the bones of plaster and stone underneath. The streets have been pounded back into the rubble they were made from and the air is fogged with the fumes of a million swarming Fiats.

Up close, face to face you have to admit, most of Palermo is dead now. Although the screaming of the cars trapped inside gives her a kind of buzz of afterlife.

We joined the swarm on the godawful peripheral road, the Viale della Regione Siciliana. It was worse, even more clogged than when we were on it before. The air was peppered with the grit and chatter of air drills and the traffic had to squeeze into one lane from both directions. We waited, crawled a little and waited some more. Evidently the Mafia does not enjoy special traffic privileges. I was in the front seat alongside the man with the delicate face and the long nose. The man with the soft eyes and bushy curly hair sat in the back with the Uzi barrel resting lightly against my spine. Anna huddled in a kind of crouch in the seat alongside him. She had not said a word since we'd stopped for the car overturned in the middle of the road. Although, when we were stuck in the fumes and noise of the stalled and endless stream of traffic, she reached forward to lay a hand on my shoulder. I reached over and laid my hand on top of hers and we rode that way in the tiny Fiat for some time.

Our motoring companions didn't seem to mind. They didn't make threats or pull faces, they didn't have to. Opening the door and rolling out into the traffic would leave Anna in the car. Even if I could pull the door handle before the hand on the trigger squeezed. And if I called out to a uniformed policeman, a Vigle Urbano who dodged by us on a Vespa, if he heard me, what could he do, if he cared to, except get shot. From the outside we were just four people jammed inside a Fiat in a herd of Fiats with people jammed inside. I wondered if these men had killed before or if they were anxious for the opportunity to move up a rank with their first brain spattering. Or if they had killed so often it was just a job. They said nothing to us and acted as if we didn't exist. We were just cargo.

In ten years, Vito could be just like either one of them. I remembered my advice to him, that he was going to have to help himself, and I felt a jolt of guilt. Big, fatherly, helpful, hero-driver Evers, extending his empty, patronizing hand to the needy. "Help yourself," I'd said, as if he could. Sitting in the front seat of this car with a gun barrel in my back I had more free choice than Vito did, even though there was nothing I could do but wait and hope.

I wasn't really worried. I was sure it would turn out fine, it always does turn out fine, doesn't it? I had often wondered what held men still in front of firing squads, or why some poor souls went to the gas chambers without making at least some last gesture of escape. Now I knew the answer. Hope. Like my friend Ullett says, what kills you in

Hollywood is hope. I sat still in the front seat, anxious not to jostle the gun in my back, and hoped.

If . . . No, not "if," when. When we got out of this I promised that I would do more for Vito than give him the benefit of my fatuous advice. I could talk to him, tell him how to tell the sharks from the pussycats at the dinner table and when the left front wheel was losing grip at 185.

Christ, I didn't know anything worth telling him. But I could buy him some decent clothes, take him to a race, get him into a school. He brought me out of my thick hard shell. I knew how it felt to be cut off from your parents, cut off from anybody that gives a damn. Under that tough-guy bluff there was an exceptionally bright kid. The least I could do was tell him. Talk to him.

The metal dashboard in front of me was scratched. Somebody had ridden in my seat with their feet up, the soles of their shoes scraping the paint. Had he been bracing himself, frightened with a gun in his back, or had he just been along for the ride, admiring the countryside?

We turned right. Three blocks and ten minutes later a tiny blue and white sign high over a sidewalk café told me we were on Via Cappuccini.

Ten minutes down Cappuccini and we turned left, down a quiet little side street. After three blocks the side street ended in a courtyard in front of a wall with a church half-hidden behind. We stopped, the driver nodded to me and before I got out of the car, Anna leaned forward and said, "Forrest, it's all right. Just relax and do whatever they say. Don't do anything stupid."

I got out of the car. Long Nose took his time getting out. No danger of me running while Anna was in the back seat. There were not many cars in the courtyard, and the sun was setting, giving the scene the rosy promise of sunset. He came up to me, facing the sun so he had to squint. "That door over there, behind you. You go first."

Three steps and I was out of the sun and into the cool shade. The door was an ancient, faded and pleasant blue against the beige wall, wide open, with a bored middle-aged monk in brown robes standing beside it. He didn't look up when we went past him, asleep on his feet. The passageway was lit by a row of single light bulbs hanging from a low ceiling. The floor was grey stone and the bare walls whitewashed with a bloom of mould showing through here and there. The air was still and humid and smelled of laundry soap. Long Nose stayed two steps behind me, our footsteps unnaturally loud as we followed the passageway down, turning left and right from time to time.

Another sharp turn and the passageway opened up into a long high gallery, its ceiling criss-crossed with arches. The red and gold light of sunset warmed the hall from windows set high up between the arches. Standing along the walls, on pedestals with their heads bowed there was a row of what I took to be men in robes, monks, praying.

At the far end of the hall, another man was walking towards me, the sound of his hard heels on the stone the only sound in the gallery. I walked towards him and as I walked I looked up at one of the praying men and found myself staring into the face of a corpse. His mouth was open wide in the frozen O of a scream, four teeth in his mouth still in place, his skin the colour of parchment, his arms crossed in front, one hand missing a few joints from the fingers, and the other hand broken off leaving a stump that looked like bone and sawdust at the wrist. These were not monks and no one was praying here, they were all dead, long dead, propped against both walls in varying stages of preservation and decay, their heads stooped forward as if they were on the verge of toppling over.

"Good afternoon, Mr. Evers." A short man in a wide-collar aquamarine shirt and cream linen trousers stood in front of me, tassels on his glossy burgundy loafers. He had a low forehead and chubby cheeks with a trim beard, his eyes merry little slits. "I know it's a little baroque, bringing you here, Mr. Evers, but I find these, ah, witnesses concentrate the mind. Walk with me a little." He held out his hand to indicate that I might walk alongside him. Long Nose had dropped back a few paces. We walked along under the rows and rows of the dead. As my eyes adjusted to the gloom I saw there were shelves beneath the standing dead packed full with more corpses stacked like logs. "If I'm not mistaken," the little man said, "this is your first time to Sicily. So maybe you don't know where you are."

"Some burial ground," I said, not sure.

"Let me explain to you," he said. He wasn't threatening, he was explaining. "In the old days, a hundred, a hundred and fifty years ago, a man of substance would choose his best suit and he would come down here and select himself a niche along the wall here. One that might be near enough to the entrance to reflect his prominence in life, but not so near as to commit the sin of pride so close to Judgement Day. And he might come down here on a Sunday afternoon wearing that best suit to stand on the niche that he had reserved for himself with the holy fathers to try out different poses, to see which one he liked best, which one conveyed his importance, maybe, or his sense of humour." The man mimed the poses as he walked, smiling.

"It was expected, nobody thought it wasn't respectable. You see, getting embalmed and put on display, it was a way his relatives could pay their respects to him, see him at his best, the way he wanted to be remembered. Except the preservation isn't always so good.

"So anyway this guy, he comes down here to try out the pose which is going to be his pose for the rest of time. And he wants to get it right, you know, try out a few he has in mind. Picture walking down here, Mr. Evers, say in 1890." We turned a corner to walk down another passage lined with frozen staring faces.

"You are going to pay your respects to your grandfather and you think it's all corpses; while you are walking past one of these characters waves, 'Hey Forrest, how ya doin'. It's me, your Uncle Luigi. You like the suit?' "

I gave him the smile he expected. I had been watching the chalk faces staring down. They wore a variety of clothes; black velvet suits with black velvet bow ties and tails must have been the height of fashion at one time in Palermo, worn with baggy ice-cream trousers. Some men wore brimless hats on their shrunken heads, like oversize upside down black saucepans, ready for a little socko comedy. The flailing arms and legs of some of them made them look as if they had been frozen in the midst of a mad whirling dance. Some had rakish scarves or the hoods of a holy father. Here and there the once fine trousers had rotted, split open and drooled an awful sawdust of crumbled flesh and bone. But it was their faces that caught my eye.

There are no first-hand reports of death. It would be nice to think that death is sometimes peaceful or at least painless. That truth is revealed along with large portions of forgiveness, understanding and beauty. And that there is rest at last for the kind, the shy and the suffering.

Or at least a fade to black.

At least a black sleep with no dream.

But all of the faces of these men were frozen in that wide open scream of horror, O, as if they had met death face to face and what they saw made them scream with the force of God or Hell blowing through their wide open mouths. O. A survey of their faces along both sides of the wall confirmed that their opinion was unanimous. I consoled myself with the thought that no doubt it was an atrophy of the jaw muscles that opened the mouth wide after death. Perfectly natural. And I told myself that time emptied the sockets of the eyes. They could not see me, could they. They were just the dust we leave behind. The little man had stopped alongside me, looking up at me and smiling expectantly as if he had asked me a question and was waiting for an answer.

The smile faded and he said, his hand indicating the men leaning forward along the walls, "These are my ancestors. They judge me. What is it that you want, Mr. Evers?"

"I want to talk to the Capo dei Capi. I want to talk to Mr. DiSanto," I said.

"A lot of people want to talk to him. Let me tell you something." His voice was quiet, reasonable. "You're a racing driver, you got a race at Monza in a few days. Go get ready for your race, Mr. Evers. Prepare, do whatever you have to do. I mean, normally, if you weren't Guido's team-mate and you were sticking your nose around, nobody would talk to you like I am talking to you now. You would not even see us coming. This is already a special favour. Normally, Mr. Evers, you could pick out your niche. Let me tell you, as a friend of a friend, just go away quietly, take that nice-looking girl with you and we can forget all this."

"I'm happy to go away. But first I want to meet Mr. DiSanto."

"You don't seem to understand. He doesn't want to see you here, he wants to see you gone. Which you can arrange or I can arrange. I'd prefer you took yourself away. I mean what's he want to see another dead man for? Besides, you think you're going to tell him something he doesn't know already? You want to see Mr. DiSanto you have to bring him something. You don't bring nothing to the party, you don't get an invitation."

"Tell Don DiSanto I can make him a prince."

The small man's face filled with creases for a moment. "That's a funny thought." Then his face smoothed. "You be on a plane tonight. Or go to a hotel, I don't care, go to the Palmes, they take a lot of tourists in there. Don't have dinner there, though, the restaurant is terrible. Catch a plane in the morning. Tonight, tomorrow morning, either way be out of here before I think of you again."

"I mean the real title. He could be a nobleman, a member of the aristocracy. Something to pass down to his children."

"What are you talking? He don't give a fuck about aristocracy. He's got fifty of them working for him. The aristocracy need him, not the other way around. This is not your game Mr. Evers and I am finished talking.''

"Tell him."

When I walked out of the passageway and into the square, I took a deep breath and the polluted night air of Palermo tasted sweet. The sky was dark blue going black, and the one car left in the lot was our Fiat Uno, sitting on the edge of a pool of light from a streetlight high overhead. The monk shut the blue door, with the clank and squeak of old wrought-iron hardware, behind me. I could just see Anna's head in the passenger seat.

"Are you all right?"

"I'm all right," I said.

"Some man drove our car in and they put me in it and told me to wait. They just left me in the car. They said to wait for you and that you would be out."

"I'm out," I said. "Let's find a hotel."

Chapter 24

The Grande Albergo delle Palme is an old and faded *grande dame*. But then if you want grandeur these days you'll have to take it old and faded. The new hotels and public buildings are too cramped by accountants and zoning regulations to lavish space on soaring ceilings, solid marble columns three storeys high and acres of mahogany and walnut to panel rooms with chandeliers and stained glass skylights high overhead, rooms that have no function other than to be sat in and admired.

Hot, frustrated, tired and stuck in traffic, Anna read aloud from the guide book, editing as she went along. "The Palms was once Palermo's most grand private mansion. When they turned it into a hotel at the end of the nineteenth century Wagner came to stay and orchestrated Parsifal in a room now named after him and Renoir came to paint the great man's portrait.

"But stories of faded grandeur are not what makes the Grande Albergo delle Palme famous. It used to be an old Mafia haunt and it played as large a part in shaping the modern world as Verdun, Versailles or Yalta." She turned the page as a large van backed out of a side alley and began the beginning of what promised to be a sixteen-point turn.

"Mussolini had nearly wiped out the Mafia. He didn't bother with trials, he just had them shot. The American Army, liberating Sicily in WWII, made the mistake of bringing back the Mafia to help them 'Fight Communism.' Once the Mafia got a little money in their pockets from prostitution, protection, racketeering, contract murder and larceny, the Palmes was their hangout. Lucky Luciano, another American export, had his own little screened off corner in the lounge, his 'little red room.' So naturally it was in the Grande Albergo delle Palme, that the Mafia held their most famous summit meeting in the 'Wagner Room' in 1957. Mafia chiefs from US and Sicily held a summit to organize the Cupola, their name for their multi-billion dollar international heroin consortium. The Americans, most of whom had been born around the corner from Palermo, in Castellamare del Golfo, were persuaded. . . . ''

"That's what it says, 'persuaded'?"

"Of course it doesn't say that. It says they 'agreed.' A little translation won't hurt you." She picked up the book again. "Were persuaded to ask the Sicilians to take over importing and distributing heroin in North America. And the Sicilians (after four days of bargaining back and forth what they would pay for it, who got a cut of what), said yes. Since then the Sicilian Mafia has never looked back. They have had their setbacks, gang wars and the occasional show trial, but they have opened the floodgates of drugs that keep the cities of the western world awash in crime. And make them the richest men in the world. The American Mafia are small-timers compared to the Sicilians. And they are afraid of them.

"One local capo in Brooklyn said, 'Hey wait a minute.' Said he didn't want to mess up his own neighbourhood by making addicts out of his friends and neighbours. Was it OK, he asked, if he just stuck with the extortion, numbers, murder and prostitution and didn't become a pusher, didn't fuck up his neighbour's kids?''

"Anna, the guide book doesn't say 'fuck up'."

"You drive, I'll read. Look, that street is empty, turn left."

"You read, I'll drive."

"OK, don't turn left. But you'd die of starvation if you were a taxi driver."

"And then?"

"Then?"

"Just read."

"That's what I'm doing. 'Don't worry about it,' the Sicilians said. And two weeks later they blew off his head with a shot-gun."

There was an opening in the double line of cars and I went for it. Made it. Fantastic. Brilliant. Ten yards closer to our hotel, the Grande delle Palme. Which, as Anna's guide book said, had a history of grandeur, corruption and decay. And like all great and ancient ladies she also had a certain faded style.

But not a lot.

We carried our bags into the vast reception rooms and waited for the one clerk behind the desk to sort out a group of Scandinavian tourists in drip-dry dresses and no-iron shirts. It had taken a Formula One racing driver, driving flat out, sometimes reaching speeds of three or even as high as four miles an hour, taking advantage of every available inch, careless of his own safety and the safety of his passenger, over an hour to drive the two miles from the Cappuccini Monastery. Several wrong turns onto one-way unmarked streets hadn't helped. There was no bellman to carry our bags up to the room.

It didn't matter. The bathtub was a huge old cast iron extravaganza. It was long and wide and gleaming white and had lions' paws for feet. The thick towels on the chrome racks were big enough to cover a dining-room table and before I had put the bags down Anna had both taps turned on full. It had been a long hot and grimy day and I couldn't shake the feeling that the mould of death clung to my clothes and my skin.

When I came in, my clothes in a heap on the floor behind me, the bathroom was full of steam, the bathtub was foaming with bubbles and Anna was leaning back in the tub, arms overhead, pink nipples like the bowls of upturned wine glasses, pointing straight out, stretching, with her eyes closed. I walked across the room to stand behind her and take her hands. Her eyes opened looking up at me. "Help," she said in a whisper. "There is a big naked man in my bathroom with an ugly weapon and he is laughing at me. Help." She closed her eyes again, I let go of her hands and she slid out of sight beneath the bubbles.

I went around to the other end, went in head first and found her underwater, first her ankles, my fingers sliding up in the slippery water feeling her calves tighten, and over her knees, and inside her soft and loosening thighs. I pulled myself along head first underwater and her thighs snapped shut around my head and squeezed hard. I brought my right knee underneath me, then the other, then one foot, then the other and reaching up to hold the tub with both hands, stood up, with Anna, perched on my shoulders still squeezing. I said "MMMMMMPH." I still couldn't breathe.

"I am very sorry," Anna said, half curled over my head, legs crossed behind my back, squeezing my head between her thighs, "but I don't believe we have been formally introduced."

I fell forward, plunging us into the bubbles and warm soapy water, sending a wave of water over the side, Anna screaming "Nooooo," and kicking wildly. From a distance we must have looked like alligator wrestling or two kids in a blender. Once I lost track of Anna and she suddenly rose up out of the bubbles and ducked me. And when we were out of breath, and half the water was on the floor, noisily making its escape through a big chrome drain, Anna wrapped her arms around my neck and her soapy legs around my hips and we began to move in slow time together, in the warm and slippery water, making waves.

Later I lay back against the tub and Anna lay back against me, her knees pink and cinnamon islands in the white foam. "Your hands are much better now," she said.

"I only used my fingers. The palms are extra." I held my hands up.

"Ugh. Disgusting. Were you frightened?"

"Only when you . . . "

She held me and leant her head back on my shoulder whispering in my ear. "No, no, dummy. In the Cappuccini, in the crypt. Were you frightened down there?"

"Not until I got back out in the parking lot. When I saw you, in the car, my knees were shaking."

"What happened?"

"In a way we were just two men talking. It didn't feel that threatening. The dead men on the walls were horrific but they were also dead. I mean when you look at them, you know you are going to die, and when you do you are probably going to look like that. You also know that they were alive once, and they were just men. So they didn't look that frightening. But rows of corpses up on the wall staring down at you don't make for wonderful company. And I thought maybe what he had in mind was to have Long Nose shoot me in the back and prop me up on the shelf along with the other corpses. I mean you don't know where the limits are."

"There are no limits, Forrest. None at all. You don't know these people. They are not normal, they don't feel what you and I feel. They are psychopaths. Please, I think we should leave now. Tonight. We can take a plane back to Rome, or I don't know where you want to go, London or Milan. I want to go back to Rome. Maybe, if there are no flights we can drive to Messina, take the ferry. I don't care."

"There's no rush," I said confidently, lying. "I did find out that there is a DiSanto. He could be your father, Anna. I think we should meet him."

She looked back over her shoulder at me for a moment then she reached between her legs and wrapped her hand over me as if I were a gear knob. "You have to teach me," she said, moving my cock up and down and back and forth.

"I know where first and second is. And third and fourth. And fifth. But you will have to show me how to put you into reverse," she said, pulling back sharply.

When we left the bathroom there were clouds of bubble bath on the walls and the ceiling and a soggy heap of towels hanging over the side of the empty tub. The cool air-conditioning of the bedroom made us shiver and as Anna reached for a terrycloth robe on the back of the bedroom door she noticed an envelope had been pushed under the door. She picked it up by the edges as if it might be a disease. Then she ripped it open. She read it and looked up.

"It says we are supposed to go to lunch tomorrow. They must have been watching us," she said, passing the little white piece of paper to me.

I picked up the phone and started dialling. "Who are you calling? The police? Forrest, for God's sake don't call those idiots."

"I'm ringing some lawyers in Rome. I have to dig up a title."

"Well, if you are going to be stupid enough to stay I better make some phone calls too."

Chapter 25

"The money," Signor Angelo Bondino said, leaning forward on his grey metal desk, "is a big problem for them." A grin spread across his wide, smooth face. He had a low hairline, deep-set eyes, and a wide nose that with his dark skin made him look more African than Italian. "There's too much of it to hide, so they spill a lot." Anna was asking the questions, taking notes, but he tended to direct his answers to me, and it was beginning to get on Anna's nerves.

"So what you do? You pick up the crumbs that fall off the table?" she said, holding her pen poised as if she expected an answer.

His office was a metal desk, a phone and three chairs surrounded by glass panels. Outside his little metal cubicle were twenty other little metal cubicles and together they made the dull, repetitive chorus of bureaucracy, a phone ringing on and on unanswered, typewriters halting along over forms that no one would read and where a single mistake would mean having to start all over again, printers screeching out pages of columns of numbers, computer fans adding their small electronic whine.

"You see, Signor Evers, we only have forty-two thousand men in the Guardia di Finanza to cover all of the financial transactions and all of the taxes in all of Italy. Italians, you may know, are not very fond of paying taxes. And our tax laws are complicated. And we are civil servants, not well paid. So what your friend, Signorina Bellini, is referring to is that not all of our Carabinieri have been totally immune to temptation.''

Anna made a little cluck of disbelief and turned to me as if Bondino wasn't in the room. "The Guardia di Finanza are notoriously corrupt, Forrest. The worst thieves. The last Chief General of the Finanzieri is in jail for a multi-billion dollar fraud,'' she said, dismissing the whole force with a wave of her hand. "Oil refining, something like that.''

Lieutenant Bondino pushed his chair back and stood up. It didn't make much difference to his height. "Signorina Bellini, I would remind you we, the Guardia di Finanza, most of us, are one hundred per cent honest. And we, the Guardia di Finanza, are the only ones, I repeat, the only ones who have success in investigating the Mafia.''

"What I wanted to ask you for my newspaper . . . '' Anna tried to interrupt. But she might as well have been talking to the desk. Bondino had momentum.

"We are the only ones the Mafia fears. You will forgive me, Signorina Bellini, before I answer your question I must give Signor Evers some background. You see, Italy is not a normal country. I'm not so sure what normal is, but whatever it is we don't have it in Italy. And we don't want it. Maybe the future will change that, I don't think so.

"Nothing in Italian finance is ever simple. Our stock exchange is the fastest growing in Europe. Insider trading, which is a big crime in your country, in Wall Street, all over the world . . . in Italy insider trading is OK, quite legal. The share prices are manipulated by the big boys like Mediobanca who usually control more than fifty per cent of the stock. And, on top of that, most of the dealing takes place illegally outside the floor of the stock exchange. And, on top of that, the state owns about sixty-five per cent of the companies in Italy, which means that sixty-five per cent of the companies are only mildly subject to the forces of the market and hopelessly bureaucratic. IRI, the state holding company Mussolini started, is the largest company in

Europe outside the oil companies and the ninth largest in the world. Then the big companies like Fiat and Montedison, Finivest, Benetton, they are privately held by families and there it is not easy for the Mafia to invest their money.

"You see what I am saying? In a pool with the very big fish of the state and the big fishes of a few powerful families and everybody else a very little fish, there is suddenly with all the drug money, another very big fish, the Mafia. They love to put their money into big business, and when they get the chance they do. They want to be members of the community, respected. And not just respected because they will blow your head off with a shot-gun if you don't kiss their ass, but respected as financial leaders of the community.

"Just now they are having a little Mafia war here in Palermo over who is going to be the financial leader of our community. Or something. To tell you the truth we don't know what this war is about, maybe control of the docks, we don't know. But there have been over fifteen murders, executions whatever you want to call them, these last four weeks and five fire-bombings within half a mile of here.

"Anyway, to return to what I was talking about, Italian law is quite restrictive about money leaving the country. Theoretically it is very difficult for them to invest abroad, so in Italy, they have tended to look for smaller local companies, of which there are hundreds of thousands. Ninety per cent of the companies in Italy employ fewer than a hundred people, and that has been a place for the Mafia to hide their mountains of money. But these little companies are little. You can only stuff so much cash into them before it starts to spill out on the street where we in the Guardia di Finanza can see it.

"So, excluded from the state companies, excluded from the large family companies, and from the companies outside Italy, the Mafia have opened up their own banks. With their own banks they can handle this cash flow, 'invest' in companies, and first and most important of all to them, they can wash the blood and the stink of death out of their money. Their banks give them some of the 'respectability' they want because they can become players on the stock market and now they have the satellite and electronic banking technology to leap over geographical borders.''

He looked back and forth at us. "I am sorry," he said. "I am making one of my speeches. Forgive me. Would you like an espresso?"

Signor Bondino made a show of pressing a button on his telephone, and then leaned back in his chair.

"You were going to answer my question," Anna said.

"Yes. Sure. I would be glad to. What was the question?"

"I wanted to know how much of their income comes from cocaine?"

"Seventy-six per cent. Fifty-seven point five per cent. Pick a number, I don't know. I don't know what their income is. Pick a number, thirty, forty billion dollars a year from drugs? You tell me. I keep reading numbers in the newspapers. Maybe their sources are better than mine, but I doubt it. All we can do is guess.

"You see the problem is, Signorina Bellini, that while we at the Guardia theoretically have unlimited access to all their transactions, they have put in some very sophisticated systems and we do not always understand their code. On top of that if there are, say, in any one bank, eleven thousand eight hundred transactions a day, and if one part of the Mafia, say the Mafia Coscia in Trapani has twenty-three banks, you have to know what you are looking for before you can find it. I am sorry, we have had some budget cuts, the service is not so good. I will bring you your coffee."

He went with a kind of half-bow, edging his way around his desk and out the door.

"I have the same problem," Anna said. "Unless I know what I am looking for I don't know where to find it. I mean it would be good to have some hard figures and some names. But I think he is just giving us the little waltz he gives all reporters who come asking questions. It's the modern equivalent of the Sicilian shrug, 'Don't ask me, I don't know nothing'.''

"I know exactly what I am looking for," I said.

Bondino returned balancing three tiny cups and saucers of espresso, tiptoeing behind us, holding the cups high and setting them delicately down on his desk with a sigh. "I don't know why it is not possible to get good coffee outside of Italy," he said, unwrapping a sugar cube and placing it in his cup being careful not to splash. He unwrapped two others, giving the coffee his full attention, stirring the concoction with a tiny spoon that seemed childish in his large fingers. He leaned forward over the cup with his large nostrils twitching, and sniffed.

Then he sat up with his back straight and lifted the cup in a mock toast and said, "What brings you to Sicily, Signor Evers?" before taking a tiny sip and putting his cup carefully down and leaning back to enjoy the hit of sugar and concentrated caffeine.

"We have another appointment in an hour so I will come to the point, if you don't mind. Can I speak to you in confidence?" I heard myself say. Speaking in Italian was leading me into the same baroque linguistic convolutions as the Italians.

"Absolutely. No one has to know what is said in my office."

"I think my co-driver, Guido DiSanto, is connected to the Mafia."

"What do you mean connected?"

"I mean I think his father is the head of the Palermo Mafia."

"Well, that may be. But what do you want me to do? So far, being a relative of a Mafia is not a crime. Which is just as well because if it were we would have to put a third of the citizens of Palermo in jail." He smiled at us, taking another tiny sip of his espresso. "A joke," he added, seeing our blank faces.

"What I want to know is where Guido's money comes from. If it is drug money, then his receiving it is a crime."

"Signor Evers," he said his face tightening. "I, like most of the men in my country, am an aficionado of motor racing. I follow Formula One. Ferrari is my middle name. And even if it wasn't, and I didn't, the newspapers, especially *La Gazzetta dello Sport*, have been full of stories about you and Guido DiSanto. And I appreciate that it must be, at your stage of your career, what is the word I should choose here, I want to choose my words carefully, with all due respect." He paused for a moment looking for his words on the scarred surface of his desk. He looked back up. "It must be, ah, disappointing to no longer be the fastest man on your team. But I am not a personal investigator. And I do not think it does you credit to attack your teammate in this way." This last was said with a righteous slap of his hand on the desk.

"That is not the reason," Anna said with a smile to let him know that there was more to this than he knew.

"Whatever the reason, I am a busy man, and I don't have the resources to chase after individuals. And even if I did, you would have to provide me with the name of his bank or banks, account numbers, dates of transactions."

"Anything else?" I asked.

"It would be a lot of work," he said, "even if you could give me all of that. It would cost me a lot of time."

"Still," I said, "the rewards would be high."

"I am well rewarded for the job I do."

I leaned forward. "I would be very grateful. Say two per cent of the proven assets you uncover."

Bondino looked alarmed. Then he leaned forward and whispered, "And what form do you expect those assets, I mean, what do you estimate they might be worth?"

"I have no idea. Fifty million, two hundred million, five hundred million. That's what I am asking you to find out."

"I'm very sorry but I really am much too busy," he said, sitting back again and reaching for a pile of papers.

"Dollars," Anna said, "not lire."

He looked up, the smile back on his face. "I see. Yes, well, if you would be kind enough to provide me with the information I indicated . . ."

Chapter 26

"How do I look?"

"Not as good as you did sixty seconds ago," I said, making a show of looking her up and down. "Definitely much worse now."

"Forrest, this is serious."

"Very serious. This is about the fifth time you've asked me how you look since we got in the taxi."

"Not too tarty?"

"Not too tarty."

"But sexy?"

"You look just like Daddy's Sexy Little Girl."

I've always wondered if there is any truth to the rumour that little girls secretly want to seduce Daddy. Looking at Anna I could believe it. Anna was wearing an Ungaro suit a few shades more coffee than her cinnamon skin. Nicely cut, with a shrinkfit miniskirt. Her ear-rings looked like antique ruby chandeliers, a touch of the Saracen glitter, with her gold and copper hair down to her shoulders for backdrop. Daddy's pouting little redhead girl was all grown up. Daddy, I thought, doesn't have a chance.

"What'll I say to him?"

"I don't know, maybe nothing. Meet him first, then see if there's anything you want to say. You might not like him."

"What difference does that make?"

It was a long drive out to Mondello, Palermo's mini Riviera. Mr. DiSanto would expect us around one, the scrawled invitation said. We crept out to the edge of the city stuck behind a number 12 bus which was exhaling hot oil fog. Our taxi driver evidently hadn't got to the part of the driver training course that included passing. Or maybe the bus was the only one who knew the way. Our driver was sorry, he said, but passing the bus was just not possible. This was a no passing zone. It was just bad luck, said the one law-abiding driver in Palermo.

"Don't you think you are just a little obsessive about Guido?" she said, taking my hand. "You don't really have to do this."

"It's nothing to do with Guido."

"Ah yes, you promised Rossella. For the baby," she said, dropping her voice a couple of octaves. "Now sit up, now beg, now roll over. Good doggy," Anna said with that wide grin, just having fun.

"She was your friend."

"She was my friend, like a sister, and you are being very brave for her. I just don't think you are being very smart."

"You don't have to come," I said. "You could stay in the car, have Fangio here take you to the airport."

"Of course I have to come. I am not coming for you, I am coming for me. You stay in the car if you want to."

We looked out the window for a while, at the trees in the park. "Who says the Italians don't read," I said. "There's enough newspapers out there for half of Europe." The roadside was littered with layers of newspapers deep enough to interest an archaeologist.

"That's not reading, that's romance. They're Italian curtains. Young people can't afford an apartment of their own so even when they are in their twenties they still live with their parents in some tiny little flat falling all over each other and there is no place they can make love. So they take their car, their father's car, they steal somebody's car and drive out to the park to stop along the side of the road and make love. They put the newspapers up to keep out the peeping Toms. You can play a game, sometimes, see who can see the most cars rocking.''

She paused for a while looking out the window and then she turned to me, ''What are you going to say to him?''

''I don't know. I don't have any leverage and he knows it. The only thing I have is the boy's title.''

''Rossella's boy?''

''I talked to the lawyers and they said the child inherited the title from Rossella and as his godfather I hold it in trust for him.''

''What, you are his godfather?''

''It's something Rossella fixed up with the priest. It's not just something she asked, I have a legal obligation.''

''You know what a legal obligation means in Italy? It means don't worry about it. There's still ten thousand claims for WWI pension claims in the courts.''

''I'm learning about the courts. The lawyers say if I bribe enough people, I can sell the title. Or give it away.''

''Sure, OK, you can do that. But that's terrible. It's not your title. It's like stealing from the baby. You can't do anything with that.''

''The lawyers said it would cost a few million lire to transfer it. Nobody cares about it.''

''OK, maybe nobody cares, but it is not yours to give away. It is the boy's.''

''What else do I have to bargain with? Of course it means giving away part of the child's inheritance. But you tell me, Anna, which would you rather be? A poor orphan with a title or a rich orphan with no title? Maybe a title might get you a few dinner invitations from people you don't like. But like it or not, money is power. Money is an education, doctors, food, clothes. A good house to live in. I don't want to give anything away, but if I have to make the choice for him I'll choose the money. If he wants a title he can always buy one later.''

We finally passed the bus, accelerated all the way up to twenty miles an hour and finally the road came out from behind Monte Pellegrino and we were at the beach. We drove along past rows of little beach huts. In the sea, swimmers, boats and inflated alligators were suspended on the glittering surface of water so clear we could see the golden sandy bottom.

The driver stopped in front of a high, cream plaster colonnade that looked like the entrance to Caligula's Funhouse. Two steps inside the columns and you forget about carnival comedy. Two steps inside and the entrance doesn't matter any more, the columns just fall right out of significance. For in September, when the sting has gone out of the Sicilian sun, the setting for the Charleston Terrazza makes it the most beautiful place in the world for lunch. They could serve peanut butter on palm fronds and it would still be the best.

For most of the year the Charleston is an expensive conservative restaurant adding a little class to the middle of Palermo where the rats in the back alleys swallow Fiats whole. But from June until late September the Charleston skips town and goes to the seashore at Mondello where it transforms itself into the Charleston Terrazza and graces a wide terrace outside the old casino and bath house, hovering just over the surface of the sea with the Aeolian Islands in the far distance. The Charleston Terrazza has the aquamarine sea for a floor, the deep blue sky is the ceiling and the crags of the mountains are the walls. The grandiose columns out front are just man's puny doorway.

We walked out on a gangway over the water, like boarding an ocean liner, and the maître d' led us through the grand hall and out onto the terrace, a mild breeze just ruffling the water so it glittered. The waiter led us through the islands of white tablecloths to a table at the edge. Don DiSanto stood up to greet us. He was in the shade of the umbrella over his table and sunny reflections from the water played across his face.

Normally I like it when gangsters dress up, they look like toads in ballet slippers. But he didn't look like a gangster. "Glad you could make it," he said, opening his palms to indicate the chairs at each side of him. There was nobody else at the table.

I had pictured some display of power. Something like a weak and sick old man, a little green at the gills, lifts a finger and a whole family is fire-bombed. But he didn't look like Marlon Brando with oranges in his mouth or Al Pacino looking off camera. He looked like what he was, a businessman. A very successful international businessman. A precision-cut grey suit, white Oxford button-down shirt, a conservative silk tie with mild, watery colours in a paisley pattern, and high-gloss oxblood loafers with the little tassels that middle-aged businessmen wear. A corporate golf-cart rider on the weekends. A tired and grey-faced businessman with lines on his forehead and watery eyes in the middle of his fifties who tried to look after himself, tried to be careful what he ate, tried to get a little exercise. But the business kept getting in the way. The business hung bags under his eyes when he wasn't looking and strapped on a little roll of fat over his belt. It must have bothered him because he kept pinching it when he thought nobody was looking. Well, every businessman has his problems, no doubt he had his.

The morning papers were full of the problems he might have. Full of what might occupy his voracious mind. Problems like: the local papers had been making a big deal over a few kids the Mafia had shot because the kids were witnesses. They didn't used to shoot children, but children had lost their exempt status. It was just one of those things. Some wiseguy, they take him at his home and his family is there, his family sees the action, so there's no choice. They have to take the whole family. Then everybody starts screaming, "child killers." "Baby rapers." That never should have happened. They should have put the bodies in the lime pits over in Trapani, in the sea. Something. And the crap they were getting from Bulgaria these days. When the communists were in power there was a bureaucracy in place, you knew who you were dealing with. Now it was a fucking zoo and they were shipping in crap. You can't make good products from crap. They had to shake out the line all the way back to Sofia, straighten out those assholes. There was no percentage in all those hard-ons in Salerno OD-ing. They were consumers. It was bad PR. Bad business. Every time some asshole ODs you have to win a new consumer just to stay even. So it doesn't add up. Nobody ever had to OD, not if the stuff was clean. He had personnel problems, he had supply problems, and he had production problems and now there was this war with the Cosca in Castellammare del Golfo. He handled shipping, he controlled the docks and if they didn't want to meet his price, if they wanted to try shipping product out of Trapani, fuck them. Fuck all of them. He would kick ass. He would solve his problems.

Or maybe his problems were on a larger scale. Just looking at him, it was hard to know where he fitted in the Mafia hierarchy. Maybe he was worried that the yen was falling against the dollar, or the effect of the entrance of East Germany and Poland into the European Common Drug Market. A whole new market opening up, but you couldn't just walk in without distribution and enforcement in place. You needed nationals in the field and they never knew how to walk through the fuckin' door.

Maybe something else was going through his mind. What he said was, "This is going to do you more good than it's gonna do me."

We sat down.

His eyes were sharp as razors, like he didn't care whether we were there or not. But as long as we were there, forget the other problems. While we were there we had one hundred per cent of his attention.

"How's Guido?" he said to me just to get the conversational ball rolling. "You're his team-mate. I hear you

don't get along. Like you killed his wife.'' He was a businessman, he didn't make conversation, he scored points.
And when he made points he had a little skeleton of a grin
that came and went.

DiSanto turned to Anna, speaking in an undertone, explaining, ''You see, you sit with me, people see you. They
respect you. They want to do things for you.'' Two waiters
hovered at the table. He waved them away.

''Guido's OK,'' Anna said, her hands in her lap like a
schoolgirl on good behaviour. ''He sends his respects.''

''What's this shit I hear,'' he said, ''he has a kid?''

''Guido hasn't told you?''

''Told me what, Mr. Evers?''

I looked around, changing the subject. I thought he
would get back to the possibility of a grandson. But I didn't
want to give him anything before we'd even started. ''I
thought you would have bodyguards,'' I said.

''I do. I have them all around me all the time. All the
time, a perpetual pain in the ass,'' he said, nodding his
head, slowly. ''It doesn't mean I have to eat with them.
Look around, take your time. If you see them, they're not
doing their job, know what I mean?'' His eyes ranged over
the other tables and the waiters, went to the casino behind
us and came back to me. ''Why are you fucking around
with my business Mr. Evers?'' He had a plate of shrimp in
front of him. He took a bite, and chewed carefully as if he
might be afraid of slivers of glass in the little pink and
white bit of sea flesh.

''I'm not interested in your business,'' I said, ''I'm interested in Guido's bank. I'd like some financial advice.''

''You came to Sicily for financial advice?'' he looked at
Anna with his eyebrows up a notch.

''Go to the top, I always say. I earn money in sixteen
countries. Not a lot by your standards, Mr. DiSanto, but
enough to want to keep some of it. When Guido was still
talking to me he said he never paid tax. He said he had this
very smart bank that knew its way around borders and

taxes. Guido said it was the same one that handled Vini Cristalli. I thought as long as I was in Italy it could be worth talking to this bank.''

"Forget the bank. What have you got for me?"

"Rossella's title.''

"That's it, Rossella's title? If I wanted a title, I'd have one. That's the first thing they want to sell, their fucking title. Guido likes that shit, but I never felt the need. You are who you are, you know? If people don't respect you, you got a problem.'' He lifted his right index finger a barely perceptible quarter of an inch from the white tablecloth and a waiter was taking the bottle of Cristal di Cristalli from the silver ice bucket and filling DiSanto's glass and putting the bottle back into the ice bucket, giving it a twirl before replacing the starched white napkin that kept out the sun. "Anyway I heard you had that, and that is not why you are here at this table talking to me. That title bullshit wouldn't get you a ride on the bus.''

He turned to Anna and he took her hand, just holding her fingertips. "You are here because Guido tells me you think I could be your father. You believe that? Half the bastards in Palermo think I'm their father. Who's your mother?''

"Was,'' Anna said. "She's dead. Her name was Anna, like mine. Anna Bellini.''

"A redhead, right?'' He looked at her closely with those sharp, indifferent eyes and no expression that I could read. Seeing the two of them side by side it was hard to tell if there was a resemblance. Maybe something about the shape of the eyes.

"Could be,'' he said, leaning towards her, inspecting her fingers. "I knew a lot of redheads, know what I mean? You tell me, what do you expect from me? You're grown up, I'm gonna be an old man before too long.'' He put Anna's hand down and took a sip of wine. "If I live that long. So what do you want, money? Forget money. So what? You want to play Daddy and Daughter, you want to act it out?

I'll give you some fatherly advice. You want some fatherly advice? Stay off your back.''

Then his head came back to me, to the unfinished business. "You want to do a favour for yourself, tell me. Am I a grandfather? Does Guido have a son? He told me about you. He says you are a stupid prick. But he doesn't say nothing to me about a grandson.''

"I don't know what you've heard, but Guido's never said anything to me about a son.''

He waved his hand, like shooing a fly off the table. "OK. That's all.'' He bent back over his plate; he'd asked his question. The audience was over.

Then he looked up again. "Wait a second, I got an idea. I'll give you the name of something better than a bank. You want financial advice this is the guy to see. He's also Guido's accountant,'' he said pulling out a card from his jacket pocket. "From what I hear it's not gonna do you much good. But you might learn something.''

He studied his plate and speared three shrimps on one fork. "By the way,'' he said taking a tiny bite. "I hear you wanted to see the Capo Dei Capi. You've seen me but you ain't seen him. Now piss off.''

He was starting to lean back in his chair, his head back, smiling a half self-satisfied smile. And it was like coming off the brake and back onto the accelerator, a flick of a move in a fraction of a second, my foot lifting off the floor, and just touching the tip of the front leg of his chair and gently lifting, keeping the momentum going, as if he had done it himself, my foot back on the floor as his arms waved for balance and he fell backwards into the sea. I jumped up, knocking the table forward, the shrimp and wine sliding away with the white table-cloth to crash on the floor as Don DiSanto did a backwards arm-waving cannonball into the water, sending up a wave of water onto the deck.

I am reasonably quick and I was moving fast but I was fourth in line to pull him out. So I waited with the others behind me. Some of them, including a teenage bus girl with short curly hair, had drawn their guns, looking for something or someone to shoot at. But there was no one to shoot at. For all they knew and for all he knew, he had just lost his balance.

A waiter and a soft, middle-aged woman in a purple silk dress from a table next to us were pulling him back up onto the deck, seawater running off him. They pulled him up, held him so his face was inches from mine. "Get the fuck out of here," he said, coughing. Spitting water onto the deck.

Chapter 27

"Will you stop looking over your shoulder?"

"Those two motorcycles are following us."

"If they're not, somebody else is. What the hell do you expect, Forrest? And what the hell do you think you can do about it? They are probably going to kill you and for all I know they will kill me too."

"Your father is not going to kill you."

"He's not my father."

"How do you know?"

"I know. What difference does it make how I know? And what do you care? He's a bastard. I know, that's all. Goddamn it, Forrest, let's turn around. We're not that far from the airport. We could make it."

"If we can find Guido's accountant, we'll have him."

"You'll have your face in the street. For God's sake Forrest, get this stupid taxi to turn around. Believe me, what you'll have if you find Guido's accountant will be an accountant. Terrific. What did an accountant ever tell anybody? You think he is going to tell you something? Nothing in Italy is that simple. And even if he decides to make you the one big exception in his whole life and he tells you something . . . or maybe you inject him with some magic truth serum or something and a miracle happens and he tells you everything, what difference will it make when they shoot you?" The traffic had stalled again and we were stopped in the middle of the park on the way back into Palermo. Behind Anna's head a Fiat Panda, its windows blocked with newspapers, was rocking.

"There's a taxi over there, headed the other way. I'll put you in it and he can take you to the airport."

"NO! I mean, no. I'm afraid to be alone, Forrest. And I don't want you to do this. Please, for me?" Anna's vast lower lip was sticking out and her face was starting to crumple.

"I don't think he could be your father either," I said. "He's got skinny lips."

Six blocks away from the address DiSanto had given us, the traffic was locked solid. We paid the driver and got out and walked down the broken sidewalks towards the sound of the fire engines.

When we turned the corner onto Via Candelai, they were cleaning up, trying to get the traffic to move again, trying to get a crowd of gaping pedestrians to move on. The street was a tangle of firehoses, rubble from the blasted building, and fire engines. Miraculously a computer video screen had survived intact, its dead eye looking up at us from a pile of bricks and charred and twisted fragments of office furniture. Looking up at number 57, we saw a piece of the building, about four floors up, had been blasted away. What had been a solid brick and concrete wall was now a curtain of smoke that blew away from time to time to reveal an empty bleeding socket where there had been an office. I read the name on the card DiSanto had given me, checked the address, and hoped that Salvatore Dellacroce was out somewhere enjoying his lunch. The front of the building was stained with water from the firehoses. Except for a few places where it was still smouldering, the fires had gone out, and through the wisps of smoke, you could see an open door, swinging in empty space, leading into a hallway.

"God damn you, Forrest, I told you. This is DiSanto's lesson for you. For you to learn something."

"This isn't just for us."

"Of course it's not for us. It's nothing to do with us. He just sent you here to frighten you. There's nothing here for us. Please, Forrest, let's get out of here. Take me home."

"Would you like to have a look, Signor Evers?" Signor Bondino was smiling up at me. He had put on his green beret with the yellow flame on the front, the John Wayne di Finanza. In his office he had the compromised look of a government clerk, apologies all around for giving up on life. But out on the street, his short figure had a presence. Out here, he was in charge.

"I didn't see you following us," I said.

"Difficult as it may be to believe, Mr. Evers, I do have one or two things to do beside follow tourists around our city. When an accountant is fire-bombed, I generally like to join in the poking around in the ashes. And, what a surprise, here you are. You do not exactly blend into a Sicilian crowd, Mr. Evers. Although I do admire your canary yellow pullover. Is it cashmere? I imagine it's visible for around five miles. By the way, did you have a pleasant lunch with Mr. DiSanto? I hear he went swimming."

"You have been following me."

"Not personally, no. But apparently you have attracted quite a devoted little fan club. Shall we go inside," he said, smiling at some joke I didn't see.

"Why don't you lead the way," Anna said to him.

The building had been evacuated and smelt of burnt wood and sweetened plastic. We followed Bondino up a stairwell clogged with firehoses and running with water. On the fourth floor, the firemen were still spraying a couple of smouldering spots, but most of them were packing up, talking on their radios, waiting for the signal to go.

"These are the days of overkill," Bondino said, looking through the doorway with the shattered door that said *Dellac . . . aglia, D . . . roce* on the remaining shards of glass. Down in the street people looked up at us suspiciously as if we were acrobats who had refused to jump. Two water pipes drooled onto the floor below forming a small lake of dirty water that ran in a stream down the front of the building. Other than that and the smoke nothing moved. "They could have done this with half the blast, but plastique is cheap. This way they leave us nothing, not a single scrap of paper. Just a hole in the wall."

"Was anybody in the office?" Anna asked.

"There was some evidence that there was, yes. But it is hard to identify a man from a piece of a nose or a portion of what the medical officer tells us is a kneecap. We can do it sometimes, but it takes time. There is also some evidence of a woman but again, I'm afraid it may be a little while before we are sure of that."

"Do you have any idea why?" I asked.

Bondino made a snorting sound through his nose. "This is the second fire-bombing this week and the fifth in the last four weeks. In that time, in Palermo, we have had twelve homicides that we believe are Mafia killings. They are having some damn war about something. We think it's over the docks but to tell you the truth I don't know. To tell you truth I wish they would hurry up and finish killing themselves so we don't have to keep on cleaning up their mess." He took off his beret and wiped his face with the back of his sleeve.

"So no, I don't really know, Mr. Evers and I am very close to not caring at all why or who. I assume because you are here and you have just come from lunch with DiSanto that he is connected to this. But as you see, they have left us nothing but ashes and stink."

I looked into the empty space where, while DiSanto had his lunch, people had worked. Where now there was only dust and smoke. An accountant might have been looking into a video terminal over there, a phone tucked between his cheek and his shoulder while he talked to a client in Messina about the opening and closing exchange rates in Tokyo. A secretary might have been typing a fax there, her desk an orderly landscape of files in a stack, a word processor terminal and keyboard, an ashtray with a cigarette burning, a leather cup to hold pencils and ballpoint pens, a white telephone and a small framed photograph of her husband holding their two-year-old boy, Paolo. Now there were only wires hanging from the naked walls, their connections broken. "What about their faxes and telexes. And their telephone calls?" I said. "There must be records of them somewhere."

"You think the bomber rang for an appointment?" Signor Bondino was staring down into the crowd as if he had seen someone he knew.

"DiSanto told me that this company is, was, Guido's accountant." I handed Bondino the card. "You might not find out who the bombers are by tracing their telexes, faxes and phonecalls, but you could find out a lot about Guido."

"Ah, yes, Guido. Mr DiSanto's second son."

"I didn't know there were others."

"There are several. Some legitimate, some not."

Anna had been standing quietly behind us, staying away from the edge as if she were afraid of heights. "What about his daughters?" she said almost under her breath.

"There are two from his first wife and one from his second, all grown up. I think we have addresses for them, but I'd have to look them up. There could be others, I don't know. If you like I could give you their addresses."

Anna said, "It doesn't matter."

"You were going to tell us something about Guido," I said.

"Yes, well the Carabinieri sent me a fax of his record. It's not much, I can show it to you, just one entry. When he was seventeen he was arrested with five other boys. They were charged with shooting at and wounding a child of a prostitute. The record alleges that they were using the child for target practice. But both the child and his mother disappeared so the charges were dropped. Don't look so shocked, my dear," he said to Anna who had turned away. "It's become a not uncommon sport among the youngsters in Palermo who want to join the Mafia. It sharpens their skills . . . demonstrates their courage and their honour. As you can imagine, the mother is rarely brave enough to complain.''

Anna was shaking with her face in her hands. I held her and she looked up at me, pleading, ''Please, Forrest, take me out of this horrible place. Let me go.''

''Can you arrange for a car to take Miss Bellini to the airport?'' I said over her shoulder.

''Of course. No problem.''

''God damn you, Forrest, I told you. I'm not going without you.''

''Unless Miss Bellini does not wish to go.''

The firemen had reeled in their hoses, and the stairs were no longer a running stream when we walked down. Outside, most of the crowd was still there, looking up, as if they expected a second act.

''Can I offer you a lift someplace,'' Bondino said, pausing at the door of his car. ''Back to your hotel?''

''How long would it take to get a printout of Dellacroce's communications for the last two weeks?'' I said.

''Normally, I suppose if we put a couple of men on it we could have something like that in a couple of months or so. We could do it faster, but that would be expensive.''

''How about by this evening?''

''Not possible. Unless you were willing to spend a lot of money. The clerks at the telephone exchanges get a lot of requests like this. It would take a great deal to get their attention.''

''Tell them Mr. Evers can turn them into a prince,'' Anna said. ''Or a princess. Give them a choice.''

''I don't mind spending the money,'' I said. ''Whatever it takes. Do you think someone at your office could make a reservation for us on the last plane out to Milan this evening?''

''It could be arranged,'' Signor Bondino said, holding open the door, ''anything can be arranged.''

Anna got into the car first. "Bastard," she said to me as she ducked her head.

By five o'clock in the afternoon, Bondino's office was awash with streams of printouts, soiled coffee cups, and the stale air of three people who have been cooped up together too long. And I had my answer. Dangle ten thousand dollars in front of an Italian telepost clerk and he is transformed into the most efficient intelligence gathering machine on earth. What we were doing was inefficient and noisy. We wanted the word to get around and we knew we were wasting money. If the Mafia ever had any doubt about what I was doing in Sicily they certainly knew now. But it had been worth it. We had found Obsidian. And as we watched the computer was printing out a ream of telephone numbers and dates. Another printer that the Guardia had patched into an Obsidian computer was printing out, more slowly, payments, credits, transfers and debits.

In the past sixth months, a privately held offshore corporation based in Georgetown, Grand Cayman Islands, called Obsidian, had received a total of $875 million in cash payments into its account, those payments received from various banks in Peru, Colombia, Palermo, Trapina, Agrigento, Sofia, Switzerland and Jersey. Copies of these transactions had been faxed to Guido's accountant, Dellacroce. And Dellacroce had faxed several of those banks, possibly requesting those transactions. Obsidian listed the board of directors of its Cayman Bank as its board of directors along with two other unnamed board directors. There was no knowing, without accessing Obsidian's Cayman account key number code, what their total assets were. But Obsidian had made payments of $6.4 million to Giambatista DiSanto in the last six months and $4.1 million to Guido DiSanto in the same period. Our guess was that those amounts were interest payments on the capital. Obsidian's Italian offices were in Palermo and the Guardia di Finanza had sealed the building and were seizing their records, sending us the news as they found it.

Signor Bondino closed his eyes and smiled the smile of a fisherman who has finally landed the local Moby Cod. When he opened them he was looking at his watch. "You just have time to catch your plane," he said. "If you don't mind I will have one of my cars take you to the airport."

"That's not really necessary," I said. "We have a car."

"Under the circumstances," he said, "I insist."

Chapter 28

I wanted to drive us to the airport. I wanted to return our damn rentacar. It didn't matter what I wanted; we got "Alberto Willtakeyou to the airport." A nice man, with a lush droopy moustache, a careful man, Alberto Willtakeyou, a polite and friendly man.

I didn't want him. Normally I don't mind being driven by a professional. I can relax, think of something else besides the frustrations of being stuck behind a delivery van. But I was edgy, impatient, anxious to get out of the city, out to the airport and up, up and away. Alberto took off his dark green beret with the flaming torch in front and tucked it under his arm before opening the rear door for us, bowing slightly.

Anna was even more nervous than I was, biting her nails, looking out the side windows, peering up the street over Alberto's shoulder, and turning around in her seat to see who and what was behind us. If I couldn't drive this blue and white Guardia di Finanza Alfa Giulietta ("I'm very sorry Signor Evers. Of course we would be very honoured, but regulations . . . ''), I wanted a Nigel Mansell, foot to the floor and over the kerbs and the rooftops to the departure lounge.

Alberto was just a bit more cautious. Alberto wanted to be absolutely sure that there was no traffic coming before he pulled out of the Finanzieri compound, coming to a complete stop then looking both ways up and down the one way street. Nothing coming, pause, check again, pause, then we pull out. Here was a man who knew his Highway Code. We proceeded at parade escort pace down the street. Not that it made any difference. When we reached Via Roma he could have been Ayrton Senna and we wouldn't have gone any faster. It was the beginning of rush hour and the traffic was set in concrete. He turned to roll his eyes at us and shrug. Nothing anyone could do. "Did you enjoy your stay in Palermo, Mr. Evers?" Alberto wanted to know.

"Smashing."

We inched along. My watch said 5:32, just over two hours before our flight was due to take off for Milan. One inch, another inch, stop. At this pace we would get to the airport a week from Tuesday. Nothing to do but sit back and enjoy the fumes.

Alberto turned to look back at us again, his shy calf's eyes with their long lashes, apologetic. "I guess you are used to going a little faster than this, Signor Evers."

"Are there any short cuts to the airport?"

Alberto peered down the blocked avenue, then settled back in his seat, head tilted back like the captain of a great ship.

"This is the short cut. The shortest way. You are going to drive at Monza this Sunday?"

"If we ever get to the airport."

"Have patience, Signor. We will get to the airport in plenty of time for you to give me your autograph to take home to my son."

"Have you been driving long, Alberto?" I asked him.

"Not long. About seven years for the Finanza. One time I drove the Mayor to his house."

"Was it always this bad?"

"I think it gets a little worse every day. But in the winter, it is not so bad as it is now. A lot of people go away in the winter. We will get to the airport in plenty of time," he added.

"We" did not get to the airport.

Anna's nails dug into my arm and she pulled me to her. "Forrest," she whispered in my ear, "look behind us, over there." She was pointing through the rear window.

Three cars back, in the next lane, there were two men on a beat-up Moto Guzzi. The front rider looked around eighteen with long dark curly hair, a grey T-shirt that had a big red cartoon tongue on the front, and torn blue jeans. He was looking around, this way and that, turning his handlebars, trying to find a way out of the box they were in but so far, wasn't having any luck. The cars around him had closed the gaps. The man sitting behind him on the back of the motorcycle was looking directly at us. He was taller, and thin, thirty maybe, with mirrored sunglasses and a long thin sharp nose. It was at least 85° out there, and his arms were crossed over the front of a bulky white jacket. When he saw us looking at him, his look didn't change and he didn't look away, he leaned forward and said something to the man with the long dark curly hair and then straightened up again, still staring at us. Then his mouth widened in a smile, as if we were friends he hadn't seen for a while.

Our car inched forward and stopped. Inched forward and stopped.

"There are two men, Alberto, three cars back on a motorcycle. I think they are following us," I said.

"I don't see them. How far back?" Alberto said, looking up into his rear-view mirror.

We turned to look again so we were turned away from the blast when it hit the front of the car, shattered the windscreen, tore Alberto's mild face off his skull and sprayed blood and flesh and shattered glass across our backs and spattered the rear window. Anna may have screamed, but I don't remember her screaming, I don't remember any sound at all, not even the blast of the shot-gun, except the non-stop blare of the horn. I turned towards the sound of the horn and Alberto was slumped forward over the steering wheel. I pulled him back against his seat, the horn stopped and there was a gaping spurting hole in his neck. He was still alive. In that silence I heard a metallic click, click. I looked up and framed through the jagged hole in the windscreen, four feet in front of us, a man with black training shoes and yellow cotton socks, with grey slacks, with a white nylon short-sleeved shirt and powerful forearms was sighting down the barrel of a sawn-off shot-gun. I could feel his finger begin to squeeze the trigger and I squeezed forward between the front seats leaning down on Alberto's leg to mash down the throttle and pull his left leg off the clutch. The car jumped forward, spinning its wheels, mashing the shot-gunner into the back of the little blue delivery van in front of us, as the shot-gun went off, harmlessly into the air.

I heard the back door click open, and Anna was on her knees beside me, her hand on the door handle, swinging it open. I pulled it shut.

"Goddamn it, let me go," she said pushing against the door.

I pulled her up to face me. "Look at me," I said. "Look at me."

"I can't." She was crying, tears squeezed out of her tightly shut eyes, her wide lower lip stuck out. "Let me go."

"You won't last thirty seconds out there."

"Goddammit let me go. You don't know anything. Let me go."

"They will kill you."

"Just let me go."

"You think they won't kill Guido's sister?"

"I am not his sister. You don't understand. Let me go."

"Why won't they kill you?"

Anna shook her head, no.

It had gone quiet outside. The drivers and passengers had run from the cars and trucks around us. This was a Mafia fight and there was no way they were going to become involved.

Behind us, the man from the back of the motorcycle was alone, walking towards us down the sidewalk, his mirror sunglasses reflecting the stalled traffic, his Uzi in his right hand.

I leant forward. Alberto had stopped bleeding. Had stopped breathing. I put my hands under his arms and hoisted him into the passenger seat. Lifting his legs I didn't have time to tuck them neatly in the footwell, they stayed bunched up in front of him, knees against the dashboard like a kid on a joy-ride. The engine had stalled and the shotgunner was bent over the front of the car, arms splayed out towards me.

I slid into the front seat, turned the key in the ignition while I pushed in the clutch, shifted into reverse, mashed the accelerator to the floor and looked in the rear-view mirror to see Whitejacket start firing, making the rear window explode as the car started. I bent forward and I let out the clutch and the car, spinning its wheels wildly, lunged backward towards the gunman. The car bounced hard against the kerb onto the sidewalk, the gunman stepped aside and the car smashed a plate-glass window of a men's store. Inzerillo's it said, in the instant before it fell like a slow-motion waterfall. Whitejacket had stepped between two cars as we went past him. Now he stepped out again, facing me through the big hole in the windscreen as Anna opened the rear door. Before he could bring his gun up again, I was in first gear, accelerating towards him and he had to jump back between the cars as we went roaring past down the sidewalk, the force of acceleration slamming the rear door shut again.

I found the switch to the siren on the dashboard and flicked it on. The car wouldn't shift out of first gear. So with the siren screaming and the engine roaring flat out, the windscreen and the rear window shot out, the shotgunner still impaled on the front of the car, and the poor dead Alberto lurching from side to side in the front passenger seat, his red stump of a face lolling side to side, we proceeded down the sidewalk bouncing down off the kerb at the cross streets, and bouncing back up again. After three blocks, there were pedestrians on the sidewalk again and we ploughed through as they parted to make way for the horrible screaming wounded four-wheeled beast.

After four blocks, we shed our ghastly hood ornament when we hit the kerb, the man bouncing up and rolling off to the side, still deathgripping his sawn-off shot-gun. After six blocks the traffic began to thin a little and I drove back onto the street. First gear was just fine for free-flowing Palermo rush hour traffic. Speed to spare. "Anna," I said, not seeing her in the rearview mirror.

Her head rose up behind me, her red hair tangled and dirty with drying blood turning brown. She had bruised her eye and her lower lip hung loosely as if she was gasping for breath.

"Please," she said, "let me go."

"Anna, look out behind us and see if there is anybody else."

"There isn't anybody else," she said, not turning around.

I slammed on the brakes and turned off the ignition, stopping the car in the middle of rush hour traffic. I took a handful of Anna's silk blouse and pulled her up to me. "Who are you?" I had to shout over the sound of the siren and the horns protesting behind us. "Not Guido's sister?"

She shook her head no. "Let me go," she said, "I cannot stand this."

"Who?" The noise from the horns behind us was growing.

"Will you let me go? If I tell you?"

I let go of her blouse and she slumped back against the seat cushion. I looked at her.

"I am Guido's friend," she said, looking down, her hand brushing the front of her blouse like a guilty child.

"I don't understand."

"No you don't understand nothing. You will let me go?"

"Anna, you can go anywhere you damn please." She

started to open the door to get out and I took her face in my hand, squeezing her face. "When you tell me."

"I will tell you," she said, her eyes still avoiding me. "I am Guido's lover. His mistress."

I looked at her, still not comprehending. "He pays me," she said. I let her go and she slumped back into the seat, crying.

"Anna, you can't go out in the street like that," I said. "You might as well let me drive you to the airport."

We crawled along, roaring in first gear, the fifteen kilometres to the airport. Anna sat crying quietly in the back seat. The dead man alongside me did not bear looking at. After a while, Anna reached down into her handbag, pulled out a mirror and set to wiping away the spots of blood and combing her hair. There wasn't much she could do. But as we drove out the causeway, the sea glittering behind her, she stopped crying. I looked at her in the rear-view mirror.

"The stories I told you about Rossella," she said. "They were true. She really was like a sister to me."

Anna had come to Sicily with me because Guido paid her. They always knew where I was and what I was doing because Guido paid her. She had to stay with me when I came back from lunch with Don DiSanto because Guido paid her. She made love to me because Guido paid her.

And what really had I accomplished? At the most, Guido and his father would have some heavy tax bills and fines. But the trials could take years. They could and probably would buy their way out. And although I had found a source of Guido's money, his son was still as far away from it as ever, and in as much danger. And Alberto, beside me, whose mother was probably so proud of her son who had left the little village in the hills, who had a son of his own waiting for Daddy to come home, Alberto was dead. I felt dirty, cheap and profoundly stupid.

The reason we had not seen any Poliziotti or Carabinieri on the way out of Palermo became clear when we pulled up in front of Alitalia. They were all at the airport, lights blazing, guns drawn. They surrounded the car, dragged us both out and had us leaning into the wall of the Alitalia building when Bondino intervened. A few words, a few waves of his hand, and the Polizei and Carabinieri backed off. They strapped Alberto to a stretcher, covered him with a white blanket and carried him off in an ambulance, sirens wailing. As if a siren made any difference.

Bondino ushered us in to the check-in counter. "Milan?" he said.

"Where do you want to go?" I asked Anna.

"To Rome. I have an aunt in Rome."

"Miss Bellini is flying to Rome," I said. Anna looked up at me surprised, but she didn't say anything. "I'm going to Milan."

"Wherever you are going, Signor Evers," he said, "I should be extremely cautious. One way?"

"One way," I said.

"Thank God," he said.

When I saw Anna to her gate for her flight, she put down her carryon and put her arms around me. "I am very sorry," she said. "I like you very much. It's the truth."

"I'm sorry too," I said.

She joined the file of travellers getting on the plane and just before she went through the gate she turned and waved and I waved back.

Part 3

Chapter 29

L'Autodromo Nazionale di Monza is the Great Italian Open Air Operatic Theatre, La Scala under the skies. Listen and the air still vibrates with the arias of Nuvolari, Ascari, Villoresi, the tenors of Stewart, Andretti, Surtees, Moss, and the fine baritone of Fangio in full song. Varzi, Caracciola, Farina, Villeneuve, Clark, Rosemeyer, Campari; all of the greatest Grand Prix racing drivers of all time have driven here. Monza is the greatest and the oldest Formula One circuit in the world, and if I could drive on only one course and no other, it would be here.

At Monza I walk the track.

I walked the track to get away from the fumes and the chaos of the paddock on a Thursday before a race. Away from the fleets of massive diesel transporters pulling in, painted in flamboyant corporate livery: Ferrari—scarlet; Benetton—green, yellow and red; Tyrrell—blue and white; Williams—yellow, blue and red; Marlboro—red and white; Leyton House—aquamarine . . . thirty teams from all over Europe. And Goodyear's seven blue and white fifty-foot long articulated trailers bringing in three thousand racing tyres, and Honda, Pirelli, Ford, Renault, Shell, Agip, Longines, Canon, and all the other tractor-trailers from all the corporations who have spent their millions to be here, and even more important, to be seen here.

I walk the track to get away from the hundreds of computer technicians in white socks downloading their software, staring as they will stare all weekend, into their video screens; away from the army of mechanics, aerodynamicists and designers, assembling and setting up the cars for Friday's practice sessions: and away from the journalists who are as persistent as wasps on a picnic because it is Thursday and nothing is happening so they need an ''in depth'' interview to fill their insatiable media machines. And I walk the track to get away from the officials of FISA, the Monza circuit officials, from the friends and the friends of friends (''Hey, Forrest, great to see you. I want you to meet . . . ''), away from the clients and the marketing men, away from the hangers-on and from last year's drivers hoping for another chance to drive.

I walk the track at Monza to learn it again. This is the stage whereupon I perform my simple act in my old soft-sole Nomex shoes. And it pays to walk the boards before the lights go up because every year they change the stage. It may be as simple as a fresh patch of paving on the apex in Lesmo One or a new and steeper kerb in the chicane at the end of the main straight or as subtle as where the racing line has worn the track smooth in Lesmo Two. It's not as if they are surprises, the track turning left instead of right, although they have done that in the past, it is just that there are always changes, nothing is ever quite the way you remember it and every change affects the car and some of them, unless you walk the track, you will never see.

But even if nothing had changed, even if they had put the whole place under a glass case in a museum, I would still walk the track because at Monza it is a wonderful track to walk, and it gives me immediate relief from the Sixteen Ring, Worldwide, Grand Prix Circus setting up its Billion Dollar Tent.

Walking the track reminds me why I am here, to race my car against the other men who race their cars. The rest are the props, the scenery and the chorus.

I found Vito in the Arundel garage, his small figure bent

over the gleaming surface of a nose-cone, polishing our image. I asked him if he'd like to come with me.

He stood up, grinning, glad to see me. "Hey man, that's six clicks a lap. What do you want to walk for?" he said. "And, I thought you were going to teach me to drive. I already know how to walk."

"I am teaching you to drive," I said. "Before you drive on a race track you have to know it like your own hand."

"I know this track better than you do."

"Show me," I said.

The track at Monza runs through what was once a royal park, part of the old Monza Palace. Trees arch overhead and the great open space of the black asphalt track disappears in the distance, curving away like an invitation. We were two figures with long shadows slanting behind us in the late afternoon light.

"You are going three hundred feet a second," I tell Vito as we walk towards the first chicane, "and you start thinking about getting on the brakes right here where the old banked track goes off to the right and this old tower rises over the track." A hundred yards later I say, "Here, this is the spot you want to hit on the track with the brake pedal."

"Ascari would have got a little closer," Vito says.

"Ascari wouldn't have been going as fast."

"Maybe faster, there wasn't any chicane then, you know? In those days they went all the way down the straight and into the Curva Grande. You had to have a lotta balls to go through the Curva Grande without touching the brakes."

"How do you know so much about it?"

"Is the Pope a Catholic? This is Italy, man. Who has won over a hundred Grand Prix races? Ferrari. Who was winning Formula One races since before you were born, and you are an old bastard? Ferrari. What happens when Ferrari wins? They ring the church bells all over Italy. I got friends who could tell you Ascari's lap times. You think you know this track? You don't know this track. I'll show you.''

Vito walked on, his hands gesticulating, shaping the air as he talked, his shadow following behind him like a giant magician waving hocus-pocus. ''We came up one year, around four years ago, and outside the track there is this guy with a big van, you know, like the big transporters they got in the paddock. And he puts a sign up. 'Motorcycle Parking. 20,000 lire.' And he goes, 'I'll lock the van so you don't have to worry about your motorbike getting ripped off while you watch the race.' And at Monza a lot of motorbikes get nicked so a lot of guys think, OK it's a heavy hit but at least I'll know my bike is safe. And the van fills right up, maybe fifty, sixty motorcycles in there. And the guy locks it up. And when the race starts he drives off with everybody's money and everybody's motorcycle and nobody ever sees him again. A class act.''

''You were ten years old when you first came here?''

''Nah, the first time I came to Monza I was eight.'' Vito scooped up a handful of pebbles from the trap at the chicane. As we walked down the track he flung them one by one at the fences.

''Listen, Forrest, you get up in those trees, that's where you see the race. That's where I watched last year's race up by the Curva Grande in those trees over there. We hitchhiked up, and climbed over the wall and under the fence at night. You get up in those trees and that's where you meet the guys who know something about racing. Like up in the gods at La Scala. You want to talk to somebody who knows something about opera you don't go to the dress circle or the stalls where the rich people go, you go way up in the highest balcony. That's where they know something about opera.'' He paused for a moment, lining up a sign on a bridge over the track, taking aim and letting fly.

''It's safer too. Like my friend Vincenzo's uncle, this is a long time ago but he tells the story. His uncle has this scam with some fake ticket and he gets himself into the main grandstand, you know right opposite the pits underneath where Mussolini used to have his box. Where the seats cost what, around 400,000 lire now. And these two guys in front of him, they start arguing about who is a better driver, Surtees who used to drive for Ferrari or Scarfiotti who is taking Surtees' place on the Ferrari team. And they are screaming at each other during the race, you know, really pissed off. Surtees was driving a Cooper Maserati and it breaks. And Scarfiotti wins the race. Scarfiotti wins the race and everybody goes home except this one guy who was the Scarfiotti fan stays in his seat. And Vincenzo's uncle goes up to him and the guy has a knife sticking out of his stomach.''

We walked on, under the trees, golden light filtering down to the black surface of the track.

When we reached the chicane at Roggia, Vito said, ''See, this didn't used to be a chicane here. You guys have it easy compared to what this place used to be. So what are you going to do about Guido, then?''

''You have any suggestions?'' Listening to Vito talk, I'd forgotten about Guido. Listening to him talk I wondered how he knew so much. Vito had hardly mentioned Formula One racing in the hours we were together in the cell. I suspected that he had learned all this in the few days that I had been away. He had learned all this to please me.

''Maybe you don't have to do anything,'' Vito said, squinting, the tough guy again. ''The way he drives maybe he's gonna crash and kill himself. A lotta guys have died on this track, you know? Up in the trees, I'm telling you, you can feel them. We call them spooks. I mean they were like heroes but we call them spooks. You know about that?''

I knew some of it. It's part of knowing that death is always possible. It's one of the great revelations of turning thirty, you realize that there really is more than just a chance that one day you will die. Cross the street and the possibility crosses with you. Strap yourself into a racing car and the possibilities multiply at an exponential rate. So you are aware of who died where, on what part of what corner. But you never think about it, you keep it hidden in some dark corner of your mind. But I shook my head no, as if the deaths were news to me, enjoying Vito's stories, glad for his company.

"Back where we were," Vito said, "just past the start-line there is this tree. You can see it from the track and some guys watch the race from it. But I wouldn't because this is the tree Ronnie Peterson went through the catch fences and crashed into when his rear brakes failed on his Lotus during the warm up session for the 1978 Grand Prix. Then there was this crash at the start of the race and they took Peterson to the hospital. His teammate Mario Andretti won the World Championship that afternoon, and Ronnie, who everybody thought was going to be OK, they just checked him into the hospital for observation, Ronnie died that night in the hospital."

We walked around Lesmo One and Lesmo Two and went on downhill under the old and crumbling banked track through Seraglio. When we reached the Variante Ascari, Vito stopped. He said, "You know Alberto Ascari, world champion for Ferrari for two years, 1952, 1953?"

I nodded, yes, I knew.

"Well," Vito said, "there are two Ascari curves. This one used to be called Vialone. The other one is at Montlhéry. That's in France. Alberto Ascari's father, Antonio, crashed there at Montlhéry and died driving a racing car on the twenty-sixth of the month when he was thirty-six. This one is where his son, Alberto Ascari, died. And the weird thing was, Alberto didn't have to go out, he was testing a Ferrari sports car. Maybe he was thinking he was proving something because just four days before in the Monaco Grand Prix his Ferrari crashed into the harbour where all the yachts are. Luckily he could swim. So it was four days later on the twenty-sixth of the month when Alberto was thirty-six, thirty years after his father died. Same age, same day as his old man. Nobody knows why he crashed. Spooky, huh?"

We walked down the long back straight into the southern curve and Vito stopped again, at Parabolica.

"You know about Stewart, right?"

"Jackie Stewart."

"Right. First time he has ever driven here, in his first season in Formula One, he drives inside Graham Hill in Parabolica, passes him on the inside, two laps from the finish of the 1965 Italian Grand Prix and he wins his first Formula One victory. You could try that on Sunday, pass somebody on the inside of Parabolica."

"I thought you were talking about spooks."

"I'm coming to that. You see, right here in Parabolica is where Count Wolfgang Graf Berghe von Trips just touched Jimmy Clark's Lotus, lost control, crashed into the crowd, killing fourteen spectators and himself. They kept the race going so the crowd didn't panic. And this is where Jochen Rindt died when his Lotus went out of control in a Saturday afternoon practice session. They think it was probably his front brakes went zooey. What I hear is, his friend, Jackie Stewart, stood alone in the corner of the Matra pit garage and he was crying for him. And then Stewart went out and drove the fastest lap of the whole weekend."

Yes indeed, ghosts ring the track. At Monza you don't just race against the other drivers in the race, you also race against all the drivers who have raced there since the track first opened in 1922. Your skill measured against their skill, your courage measured against theirs. These ghosts, I thought, echoing the phrase from the crypt in Palermo, are my ancestors. They judge me.

When we got back to the paddock, Vito said, "See, if you knew your history you'd know that right there in the pits is where Peter Collins gave up his car in the middle of the race to Fangio so Fangio could win the Championship. And this is where Rob Walker . . . you know in the old days they used to push the cars out onto the grid. And the Ferrari mechanics used to make a big thing of pushing the Ferrari out with their fingertips, to show how light and elegant the

Ferraris were. In 1959, this is where Rob Walker walked right past the Ferraris followed by his Cooper being pushed into pole position by Alf Francis for Stirling Moss. Right in front of all the Ferraris. And Stirling won the race. If you knew your history you'd know stuff like that.''

He was fourteen. If Vito could learn enough to be a walking Monza encyclopedia in a few days, I thought, there was no limit to what the child might learn, or could do. A typical proud parent, I thought, helping myself to a portion of pride I didn't deserve.

Then Vito looked up at the big green sign on the side of the control tower. ''Autodromo Nazionale Monza,'' he said with some deliberation. ''Track reg-u-lay, regulay-shuns. One. Crash helmet. It is compulse, compul-soary for oc-oc-occu-pants of open vehicles and sports or racing cars.''

''What are you doing?'' I said.

''Reading,'' he said. ''What the fuck do you think I was doing?'' I wanted to pick him up and give him a big hug but he would have hated that. Bad for his street cred.

I walked him back to the pit garage where the mechanics were setting up the cars, his little figure in the Team Arundel coveralls instantly at home among the men, and I went to the Arundel motorhome, back to work.

I was giving an interview to two journalists from a Brazilian motoring magazine, giving them some variation on *''No there was no truth whatsoever to the rumours that I was looking for another ride for next year because there was no truth to the rumours that I was either unhappy with or being thrown out of Team Arundel. So far as I knew''* when Ken came in to tell me that Guido wouldn't be at the track until Friday morning. Guido was tied up with business meetings. Monza was his home track, and he knew it, Ken said, like he knew the palm of his hand. Guido didn't need to walk the track. Guido didn't need to be here early. He would be here tomorrow for the first day of practice.

''Fine,'' I said.

Chapter 30

At six in the morning, the door of the Castello di Pomerio restaurant swung open and Max was moving through it, head down, a man in a serious hurry. Encased in a dark blue XXXtra Large Team Arundel T-shirt, and in dark blue sweatpants stretched to the limit he looked like the Michelin Man's fatter brother. Big Blue Michelin headed straight for the buffet table, his beady little eyes taking inventory, calculating the best line of attack and he takes a large plate in his left hand and a fork in his right. He knows exactly what he wants. He wants everything.

With the delicacy of a fat man stepping on the scales, Max carefully placed on his plate, slice by slice, several slices each of Genoa Salami, Milano Salami, Carpaccio, Bresaola, Prosciutto Cotto, Prosciutto Crudo, Mortadella, Gruyère, Emmenthal, Bel Paese, Provolone and I stopped watching. This was Max's breakfast *hors-d'oeuvres* plate. The scrambled eggs, sausages, bacon, grilled tomatoes and hi-rise pile of buttered toast with pots of jam on the side would follow. Max doesn't eat, he engulfs. As the chief designer of a Formula One team, Max balances the battle to shave weight off the car (the tubes that carry the coolant on the Arundel are made of an exotic material so light they float in your hand) by adding to his own bulk. Ten grams off the car. A kilo on Max.

As Number One driver who was due on the track for this

morning's first untimed practice at eleven, I helped myself to a cup of black coffee and a dry roll of Italian bread. Even the coffee is an indulgence some drivers deny themselves, fearing the minor interference of caffeine on a nervous system as highly tuned as a virtuoso's violin. I take the coffee because a glass of water with a dry roll smacks too much of the condemned man, especially sitting at the same table as Max. What the hell—live it up, Evers, have a whole cup. Ken loomed behind me at the sideboard, grazing among the platters, spearing a helpless delicacy here and there.

For three years now, it has been our custom to have breakfast together before the practice and race days of a Grand Prix. It's our way of drawing together for the battle, pulling up the drawbridges to the outside world. Two other teams who can afford the prices at the Pomerio and a few journalists filter in and ignore us as we ignore them. The poor bastards who have to pre-qualify for the chance of joining the other twenty-six teams in qualifying are already out at the track, preparing for their 8 A.M. one hour do or die session. In fact most of the teams are out at the track, staying in their motorhomes so they don't have to fight the traffic back and forth. But I like distancing myself from the track, getting away from the ring and the high wire with no net. I tell myself a little distance allows me to sleep better.

But it is not that, I probably wouldn't sleep well on a race weekend wherever I was. The distance allows me to withdraw more, inside myself, to put everything and everybody outside to clear my mind for the race.

"Sleep well, did you Forrest?" Ken asks in a voice large enough to fill the twelfth-century hall up to the beams.

Ken always asks me that and I always lie and he knows I lie. Sure, fine, like a hibernating bear. On the weekend of a race, I don't sleep, I worry.

I worry that one of the mechanics, Ed or Steve or Richard, working all night, his eyes sore and longing to close, forgets to put Loctite on one bolt in the transmission which will vibrate loose enough to spray a microfine film of oil on a rear tyre.

I worry that when I attack the kerbs in the first chicane, I will weaken the front suspension with the shock.

I worry that maybe I am a microsecond slower than I was.

I worry that McLaren's Honda still out-powers us by thirty or forty horsepower, so they can run more wing and generate more downforce so they can go around corners with more grip and still blow us off on the straights.

I worry that Grouillard is not going to be watching his rearview mirrors and that de Cesaris is going to be slowing down in the middle of the track with his mind in neutral when I come out of Lesmo Two on a flyer, committed to a line that leads straight up his tail-pipe.

I worry that Guido has arranged for someone I don't know and would never suspect, to do something tricky to my car, something nasty.

I worry that Guido is faster than I am.

I worry that I worry about Guido being faster.

I worry that I still don't know what to do about Guido. That I have blown my chance. That it is completely out of control and he knows it.

Yes indeedy Ken, slept like a log on the forest floor, I did.

Ken, the espresso cup a thimble in his big gnarled hands, his head tilted back as if he is seeing a long way said, "You don't mind, do you, if I drive us to the track this morning?"

"I don't mind, but I have to drive the Ferrari this morning," I said.

"You gone off my driving then?"

"I want to give the thing back to Jack Boyce. He said he'd pick it up."

"You tell him you've crumped it?"

"I've told him I've left my mark on it."

Ken had raced his own Aston Martin in the 1940s after

the war. He got as far as driving at Le Mans with the Aston Martin factory team in the 1950s. He started a Formula One team with the idea that it would be fun, God bless him. And maybe in those days, it was. He had the immense personal fortune you needed to compete with the factory teams and his team even won some races. But when Colin Chapman introduced the idea of sponsorship to Formula One racing in the late 1960s with his Lotus painted like cigarette packs, Ken was the last to follow suit. He hated finding, courting and stroking sponsors. But the cost of racing in Formula One soared towards a million pounds a month and he had to find sponsors or quit. So painfully and slowly he learned the skills of marketing Team Arundel. "A bit of a dodo learning to fly," he called it.

Now, after forty years in Grand Prix racing, he had his first real chance at the World Championship. He wasn't doing it for the money, and he wasn't doing it for the marketing. He was doing it because he loved to race and because like everybody who loves to race he wanted to win. He was nearly seventy.

"Did you hear about March," Ken said, looking down into his empty cup. "You remember they were having handling problems qualifying at Spa."

"They're always having handling problems," Max said through a mouthful of eggs and salami.

"Both their drivers were complaining the car was going light in the fast corners. They dialled in more wing and it was worse, exactly the opposite of what you'd expect. Capelli said he almost lost it at Eau Rouge. So they added even more downforce and the car was almost uncontrollable in the fast turns. Then they looked underneath the car and they found that the undertray was scraping on the track."

"You mean on the skid plates," Max said, correcting him.

"No, I mean on the body. The actual body. What they found out was that the qualifying fuel they were getting from Texon was so volatile that it was making the fuel tanks bulge and scrape the track.''

"You're just trying to make me feel good," I said.

"Well if you are going to just sit there and brood, For-rest, you might as well brood about that.''

The fat wide modern racing tyre is so soft it "cogs" with the variations on the surface of the track, and so sticky that it chemically bonds to the asphalt. The thought of coming out of Parabolica at 175 miles an hour, at the absolute limit of adhesion, and the bottom of the car scraping the surface and lifting the car off its tyres, turning the car into a giant skateboard, didn't bear thinking about.

"You talk to Guido?" I said.

"Look up on the way to the track and you might see him. He's coming down in his chopper this morning. Should be there about the same time as the rest of us. I spoke to him last night and he was saying he thought we ought to spend our time getting our race set-up right rather than go balls out for qualifying. And I must say I agree. It's not like Monaco, Hungaroring or Suzuka, you can pass at Monza. So where you start on the grid is not quite so critical.''

"Sure," I said. "Guido says that, then he has his me-chanics set up his car for balls-out qualifying and I look slow.''

"Well, that's what he says and by all means Forrest, you can do what you like.''

"Set up for the race, Forrest," Max said leaning back. There were still a few sticky buns on the sideboards and I could feel him considering getting up and polishing them off. He decided against it and turned to me. "That way we get two sets of figures. I can factor out the qualifying tyres, the extra 20 or 30 horsepower we get from qualifying fuel, maybe learn something from the differential in track paths, ground effect downforce, velocity, angular acceleration, radius curvature and track segmentation of times for the race set up.''

Max was talking about the stream, no not a stream, the flood of statistics a Formula One car dumps into the computers in the pits every lap, precise numerical details of every corner, what each wheel was doing over every inch of the track. The rise and fall of the engine to the last rpm. The days of the driver coming in and saying "it's understeering" were long gone. Now the computer was comparing relative adhesive and downforce values on any given segment of the track with ambient temperature and humidity factored in. In the future the technicians wouldn't have to wait for the car to come past the pits to get their messages, the cars will have transponders, beam their data twenty-five thousand miles up into the sky to a satellite and back down to the pits again so the techies can see and analyse what's happening as it happens ... push a few buttons to alter the car and a few more to react to the massive slide that begins when the wrong button is pushed. And say "oh shit" when the wrong button noses the car into the grandstands. By then that's where all the drivers will be, target opportunities on the sidelines, the last remaining element of risk in the computer game.

More Pre-Race Tension making me nasty and irritable I thought. But then it's hard to feel cheerful about being one of an endangered species.

"That's great Max. The only trouble is that puts Guido up at the front of the grid and me at the back. Let's just swap that around. I'll qualify and Guido can do the grunt work on the race set up."

"Realistically," Ken said, "from the team point of view, who do you think is better at qualifying?"

"You tell me," I said, "after qualifying is over."

Ken led the way down from Lake Como to Monza, joining the first coaches and the early risers. We came into Monza and drove through the entrance in the high stone walls and into the Autodromo the back way they reserve for competitors, drove through the tunnel under the startline grandstands and emerged into a solid wall of Tifosi. Instead of making way for the car, they crowded closer to get a good look at who was inside.

So it took a while to struggle through the mass of eager fans and get to the special parking lot just outside the paddock . . . plenty of time to watch Guido descend down out of the sky in his helicopter with the red and green letters on the side "GUIDO DISANTO." You had to give the man credit. He knew how to make an entrance.

Chapter 31

I flicked on the Ign. switch, the fuel pumps, raised my hand to signal that I am ready, Vito gave me a friendly rap on my helmet for good luck, and there was a metallic clunk as the 660 volt starter motor was pushed home onto the drive nut at the rear of the transmission. Screeeeech of jagged metal scraping jagged metal and gear teeth cracking. It sounds like all the parts inside the engine are loose, flailing around, splintering and fracturing. The engine catches for a moment, there is a blast that shakes the walls. Then nothing, not a flutter. I wait while they fit the starter back on again and this time the machine starts. The mechanics push me out into the weak morning light. I turn the wheel sharp right and they push up against the pit lane wall. A Formula One car is a single-purpose machine built to hurl around a racecourse somewhere around the edge of physical possibility. When it's not doing that, it is a pig. As wide as a London Transport bus, it has an even bigger turning circle. The pit crew came around to the front of the car, pushed me back again across the pit lane, I turn the wheels on opposite lock then I slip the gear lever into drive and the car leaps forward, spinning its wheels. The green digital display screen in front of me flickers 5,500 and 9,000 rpm as I pull up and stop behind three cars in front of me waiting for the green light to go on and go out on the track, blipping the engine to keep it going.

With a moment to look around I had the feeling that if I were any closer to the ground I'd be under it. The top of my head was about the same height as the mechanic's knees in the Lotus pits on my right. On my left the concrete pit wall blocked my view with a red and white Esso sign. Up ahead my view was blocked by the wide black and yellow rear wing of a Minardi topping the Minardi's rear suspension, exhaust pipes and wide rear tyres coated with little stones. Just above the wing, in the distance, a man in orange coveralls was sitting on a chair half-way up a pole, ten feet off the ground, facing me. He is the pit marshal; with his traffic light alongside him he controls the pit lane traffic with the hand of God. When he turns the traffic light green, we will go. My little vibrating mirrors announce that Guido has pulled up behind me.

He waves.

The bastard waves to me.

The green light goes on and the Minardi bathes me in a wash of fumes, heat waves, rubber chunks, stones, grit and noise as the Minardi in front accelerates away, wheels spinnning.

The first lap is a warm-up lap, warm up the tyres, the engine and the driver so there is no hurry. No need to pound the kerbs in the first chicane. The track feels rough down the straight and into the chicane, but then, all the tracks feel rough now. A Formula One car has so little suspension travel that if you run over a coin you can tell if it's heads or tails. Guido comes alongside me in the Curva Grande and I wave him on ahead. This is his track and if he has a different line through one of the turns, I want to know about it.

A Formula One car is a large aerodynamic device, and the effect is like an upside-down wing pushing you down onto the track. The latest trick, since they outlawed side skirts, is to force the air flowing underneath the car through a narrow venturi. The underfloor rises up at the rear of the car and the resulting low pressure beneath the car sucks it down onto the track. Along with the wings on the front and the rear of the car, the aerodynamics add nearly two tons of extra downforce. Add those gumball tyres, and the car has incredible cornering power. And the faster you go, the more downforce you generate and the more the car sticks to the road. At sixty, a Formula One car has several times the cornering power of any Porsche, Ferrari or Lamborghini on the road.

Double the speed and the downforce quadruples. At 190 miles an hour the cornering power digs into the track and turns your body into a ponderous heavy thing smeared along the inside of the car, and you think you might pass out from the blood forced to one side of the brain. Indeed you might. Your head weighs over a hundred pounds pulling sideways, the blood drains to the side of the skull and you tend to lose consciousness at those forces.

Nigel Mansell's Formula One Ferrari was pulling 5Gs around Peralta in Mexico City at 190 miles an hour. That's five times the car's weight being held onto the track and five times the driver's weight squashed against the inside of the car.

Unless, and it is a big unless, unless you get too close to the car in front of you. The car in front of you is busy punching a big hole in the air and leaving a vacuum in its wake. And in a vacuum, the effect of all those elegant aerodynamic devices drops to nothing at all. One moment you have enough grip to make your teeth point sideways and the next you have almost none. It happened to Derek Warwick on the first lap of the 1990 Italian Grand Prix and he was surprised to find himself sliding upside down at 150 miles an hour coming out of Parabolica onto the main straight. He'd had his air stolen from a car in front of him.

It's also what makes passing so difficult with these groundsucking aerodynamic devices. Because the closer you get to the car in front of you the less grip you have and the slower you are around corners. Not to mention the flying shrapnel of grit, stones, rubber chunks, oil fog, and exhaust in your face.

So I followed Guido a few lengths back, around Lesmo One and Two. We were just cruising around, no more than say 100 to 120 miles an hour and there was plenty of time to settle in and see the trees overhead and see that the grandstand that curves around the outside of Lesmo Two was jammed with Tifosi, on their feet and cheering as we went by, waving Ferrari flags at 10 A.M. on a Friday morning.

They were cheering because the wild beasts had been let out of their cage to run and cheering because there were two days and four practice sessions before the race, when Ferrari would win. None of them would be here if they didn't think Ferrari would win.

They were not "fans." "Fans" is too weak a word. They were Tifosi and Ferrari was their religion, Monza the great temple where sacrifices are still made. Tifosi stands for Fanatic Italian Religious Racing Fundamentalists who worship a black and prancing horse. As far as they are concerned all the rest of the racing world, from the red and white of Marlboro to the United Colours of Benetton were the enemy.

We ducked down underneath the old banking and came up to cruise around the Ascari Variante, down the back straight and around Parabolica, the big open hairpin turn that leads into the main straight, accelerate hard, 210 miles an hour past the pits. No more cruising, now we were on it.

It's a long wide bumpy straight and the car bounces while my head vibrates to the tune of 700 mechanical horses pounding away at 13,500 rpm. We both brake hard, but Guido draws ahead leaving his braking twenty yards later than mine, nearly two tenths of a whole second. He charges hard over the kerbs and fishtails coming out of the chicane heading up towards Curva Grande.

I let him go. I don't mind if he goes faster than me now, on the first laps of the first day of practice. Let him wow the fans. I am learning and I take my first steps slowly, learning what is possible and what is not.

If you watch a Greek dancer begin his dance, with his arms outstretched, one step and then another as if he is testing the surface of the earth, and as his dance progresses, the earth shrinks underneath his feet as he grows in speed and size until the earth is a ball under his feet and he towers above it, rolling it this way and that, keeping a miraculous balance. Seated in a Formula One car I have this same godlike power to make the earth small beneath me, and on every lap on every track I am learning how to use it.

This learning is not grand or conceptual, it is fine grain, made of the smallest observations and almost unnoticeable fragments of time. If I stay off the kerbs here, just brush the edge, I lose a three thousandths of a second because the car has a longer way to go around the turn. But the car is more settled now and I can come out of the turn six thousandths of a second faster because I can be hard on the throttle two thousandths of a second earlier. This learning is hard work and it can be tedious, but it is how I find what's possible and where the limits are. And it is how I push them back. You explore, out on your limits and the limits of the car, looking for a way to push those limits back. You can't stand still in Formula One, you have to go faster every single time. Because whether you go faster or not, some and maybe even most of the other drivers will.

And of course, I set up the car, fine tune my instrument of destruction.

The car doesn't feel right. Compared to the way it felt on that brief run at Vallelunga it feels slow to turn in, mushy as if the tyres are soft. It could be it needs more front wing or less rear. I try stiffening the front roll bar with a control knob in the cockpit and that makes it worse. It's like a sled on snow and I want it as precise as a surgeon's knife.

On my second lap I come into the pits.

The team has painted a blue and white stripe that slants

into our allotted pit. Theoretically it makes our pit easy for me to find, but with Max bulking as large as a lighthouse wearing a jumpsuit he has designed for himself with large blue and white checkerboard squares, who needs stripes on the ground? I switch the engine off and take off my helmet. By the time it is off Max has put a small computer monitor on the car in front of me.

He has keyed in the times from our first two laps. "Guido is faster," he says. "A lot faster. Maybe you should concentrate on the race set up, Forrest."

"It's soft Max. I'm sitting around looking at the scenery waiting for it to turn in. And it hasn't got any power. How much more horsepower does Guido have over me?"

"How are your hands?" Ken asked, towering over the car. He was used to Max and my squabbles.

"They are fine," I said, holding up my gloved hands, "see?" They were fine. Didn't hurt a bit. But I hadn't gone over the kerbs yet, I'd been pussyfooting around. I punched in a graph that showed the G forces in each corner and laid Guido's graph over mine. The two lines, his and mine, were completely different in each corner. Guido was generating maximum Gs on the turn in and exit, mine on the apex, the middle. I punched in another graph that showed rpm along the course. He was consistently showing two to three hundred rpm higher than I was on the entrance and the exit. "Now I see what the problem is, Max," I said.

"You *finally* figured out the problem is the driver. The driver isn't driving fast enough."

"The problem is, Max, blue just isn't your colour."

"Let's try trimming the rear wing a little," he said. "And if you fuck up my car I will have you for breakfast."

I don't mind the traffic on the untimed sessions. There are always cars slowing down or warming up out there, and you cannot count on them seeing you in their rear-view mirrors. They didn't matter much in the hour and a half "untimed" session because I was breaking the track into sections, cruising at eight-tenths through most of the track and concentrating on two sections at a time: Lesmo One and Two into Seraglio, the first chicane into Curva Grande. They were pieces of a puzzle I would assemble in the afternoon for qualifying. This meant that my lap times were deceptively slow. But in exchange for that I could bring my full concentration to each part of the track in turn. I learned that if I kept just inside the line coming into the first chicane, stayed half a car-width away from the outside kerb on the entry, I avoided a bump that upset the car when I was turning in, and I could get through the curves of the chicane almost a whole tenth of a second more quickly.

Max had set the car up with a maximum ground clearance of 20mm in front and 25mm in the rear, about an inch. With the total suspension travel less than an half an inch it meant you found the bumps the hard way and you remembered where they were. And if you couldn't drive around them you spent some quiet moments of reflection, up in the air with no brakes, no power, no grip and a hard landing to follow.

Chapter 32

"Hey Forrest, good to see you," Guido says. "You having some problems out there this morning? Anything I can do to help?"

Guido is smiling like a crocodile, confident in his driver's suit. He holds up his plastic cup of mineral water to me in mock toast. The people crowded around Guido smile in my direction. I think they look like turds in silk, but I am not my most generous-spirited self at lunch. And Guido is up to something.

Between the morning practice and the one hour afternoon qualifying session that begins at one, there is a ceremony called Lunch.

Lunch is at the Arundel motorhome and marquee, a little cordoned off area under a blue and white striped awning and Lunch is where invited guests can meet their drivers. Although we do not eat, Lunch is obligatory for the drivers. Outside the paddock, the Tifosi are twenty-five deep, pressed against the chain-link fence, straining for a glimpse of a hero, or a famous face, held back only by the spikes on top of the fence and by the guard dogs on patrol. We are hidden from their view by the phalanxes of giant buses and motorhomes. This is the inner sanctum where the PR execs are fond of repeating their favourite saying; "That it is so crowded and dirty at the bottom while there is always plenty of room at the top."

There, over there, Jackie Stewart and his son Paul are talking to Eddie Jordan. The perfectly groomed figure of Bernie Ecclestone, the single most powerful man in motor-racing, emerges from his graphite grey motorhome with the dark tinted windows that match his dark tinted sunglasses. No one knows how much he makes from Formula One. It could be as high as a million a week, fifty-two weeks a year. The betting is that he would gladly spend it all to save his dimming sight.

There, in the lipstick red miniskirt and red running shoes, is that new young French pop star, Janice Corl. And over there, the well-preserved woman in lilac trousers is Michelle Byam who is rumoured to own most of Monte Carlo. Friday is comparatively relaxed and easy. The real crowds and the real pressure will come later. Now we are all feeling that pleasant tension of waiting for the curtain to rise and the show to begin.

I raise my plastic water cup back to Guido, and return his smile, wondering if he knows yet that I have punched a hole in his cash flow. Wondering what his new buddy-buddy grin means.

"Come here, Forrest," he says, with that rasp of his. "I've got some people here I'd like you to meet." In half an hour we will be back in the cars, lining up to go all out to qualify. Lunch, for the drivers and the mechanics, has nothing to do with eating.

"Hello Guido," I say, "what brings you here?"

"I thought you two weren't talking." This was a dark tall curly-haired woman in blue jeans and a heavy gold necklace over a silk T-shirt just so you didn't mistake her for one of the common herd. She had the deep-set, soulful eyes and long nose of a racing hound.

"Forrest Evers," I said introducing myself to her. "Guido and I talk all the time. We just don't happen to agree all the time."

"Forrest let me introduce you; Marchessa Sophia Campanini, Publisher of the Castellammare Group of magazines and newspapers," Guido said with his hand resting lightly on the rump of the tall woman in blue jeans, who smiled fondly down at him. "A very close friend of mine and a big help to me these past few days." She lifted his hand off her behind and intertwined her fingers with his as he went on, "And Carlo Bonventre, I think you met at my little place in Pianoro. He's the guy who runs Vini Cristalli."

"I'm pleased to hear you've been taking an interest in our wines," Bonventre said, holding out his slim bronzed hand to be shaken. He had on a light aquamarine fisherman's shirt and casual white canvas trousers over leather deck shoes with no socks. He still wore a plain silver bracelet that emphasized the fine bones of his wrist. I let his hand hang in the air.

"Forrest seems to have a little problem keeping up," Guido said.

"No problem. I've met Carlo. I know who he is."

"Well, he pays a lotta my bills," Guido said, smiling broadly, "and it pays to be nice to him. Right Carlo?"

Flashes of light announced photographers taking our picture. Guido and I had not been seen together since Rossella had died and the two of us together was news.

There is an unwritten rule of etiquette that the press doesn't bother the drivers at Lunch before qualifying or before a race. Apparently we were too good a story to miss. And in the news-hungry paddock, flashbulbs going off lure cameramen and reporters like sharks scenting blood. They surged through the cordon, ten deep, holding their little pocket tape recorders and their cameras at arm's length.

"What's happened with you guys?" A short, quiet German reporter from *Auto Motor und Sport* was thrusting his pocket tape recorder an inch from Guido's nose. "I thought you two were deadly enemies. Never going to speak to the other guy again."

Guido held up his hand to quiet them. He had a statement to make. "That was a very hard time for me. My wife was a lovely woman and I think we were all under a lot of stress and maybe we said some things we wish we didn't say.''

I still didn't know what he was up to, but I couldn't help but admire the easy and natural way he had with the press. They were quiet, obedient, privileged that he was speaking to them as if they were all his personal friends. ''Anyway I want you guys to know, and you can print this, there's no hard feelings, right Forrest?'' And he held out his hand to me. ''Long as you don't hold me up out there.'' Guido stood there his hand outstretched.

I took it and God help me, I shook it. ''Just don't get in my way,'' I said as a joke. In the background in one of the pit garages, a Formula One engine burst into life, screamed, then settled down to a dull lumpy idle.

''Now if you will excuse us gentlemen,'' Guido said dismissing them, ''we'd like to join our guests for lunch.''

A little later, I was talking to Ken, and Guido was behind me talking to another group of people. ''Hey Anna,'' he said raising his voice. ''Come on over and say hello to Forrest.''

I looked around and she was coming out of the motorhome, her beautiful copper and golden hair hanging loose around her shoulders, just grazing a simple light green cotton dress. I went over to her and there were circles under her eyes that make-up wouldn't cover. She looked pale and her wide lower lip stuck out like she had lost but she hadn't quite given up.

''I thought you were in Rome,'' I said.

Anna shrugged and looked away.

I had held her in my arms, I had kissed her and I had made love with her. She had sold me but I was hardly the paragon of knightly virtue. I had used her too. And a large part of what I had felt was still there, even though it didn't make any sense. Even though I felt that empty stomach feeling of loss, I still had the urge to hold her, to tell her it was going to be all right. Making love with her had tied me to her, and looking at her sad face and her frightened eyes, I still wanted to protect her.

"I don't understand," I said. "I thought you weren't going back with him."

"It's easy to say that. To do it is not so simple. I don't have any choice," she said, shaking her head, looking down at the ground.

A big beefy speckled hand gently laid on my shoulder made me turn. Ken said, "Shall we?" he said. It was a quarter to one. Time to go.

When I turned back to Anna she was watching Guido walk away towards the pits, a bullfighter of a man, his shape emphasized by his tight driving suit; short stocky legs, wide shoulders, he walked with a bounce, on tiptoe. When Anna saw him turn the corner she turned back to me. "He is not through, you know," she said almost under her breath. "He says he wants to kill you."

"You take care of yourself Anna," I said. I bent down and gave her a soft kiss on her forehead, my hands on her warm cinnamon shoulders. "And thanks for telling me," I said into her ear.

"You don't know anything," she said, turning away.

Chapter 33

The kerbs at Monza are heavy slabs overlapping each other like a fan of thick, concrete cards. They are almost smooth if your tyres just touch them at the bottom. But the higher up you ride those kerbs and the more you try to straighten out your line through the "S" of the chicane, the more their edges rise up one after another and the nastier they get. Two feet up on the kerb in the first chicane at Monza and you can break a wrist if you don't hold the steering wheel tight in your hands. Three feet up and it could break the suspension or bounce you across the track.

The kerbs and the chicane are meant to slow you down, to intrude into what used to be a straight run into Curva Grande. And they do. But the higher you ride them, the less you have to slow down. In other words, if you want a fast lap, you have to drive over the damn kerbs. Which isn't racing, it's just punishment. Especially if the skin is freshly healing on the palms of your hands.

I came out of Parabolica thinking about the kerbs in the chicane ahead, skittering out to the edge of the track, foot mashed to the floor, the engine screaming behind me, full roar. A red car, Guerini in the Dallara and Boyd in the blue Brabham are on the straight, both back markers, both off the racing line. Perfect, I think, because Monza has a wide straight and there is plenty of room to pass them and they are not going to hold me up. I have a clear run and this is going to be a flyer. It had better be. Qualifying tyres are so soft they only last for one hard lap, two at the most. And each car is allowed just two sets for the session, which means you get two chances to set a good time in each session and no more. No matter what happens.

I had lost my first set when I had to lock up my brakes to avoid hitting one of the Ligiers spinning in front of me in the chicane before Lesmo One. The Ligier had got too high up on the kerbs and was bouncing across the track into the stones on the other side; I didn't hit anything but my time was gone and so were my tyres. So Ken, now, is leaning over the pit wall, thumbs up. Go for it.

The car is bottoming, bouncing, sending up showers of sparks behind me from the skid plates grooving the tarmac. I am lying down, with my arms and legs stretched before me, relaxing as much as I can while the wind pounds my helmet in 215 mile an hour gusts and the vibrations from the engine and the bouncing from the track jerk my head up and down in a 14,000 rpm buzz punctuated by the hammer blows of the rough track underneath.

I am focusing on a point up ahead which I can't yet see, but I know exactly where it is, just beyond the vanishing point, at the beginning of the Ferodo sign on the right side of the track, two thirds of a mile away. My sight goes towards it now, urging the car there, with the sky overhead, a dark grey blur, and the black track below stretching in the distance to a fine point ending at the edge of the Ferodo sign.

I imagine that point where I will first touch the brakes, turn in, hit the kerb, as I will get back on the power, turning into the second corner in the chicane, hitting the kerb.

I try to bring the two together, my picture of the perfect passage through the chicane with the way it really happens as I go just past my braking point at three hundred and fifteen feet a second, cheating just a little to the inside to avoid the worst part of the bump on the entry to the corner.

As I lift off the throttle the car feels as if it hits a wall from the loss of 700 horsepower pushing forward and from the heavy drag of the wings—a panic stop in a normal car. As I get on the brakes my body suddenly gains over five hundred pounds pushing me forward, trying to squeeze me through the racing harness in separate sections and jamming my hands forward on the steering wheel. Towards the end of the second and a half of absolute maximum braking, in the second and a half that it takes to decelerate down from 215 miles an hour to a leisurely 115, I begin to lift up off the brake pedal and turn in to the corner transferring the weight of the car to the right front then the right rear. Out of the corner of my eye, the right front tyre is throwing off a black haze of rubber ground away by the surface of the track but my eye, as I finish lifting off the brake and start to get back on the throttle, my left eye is on the inside kerb where I want to hit it almost two feet up and slice off a piece of the apex.

The car is understeering, wanting to plough wide of the turn and I let off a fraction of a second off the throttle and the outside front tyre bites into the track and I turn sharply now and hit the inside of the kerb high, around four inches higher than I wanted, bouncing the whole car up in the air, tilting it to the right and I feel the shock in my hands and the skin on the palm of my hand slip loose from its healing glue. There are two more hard shocks in succession as I am thinking about getting the car straightened out and it is all right, the knock has helped point the car towards the second corner in the tight chicane and I keep my foot half-way down on the throttle as we touch down and rocket into the second inside the kerb on the right now and I hit the second kerb a little low this time, so the shock is not so bad, but my line now as I come off the jolt, jolt, jolt, of the outside-inside-outside kerbs is a little wide for the exit on the outside and I don't want to run up any higher on the kerbs on the exit so I have to wait. Wait to get back on the power hard to take me up to Curva Grande as the car fishtails and the rear wheels spin from the power coming on, the back end kicking out to the left and back again and just a little on over to the right but there is so much traction in the qualifiers I keep my foot flat down and imagine the perfect entry point into Curva Grande, knowing I have at least a tenth and maybe as much as a half a second to make up for the time I've just lost as I exit the chicane at 135 miles an hour, accelerating hard.

The rest of the lap is all right. For the first time in my life I don't lift for Lesmo Two but keep my foot flat down into that blind killer of a corner. Just touch the kerbs on the entry there and you could be in serious trouble. And when I come out of Parabolica onto the straight again, I feel it is not a bad lap. I push the display button three times, and it gives me my time; one minute, eighteen point three six five, close to an average of 150 miles an hour. Which is not bad, but a long way from brilliant. It put me fifth with twenty minutes to go in the session. Guido was third behind Prost and Senna.

By the end of the session, after Mansell, Alesi and Berger had gone out again, I had been pushed back to ninth, and Guido down to fifth. But I wasn't worried, I was sure I would do better on Saturday. All I had to do was get on the brakes a little sooner coming off the main straight. And go flat out into Lesmo one more time.

After the practice session we had fallen into the habit of having separate debriefings, Guido with his team manager, mechanics and technicians and I with mine. Max and Ken would swap around from race to race to avoid playing favourites. But after our first practice session Guido suggested we go back to the way we had done it at the beginning of the season, together. So we closed the doors of the pit garage, Guido went through his impressions of the car and the track and I went through mine.

Guido said, "There's no power Max. I get back on it coming out of the chicanes and it's chained to the ground. I feel like I want to get out and push.".

"The charts show," Max started.

"Forget the charts," Guido interrupted. "You have to have an engine with more power out there. I want another engine in my car for tomorrow."

"The charts show that you are scrubbing off a lot of speed on your exit. You make a smoother exit, you are going to be faster."

Guido picked up his steering wheel which was lying on the workbench he was leaning against. He said, "Here Max, you drive," and scaled the steering wheel backhanded at Max. Max put his hands up too late, the wheel caught him in the midsection doubling him over. Max grabbed his stomach, and then put his hand up. He was all right, he just needed air.

Guido went on as if nothing had happened. "What do you think, Evers, you got any power out there? You're not exactly melting the track."

"You all right, Max?" I said.

"In a minute. I'll be OK."

"Relax Evers, it was just a joke. You can't hurt him, he's got an air bag. What's wrong with your car?"

I started to go over to Max but he waved me away. He was fine, fine he said with waves of his hands. "It feels like we are around thirty or forty horsepower down on Ferrari, Renault and Honda, but that's been the story since the start of the season."

It was strange. Except for Guido's vicious toss at Max, we looked like and we were acting just like a normal team. There was the usual surface tension waiting to flare up into something bigger, and there was a little antagonism between the drivers. But underneath the petty jealousy there was also a total commitment to be the absolute best whatever it took. And Guido was leading it. As if he had taken the decision to make Arundel work as a team again. He took the limelight, took the lead as if it were his. And strangely enough, I didn't mind. I knew what I wanted and I knew I would get it.

On the way out Vito said, "Hey, Forrest, it's gonna rain."

"You doing the weather forecasting around here now?"

"Gimme a break. What I'm saying is that those cars out there, those Peugeot 309s are about to finish their practice session and after that the track is clear."

"And?" I realized I'd been hearing the distant fizz of saloon cars going around the track for almost a half hour without really noticing it. At Monza there is always a buzz in the air.

"And," he said, "if the track is clear and it's raining what about a fucking driving lesson in the fucking rain?"

"We're going to have to do something about your language, Vito. You can't go around saying 'fuck' all the time."

"Why the fuck not?"

"Because it makes people think you're stupid."

"I am stupid. I don't know a fucking thing about driving in the rain."

"Well, if the great good Ken Arundel can arrange for a clear track with the clerk of the course . . . "

Ken raised his eyebrows, "probably."

" . . . here's the keys. It's in the lot straight behind the paddock. You know the car. See if you can get it into the paddock without banging it up too bad."

He ran out the door, sneakers flying, dodging through the leisurely, end-of-the-day, crowd.

"Hey Evers," Guido said looking up from a conversation with Max on the other side of the garage. "You got a minute? I want to talk with you."

"It's about time," I shouted back.

The walk from the Arundel pits garage to the Arundel mobile home can't be more than fifty yards. You squeeze between the big Arundel tech van and the Arundel workshop-trailer that are backed up to the garage, turn right a few yards past the big red and yellow striped Pirelli Marquee, turn left and left again down the row of the team and corporate hospitality marquees with their awnings and little café tables and chairs and the Arundel mobile home, a converted intercontinental bus with the blue and white striped awning pulled down from the side is third on the right. The trick for a driver, on a Friday afternoon after the timed practice session, is getting there.

Guido emerged from the two big vans just ahead of me and there was the first flash. I stepped out into the alleyway along the back on the pit garages and there were two more. Flashbulbs going off alerted more photographers and fans.

Not much happens in the paddock. A driver walking alone is interesting. Two together is news. Guido and I walking together was a good story. Within seconds we were surrounded by a mob of reporters, photographers and fans. One teenage boy put his arm around Guido as if Guido were an old friend and smiled for his father to take his picture with the hero racing driver. Reporters thrust their hand-held tape recorders at us. Fans thrust programmes at us and from all sides the reporters were shouting their questions.

''What's it like out there?''

''Do you still think Guido killed his wife?''

''Which one of you two is the number one driver?'' Innocent questions like that. I felt a hand grope my bum and swatted it away.

''Mr. DiSanto and I are just good friends,'' I said trying to lighten the situation.

Guido said, ''Hey, come on, not now. You guys make a big deal out of everything. There's no hard feelings, that's all.''

''What about your contract, Guido? You going to sign with Ferrari?''

The rain saved us. It had been threatening all day and as we stood there, pushed in from all sides, rain began to spatter us first in scattered drops and then in a light and steady downfall, soaking all of us. The reporters would have stood there all afternoon if it meant a story. They work hard, but they're human too. I raised my hands. "Gentlemen, please." I said. "We just want to get out of the rain. There's no story."

Almost grudgingly the arms and hands holding the cameras and the tape recorders in front of our faces withdrew and the fans and reporters stepped back to let us through. Guido turned as we were walking away and gave them a wave. Another photo opportunity for the photographers quick enough on the trigger.

Chapter 34

The exterior of Ken's Team Arundel motorhome looks like a bus. And it is; a blue, white and chrome, smoke-window, twin-turbo diesel, 475 horsepower $300,000 Newell imported from Miami, Florida.

Inside it is more interesting.

The interior is meant to remind you of a quiet, leather-lined gentlemen's club, with framed photographs of Ken's cars and his drivers on the faded old oak panelled walls. There's a well-stocked bar (single malts a specialty), a comfortable bedroom in the back and a scattering of worn brown leather chairs. It feels as comfortable and as unstylish as an old bedroom slipper and you could picture gentlemen in pin-striped suits drowsing behind copies of the *Financial Times* and a butler carrying in large whiskies on a silver tray.

It was the image Ken cultivated, of the landed multi-millionaire gentleman who kept exquisite, high-tech toys hidden behind the ancient panelling in the room where Balfour, Wellington, Churchill and the Queen had dined. While the other teams struggled to create the image of squeaky-clean, high-tech, ultra-modern, machine-like efficiency, Ken was Olde England, green and pleasant with the confidence and effortless grace of a stately home and the wealth of an empire somewhere over the horizon. The image worked (although it panelled over the days and nights of backbreaking work he put into the team) because it was what people still wanted to believe about England. And it worked because, like all good caricatures, it was partly true.

The rain had driven the Arundel Race Weekend Party Group inside the motorhome and the beginnings of a good party was in full cry. The roar of the party with voices talking too loud over Texas on the sound system, greeted us when we turned the corner into the impromptu promenade of motorhomes. We broke into a run, arriving on the steps dripping wet.

We squeezed inside the door and the voices rang out, Guido smiling and waving to the well-wishers.

"Guido!"

"Forrest!"

"Great driving out there!"

"I want you to meet . . . "

"The bedroom," I said to Guido. He gave me a quick nod and put his head down, shouldering his way through the crowd of smoke, back-patters and congratulators, keeping one hand up in the air in a wave of acknowledgement.

I started to follow when a soft hand on my arm made me turn. Her face had a rose flush from the champagne so she looked like a young girl again, her wide mouth in a half-smile. "Forrest, please. Leave it alone. Leave him alone. You don't remember what I told you? You can't make any deals with him." Then the smile left her face as suddenly as if the puppet's strings had been cut and her lower lip started to shake. "Forrest, he has told me that he will. He wasn't joking. It's not a joke."

I suppose I thought I could cheer her up. And I suppose it is what old lovers always do, try to pull the old strings that are not connected to anything any more. She was right. I didn't know anything. I said, "Vito has gone out to get the Ferrari out of the paddock parking lot. I told him I'd give him a ride around the track in the rain like we did at Vallelunga. Maybe you'd like to come along."

Anna smiled at me, tears welling up in her eyes, as if to say you fool. "How long ago? When did he go out there?"

"I don't know, three, four minutes."

She rose up on tiptoe to kiss me quickly on the cheek. And then she slipped away and out the door into the rain and in an instant she was gone.

"You got a lotta balls," Guido said, rising up on his toes.

I had expected him to be angry. I had hoped he would be angry. But he was smiling his big wide nasty smile. It made his head seem bigger and his body smaller.

"My old man told me," he said with that husky rasp. "He thinks you tipped him over but he's not sure. He can't figure out how you could have done that. No, I admire your guts, Evers. I never would have done a thing like that. He doesn't fuck around, my old man."

I was leaning against the oak door, the sounds of the party and the music coming through, laughter and glasses tinkling. Guido was standing on the other side of the double bed, treating me to his head-tilted-back, confident, *fuck you* look.

"What else did he tell you?"

"What I think it is," Guido said, "it is stupidity. It has to be stupidity. Or maybe it is ignorance that gives you this courage. Like a bull in Spain. You ever go to a bullfight in Spain, Evers, see the bull when he first runs out? He runs into the ring, charges around, pees a couple of times to let everybody know it's his ring. And you sit in the stands and you think this is one ignorant fucking animal. If that bull knew what everybody in the stands knows he wouldn't be pawing the ground, he'd be climbing the walls, trying to find a way out, maybe try to work out a deal with the matador. With somebody. And they always do this funny thing, they always announce the bull's weight when he comes charging out. And it doesn't make no difference. It never makes no difference. It doesn't matter what the bull weighs, doesn't count how big and strong he is because you know that in a few minutes the bull is going to get whacked and they will come into the ring with the old horses and drag the fucker out by his heels with his tongue dragging in the dirt. When the bull comes charging into the ring the horses are already outside waiting to drag him out like dead meat. You hear what I'm saying?''

"Guido, if you want to say something, say it."

"Let me ask you, Evers, you think you found something?"

"I don't know about Italy, and I don't know if you will even miss the money. But along with cutting off your money I think I found enough to have you banned from driving in most countries."

"Hey wait a minute. Let's skip the trivial shit, OK? You don't even know what's important around here. There's a lot you don't know. Like you think you did something noble or maybe you just want to fuck her, I don't know. But you think I am just going to stand around and watch you take my wife out of my home and do nothing? You think I have no honour? You think I have no pride?'' He was on his toes now, shouting, his face red.

"I think you are a lot of things, Guido. A pimp, a murderer, a thief. A nasty little shit."

He calmed down at that, forcing his grin back. "What you think does not count around here."

"What's on your mind here, Guido? You working up to taking a swing at me? You have a knife? You want to threaten me? I mean this talk is your idea and I still don't know what you are trying to say. You want to fight, good. Great. I'll start with your nose. I'll bet half the weight of your face is in your nose. I'd like to spread it around a little."

"You better look after me, Evers. If it wasn't for me, you wouldn't even be alive now.'' He was smiling easily again. "But I wanted to thank you first. I mean I really wanted to thank you about Rossella. I'm clear now. I can establish my name. You see there is no problem with the church now. You have no idea, and maybe to you because you have no family you don't understand, but I am founding a dynasty here. I am talking about a whole other level here. Another level of experience. This money is no accident. It didn't just happen by luck. Luck has nothing to do with it. It happened because we took it. We took it and that is how the world works. And let me tell you, it works for us. It works for us. Those assholes that go to work every day and once a month they bring home a paycheque. They work for us. We're talking about another level of existence here, an existence you can't even comprehend.

"So don't worry about that kid. I'm not even going to ask you. I'll find him. I'll find him eventually. I'm in no hurry, but I have a lot of lawyers and a lot of guys who are."

"Even you, Guido, even you, I'm surprised would want to kill his own son."

"He's not my son, you fucking son of a bitch. He's Rossella's. Who says I have to kill him? Who said anything about killing him? Move some papers around, change his name, nobody has to know. But that's not even the point now. The point now is that thanks to you I can start a real family. One that isn't based on lies and whores like that bastard, Rossella.

"I mean, do you blame me? Any man with any pride would have to do the same. And I am not any man. Anyway you have no idea what a favour you did for me, getting that bitch out of the house." Guido was looking out the window. Then he walked over to the bed, sat down and lay back, arms behind his head, and closed his eyes. His red boots streaked the white bedspread with black mud.

"You see you think you caused me a little irritation in Sicily. But it is really nothing, Forrest. Let me tell you it is really nothing. What you got, that company you found, that is less than one per cent. Not even that. Besides the Guardia have to prosecute us, it'll take years. We'll make a couple of payoffs, forget it, it's nothing. It's just a pipeline. We got a lotta pipelines.

"Let me give you just one figure. Improve your perspective. Total world trade, that's cars, that's oil, that's travel, that's food, all that shit, that's around two hundred billion dollars a day. Total for world international money exchanges is two *trillion* dollars per diem. You see what I'm saying? That two trillion is ten times the two hundred billion. And that is where our money is Forrest. That is our money, Forrest. You see the real world doesn't turn on the manufactured shit or trade no more. The real world turns on money. And you know where the big money is?" His eyes were still closed and he raised his arm and pointed straight up. "It's up there. In the sky. Bouncing around the satellites. The piece you saw in Sicily isn't even small change. It isn't even a crumb. And you know who is regulating all that? Nobody. Nobody nowhere. Because we own the game. We own the money."

He stood up, taking his time, going over to look out the window. Then he turned again. "You know that book they made into a movie, what was it? Bonfire? That's right, Bonfire, *Bonfire of the Vanities*. And the stockbroker, he makes a million a year and he calls himself one of the Masters of the Universe. No shit, that made me laugh. Masters of the Universe. Those fuckers work for us.

"And I'm glad to tell you this, Evers. I want you to know the size of what you have been poking your little stick at. I want you to know how deep you are over your head. You are so far over your fucking head you don't even know you are about to touch bottom."

When he said that, I don't know why, but I knew. The hairs rose up all the way up my back to my scalp and I knew it was too late. When the walls reddened and the room illuminated with the red fire I knew what it was and I wanted to scream "no" but I couldn't scream and it didn't matter. There was no noise that would make any difference. And no noise I could make would have been heard in the blast that followed, the walls of the motorhome shaking in the concussion.

When the noise of the blast hit I was already flinging open the door to the bedroom and charging through the stunned crowd, Texas still pumping through the speakers, "I don't want to be your lover," knocking over drinks and forcing my way through the door and into the rain and running down the promenade and turning the corner, running along with the growing crowd, the mechanics, reporters, marketing executives, public relations officers and photographers, running towards the dying fireball in the paddock parking lot.

Chapter 35

The rain went on into Saturday, a grey, dull drizzle that is the National Weather of Great Britain. But apparently it is rare in Monza in September and it seemed to throw the Monza Poliziotti and Carabinieri into a low grade, surly chaos.

For almost all the drivers there was no point going out on the track, apart from doing a few laps to get the feel of the car with rain tyres, the wings set on maximum downforce and the streaming track. Rain was forecast for Sunday so they all went out and came back after three or four laps, hating it and hoping for a dry Sunday. None of the practice times were anywhere near what they had been in the dry on Friday, so Friday's grid would stand. But still, some poor souls, back markers who hadn't made the grid on Friday, struggling with balky, uncompetitive machinery had to go out on kamikaze runs, hoping for a miracle and a time fast enough to take somebody else's place in the race on Sunday. They went around in clouds of spray and fury and spun before getting anywhere near Friday's slowest times. The fans who had turned up in the mud to watch the jousting match they call qualifying spent most of their time watching a wet and empty track.

Guido had made a statement to the press after the bomb went off, said how sorry he was, and how the monsters who could do this unspeakable thing must be caught, and flew away in his helicopter. Back to his castle. Safe.

He did not come to practice on Saturday. There was no need, he said. He knew the track like the back of his hand. Set the car up for rain, he told Ken. He had won at Spa and he would win again at Monza. He was going to be the World Champion. He would be there first thing Sunday morning. Bright and early.

And because there was so little to do for the race except wait, the rain washed away the layers of protection that would normally have kept the Carabinieri and the Polizei out of the pit garage while the hero driver did his laps in preparation for the big race. Now there were no excuses and I was in the middle of the horror and the mess. The bomb had killed nine people, two more were in the hospital near death and another thirty-seven had suffered serious injury. The police had come to expect these catastrophes in Palermo. But here in Monza they were amazed. They repeated their questions from the day before as we stood in the dank and cold pit garage, the rain drawing a veil over the crowds in the stands on the other side of the track.

Yes, I had been driving that car. It had been a Ferrari 365 BB Boxer, number plate FOR 2, registered in Britain. And yes, it is the same one you have a record of from Castelnuovo, the one loaned to me by a friend. No, I don't think he owns it, exactly. Yes, I knew the woman. Her name was Anna Bellini. "B E L L I N I," I spelled as their pencils slowly formed the letters. I could tell by the singed and tangled red hair and the horribly soiled green dress. No, I didn't have an address for her. Ask Guido, I almost said. And then thought why send her to Guido now. She deserved better than that. She had been, they said, no more than ten feet from the blast. No, I wasn't sure. It could be Vito's hand, but I could not be sure. No, I couldn't identify any of the other victims. Yes I would make arrangements for the remains of victims Guzzetti and Bellini.

And no, I said to them, I didn't know anybody who

would want to do this. There was no point in telling them, there was nothing they could do.

Guido had not soiled his hands, they would never trace it to him. The professionals who had done it were probably in Palermo now, or Mexico City. And Guido had the extra insurance of all those pictures of the two of us together, he and I looking like friends. We were friends in all of the morning papers and on the evening TV news.

A Formula One car is a clumsy weapon. It weighs about a thousand pounds without the driver, fuel, lubricant and coolant and has more than enough power to punch a hole in a brick wall big enough to walk through.

It is also a frail and capricious beast, stripped of every nonessential ounce of reinforcement, and nothing is stronger than it has to be. Unlike most weapons, you sit inside it lest it wander off and rip off its wheels harmlessly against a barrier fence or another car.

Yes indeed, the Formula One driver is protected, layered with systems designed for his safety and survival. The carbon-fibre tub which surrounds his body like a hard shell can withstand impacts of up to eighteen tons per square inch. There are two foam fire extinguishers on board, one in the cockpit and one in the engine compartment, set to go off automatically if the heat rises suddenly past the usual oven temperature of a Formula One cockpit. Non-flammable medical air comes in a tube direct to your helmet in case of oxygen-eating flames. The fuel lies in "burst-proof" bladders, connected to the fuel lines by self-sealing breakaway valves. The fuel lines themselves are designed to withstand pressures up to a thousand pounds per square inch and temperatures up to 500° Fahrenheit. The driver sits inside a multi-layer non-flammable flame-proof suit, his head cocooned in a foam-filled Kevlar helmet. So he is, for a man sitting inside a 200 mile an hour projectile, reasonably safe.

Reasonably safe.

In a heavy impact, nothing is safe.

While the other drivers sat in their mobile homes, talking to reporters and watching television, I spent nearly forty laps out on the track in my car, getting the set up right. The forecast for rain suited me just fine. I went over my entry lines and apex points, laying them over Guido's on the computer and eventually I chose my spot.

Ken was understanding, thinking those laps out on the track were a way of working off my grief.

I wasn't working off my grief. I was feeding it, worrying it, holding it to me like a knife. Poor little Anna, she must have known, she must have been running to save Vito. Poor girl, always running to somebody else's tune. Pulled by puppet.

Vito was a child, a boy. Thank Uncle Forrest for bringing you out of jail, thank him for the promise of a new life. Thank him for the ride.

Rossella, Rossella, Rossella. Thank Forrest for the ride.

I turned into the corners with the spray and fog hiding the track, the brake points invisible, and occasionally some other cars blocking my vision and my way. I turned into the corner in a rage, finding the sharp cutting edge of the limit and balancing there.

"Why don't you let me drive you back to the hotel," Ken said, his large comfortable arm around my shoulder. He wanted to be kind and I wanted him and everyone else to go away. "Have a hot shower, a quiet dinner, get to bed early. Be just the ticket."

"If you don't mind, Ken," I said in a voice that sounded like a hollow version of mine, some distant echo, "I'll stay here, in the motorhome. I don't want to eat and I don't want to talk to anybody. Not even to you. I'm very tired, I'll just sleep."

"You're sure? I don't like leaving you alone."

"Positive," I said.

At night, through the window of the motorhome, I could

see the windows of the other motorhomes of the other teams and the corporate players, yellow squares in the dark. And beyond, in the park where the thousands of campers huddled inside their tents and caravans underneath the trees, there was a scattering of campfires struggling to stay alight in the rain, flickering, like candles for the dead.

I went to bed early and slept as deeply as I have ever slept, the rain a muffled drum on the aluminium roof of the Team Arundel rolling country home.

Wall to wall black.

Chapter 36

Normally I am wired tight before a race and it takes a concentrated mental effort to wind down, completely relax and exclude all of the noise and the pretty girls who smile their sexy promises at me. Normally it is an effort to exclude all my thoughts, all of the other cars and drivers and let my mind settle into the car until there is nothing but myself and my car. And then there isn't even that, the car and I are one and the same. I don't drive a Formula One car, I wear it.

But on that Sunday, the day of the race at Monza, I was perfectly relaxed, all the emotional switches had been switched off. It was still raining, which was fine. And when people asked me how I was, I said, "fine." I had no breakfast as usual on a race day, and it didn't matter. I didn't want any. There was no need to wind down, none at all. I felt that special calm from knowing all the decisions and all the choices had been made. As long as time continued to move it would happen. The only emotion I felt was impatience. I just wanted to get started.

I heard Guido's helicopter arrive just after nine. And I was in the garage straightening the wreath for Vito that the mechanics had put up, when Guido walked in. So I heard him spreading good cheer before I saw him.

Guido looked good; tanned, rested and relaxed—carefully tailored cream-coloured trousers, bright red billowing shirt like a pirate, bright green wool pullover hanging down his back with its arms draped over his shoulders—a star come down from the sky. He said hello to Ken, and to Max, he talked with his mechanics, squatting, scrutinizing the settings of the car, running his fingers over the grooves of the rain tyres, smiling in the flash of the photographers who had the special FISA passes that allowed them into the pit garages. A normal race day for Guido. As far as he was concerned, I did not exist.

As far as I was concerned, he was already dead.

He was anxious to get going and when the warm-up laps began he was one of the first cars out on the track, testing his race set up on full tanks. He was in after one lap, screaming. This was wrong, why hadn't they set more wing, fucking car wouldn't handle. And he was out again. He had half an hour to get his car up for the race and he would be wall to wall fury getting it right.

Five minutes into the session, when the track had partially cleared with half the field into the pits for some adjustment or any excuse to get off the track, I went out.

Driving in the rain is not so difficult. True, you have to be especially sensitive to the car and fanatically precise and smooth in your driving. It is simply another level of concentration.

Driving in the rain with other cars on the track, though, is something else. Driving in the rain with other cars on the track isn't difficult, it is impossible.

It's impossible because each car squeegees water off the track with its rain tyres, channels it into the tyre's grooves and flings it skyward, thirty-five gallons a second, in a fine, impenetrable fog. At the same time, the high pressure venturi suddenly switching the rain-soaked air passing under the car from high pressure to low pressure at the rear of the car, combining with the near vacuum of its wake sucks another twenty-five gallons a second off the track and leaves it hanging in the air in a fog of microdrops. Visibility zero. So if there is traffic out on the track you spend a large part of your time wondering where you are and where they are. Is there another car inside that vague cloud of spray twenty feet ahead? Or, as you close in at, say, 50 miles an hour faster, are there two? And if there are two are they side by side, or one in front of the other? Your guess in the grandstand is as good as mine and probably better.

All Formula One cars are required to have a round red rain light at the back of the car. And we are required to switch it on for a wet track so that we may see each other. The regulations state that these warning lights must be at least 25 watts intensity. If the track is really wet and the spray is intense you can see one from at least four feet away.

Out on the track, in a cold water blender of noise and confusion, you find yourself asking questions you cannot answer. Questions like, ''Is there another car in the fog in front of me, spinning across the track because it hit a puddle I can't see ten yards in front of me?'' And ''Am I about to hit the puddle or the car that may or may not still be there?''

It is always possible that there is, first the puddle and then the spinning car suddenly looming out of the mist. And there is only one way to find out for sure and that is to nose into the fog and maybe into the spinning car, presented to you broadside, say, at 130 miles an hour.

Racing in these conditions is impossible, but we do it anyway.

Still we go out and we put our feet down on the go-faster pedal and we commit ourselves blindly to corners because we can't slow down. If you let up and slow down you lose downforce, lessen the grip of the tyres, and risk spinning off into the unknown. And worse, you run the risk of being smashed from behind from some other driver who has more courage or stupidity than you.

There are worse tracks than Monza in the wet. The Monza straight is long and wide and the grey fuzz balls up ahead when you come out of Parabolica give you some idea of what to expect in the way of traffic. You guess how fast you are catching this one and that one (or maybe two) and estimate where you will catch them on the back of the track. And you guess where, checking your rain-spotted vibrating mirrors, the fuzz balls creeping up behind you will catch you.

But on that rainy Sunday morning I didn't feel fear, I didn't feel anything. My time was the fourth fastest of the morning behind Senna, Alesi and Aral. But then, as the commentators were quick to point out, the Arundel chassis is especially nimble in the wet. Guido was twelfth quickest.

At 2 P.M. we roared out of the pit lane one by one in quick succession to trundle around for a lap in the rain, spinning our wheels, whipping from side to side, trying to keep from doing anything stupid on what the race officials are pleased to call the reconnaissance lap. Even at slow speed, we can't see much beyond our front wheels in the rain and spray.

As we come around Parabolica, the poor shivering Marlboro Girls, standing under their red and white parasols to mark the starting positions of each car, are sopping wet. And the thought strikes me, and probably most of the other drivers, that this is ridiculous.

At the drivers' meeting in the morning, the former World Champion, Marcel Aral had suggested that the drivers boycott the race. It is too dangerous, he said. He is right, it is too dangerous. But the TV cameras are pointing at us here on the grid, all twenty-six drivers present, because those cameras are beamed via satellite to an audience of over five hundred million people. Five hundred million people represent money so huge (so many potential consumers) that the economic Titan cannot be deflected by an Italian rain storm or anything so small as the life of a racing car driver.

The show will go on.

The Marlboro Girl who stands at my starting place, ninth on the grid, has dark roots under her bleached blonde hair, the rain blowing in her face has made her mascara run down her cheeks and her legs have goose bumps. She is shivering visibly as I pull up and stop in front of her. She will have to stand there, her feet in a pool of water, for another twenty-five minutes. Ridiculous.

I switch off the engine and Ken is leaning over the cockpit, as one of the mechanics, Richard or Steve from the size of him, I can't see who, holds a big umbrella over us. Water has crept under my visor and trickled down my neck inside the Nomex balaclava that covers my head like a sock.

Ken is talking to me but I don't hear him. I nod my head from time to time, thinking that I am on remote control, thinking that there is bound to be some bumping at the start and maybe the best thing would be to go wide, out of the slipstream of the eight cars ahead of me where I might have a chance of seeing a few yards.

After thirteen minutes of waiting in the rain they sound a horn to signal that the pit lane will be closed in two minutes. All the cars are out on the grid so it doesn't matter. Close the damn pits.

The five-minute warning sounds and mercifully the Marlboro Girls are allowed to squelch off the grid as the grandstand loudspeakers blare the Marlboro theme from *Bonanza* for the several thousandth time. At the three-minute signal the dripping crowd of celebrities, sponsors and anybody else who can wangle a pit lane pass runs for cover. At the one-minute signal they push the starter motor into the back of my transmission and the engine won't start.

The two mechanics lift up the back of the blue fibreglass bodywork of the car and hold it up while Ken is on his knees, in the rain, blue anorak over his pin-stripe suit, bending over the engine squirting ether into the intake stacks. The engine starts as the thirty-second horn sounds, and they latch the cover back on and run for the side of the track as the green flag is displayed and we all set off in order, no passing allowed, for the final parade lap.

As we parade around, through the chicane, a long sweeping right around the Curva Grande, through the chicane and around the two Lesmos corners I realize that I have not noticed who is ahead of and who is behind me and I can't remember who they are. And I realize that I don't care, it doesn't make any difference. Guido is up ahead, third where he qualified on the grid. Six places to pass.

We line up again, on the grid, the red light goes on over the start line, I hear the sound of 18,000 horsepower like distant surf on a beach a mile away, the light goes green and I am in a hurry squeezing the power and jinking left, to the extreme outside edge of the track. In the blast of water, spray, exhaust I can't see anything else, there must be at least one car ahead of me from this much spray, and I keep my foot down heading straight into the fog bank.

The track ahead clears for a moment, and the fury and fog is on my right as I keep way over to the left-hand side of the straight past the end of the grandstands. Water shoots straight up in jet streams off the front tyres and plumes past my head. Way off the racing line I hit a shallow puddle on the track and for the moment the car skates across the surface threatening to rotate but the aerodynamics keep the car pointing straight ahead and in an instant the tyres grip again. The three-hundred-yard marker looms on my left and I am on the wrong side of the track to get through the first chicane.

I move right, into the moving fog, keeping my speed up, filtering right into the maelstrom at close to 200 miles an hour, and there is, to my great relief, no one there. The car is skittering, light on its feet, feeling unstable in the boil of wind from the cars in front of me. Tiny droplets accumulate inside my visor, speckling my vision. I see in the far distance first a glow, then ten feet in front of me a red light and I begin, gently easing on the pressure until I am standing on the brakes. We almost touch, the car looks like the bright red of a Ferrari, but I'm not sure.

The light moves left and I follow it, feeling but not seeing the kerb on my left slam into my left front wheel, shock the whole car and bounce my shoulder against the side of the car. But it's not too bad and I keep the red light in front in sight, feathering the throttle, slamming into the kerb on my right, easing back onto the throttle and accelerating after the fast-disappearing round red light.

His tyres leave tracks on the wet track and when they begin to bend right, I follow, keeping a step to the left to stay away from the dirty, boiling air behind him and give my car a clean bite.

This is sensory deprivation, and all of my senses are screaming for information, my eyes noting the opening in the overarching trees describing the bend in the track, the beginning of the red and white striped kerbing on my left announcing the beginning of Curva Grande, my nose sensing cut grass, telling me I am passing a car (or more than one car?) that has just gone off. The grandstands appear in the mist on my right marking the inside of the corner. My ears listen for the sounds of the other cars, shifting, letting up for an onrushing corner, the swishing sound of another set of tyres alongside.

I follow around in the semi-blindness, sometimes able to see for twenty or thirty yards, sometimes barely able to see my front wheels, all the time treating the car delicately, keeping it balanced. With a full load of fuel (150 litres at the start of the race, just under 140 now) it feels heavy, sluggish, reluctant to slow down or turn and slow to pick up speed again. And when I come down the main straight again this time I keep to the right, to be sure I can see the lap board Ken holds out for me so I can tell where I am. Because if someone went off in front of me, and if I passed a car or two on the straight, I could be up into the points, among the first six. But if I got it wrong and there was a stream of cars passing me on the straight, who knows, I could be fifteenth. I have no idea.

I also want to see Guido's lap board. I need to know where he is. Nearing 195 as I cross the start line, I don't have time to see who is holding the yellow boards. Mine tells me I am sixth, Guido's says fourth. I must have passed some cars at the start on the straight. Or more than one car went off.

I've moved up three places on Guido. He has dropped back a place towards me.

I have to pass the car in front of me, I have to pick up the pace. If I'd had more time, my board would have told me how far ahead of me the next car is, but I was too busy looking for Guido's board. For all I know, although I am four places closer to Guido than I was at the start of the race, Guido could be pulling away from me. I don't know. I don't hear the radio from the pits and I don't talk to them. I don't want to hear them or talk to them.

I do know I have to pick up the pace, I tell myself again as the red and white kerb on my right announces the chicane is coming up. This time, instead of tentatively following another car, I attack the kerbs, a hard bang as I hit the first one high with rap of the slabs following knocking me back on the track and into the second one on my right, bang again, bruising my shoulder and squeezing on the power as quickly as the car and the tyres will stand it.

Cars tend to string out in the wet. You can't really see well enough to pass but if you concentrate you can see, sometimes quite clearly, sometimes not, the path of the cars ahead of you, a path one car wide, showing you where to turn and the line through corners and down the straights. It's inherited from the lead car, who doesn't have the fog bank of cars in front of him for the first laps before he runs up against the back markers. So he has the advantage of seeing where he's going and we all follow blindly in his footsteps.

Except.

Except the leader tends to stick to the conventional line through a corner, the one line that leads you from the outside of the turn into the apex on the inside and back out again to the exit. It is the line everybody takes, wet or dry, so over the practice sessions and the races it gets worn smooth. So the perfect line through a corner, in the rain, may give your tyres less grip than another way around, where the little stones sticking up out of the surface compound have not been worn flat and polished.

I caught the Ferrari two laps later, nearly running into the back of him coming into the Ascari chicane and I have to get on the brakes hard, the car starting to drift sideways, but he turned into the corner and I had a little room to go wide on the entry and get my balance back.

I followed his glowing light down the back straight, keeping tucked up behind him even though the air is full of grit and exhaust, and my car feels loose, riding much harder as it rises up on the springs from the loss of downforce and the suspension turns to rock. But I want the tow, I want the extra little pull of speed I get from following close behind to pull me forward as I move alongside him on the inside.

We brake together but I am inside him and I have the track. He starts to come across me, we are both on the power now in this long sweeping 180° turn and I am just hanging on depending on the extra grip from being just inside the line. The Ferrari starts to drift wide and he has to back off and when I come around to slingshot up the straight I can see, in the distance, a grey fuzzy mass of spray. Guido.

My board says I am fifth, three point five seconds behind Guido. If I have been gaining on him, it is not enough and I strain forward against the harness that straps me into the car, urging it on.

Three laps later, I have caught him. I sit behind him and in the whirl of mist and rain, study his style.

Guido is not at home in the rain. He is smoother than he usually is going into the corners and smoother coming out. He has to be to stay on the track. But fundamentally he is driving it the same way that he drove at Vallelunga and the way the computer charts showed his driving here in practice. He is waiting for the last possible moment to brake, braking hard and throwing the car into the turn, using the turn itself to scrub off speed. Then he tiptoes through the corner and stands on it at the exit, often banging up the kerbs, fishtailing and losing a little traction.

Perfect.

When we pass the pits his board tells him I am behind him and his head moves to look at his mirrors. Good. I want him to know.

I follow him carefully through the first chicane, keeping off the kerbs and keeping a little distance. I lose a little time but my exit out of the chicane is smoother and I can put down the power sooner. So by the time we are turning into Curva Grande, I am just one step behind, a little to his left.

I follow him for two laps like this, stalking him, learning his moves. And then, when I follow him into Lesmo One for the third time, staying just underneath him, as we are accelerating as hard as we can, he waits for the last possible moment to lift and dab at his brakes and I begin to take him.

I enter the turn a little more slowly than he does, and he draws a little ahead, out of visual range. But my car is settled and I take a tighter line and I come out of the corner early, high, accelerating hard. The track has more grip here and I am on the power a little earlier and I close up behind him, close enough to see him. His backwash blinds me for a moment and I have to go on instinct as we go down the straight between the two corners until he starts to turn in to Lesmo Two. As he lifts to turn in I stay on the power and I stay high, the car in clean air again and the tyres getting good grip from the rougher track off the line. And when I turn in I am late, and I stay high, giving myself room to pass on the outside as Guido waits for a micro-second until he gets to the apex to get on the power. Again I am alongside him, passing him and he sees me and he has to lift for a moment to keep from hitting me.

By the time he has risen up out of the turn up to ride on the kerbs on the exit I am inches in front of him.

And I have stolen his air.

At the critical moment, when he needs maximum grip he loses almost all of his downforce and like a cannon ball swinging at the end of a cable, the cable is cut.

At the same time, I lose control. I have pushed my car too far and my attention has wandered away to Guido for a microsecond and I am too high up on the kerbs. I ride for a second with the bottom of the car on the concrete slabs, skittering like a flat-bottom sled, wheels off the ground and the car spins a half spin. And I am going backwards, a passenger, so I see Guido's left wheel touch the kerb and start to launch his car, shifting all the weight onto his right front, bouncing the car hard and up. He is up in the air, going straight off the track at a right angle, turning, banking in the air like an aeroplane, the wings catching the air now that he is off the ground and banking in alongside the edge of the grandstand and hitting the unprotected Armco barrier head on.

My car begins to turn again, spinning slowly as I am rocketing down the track, my foot hard on the brakes but not scrubbing off much speed on the wet track and as I spin around and around I see, like flickering shutter frame images, snapshots of Guido's car compress against the Armco, the rear wing and wheels of his car still moving forward after the nose of the car has shattered. I see the splintered mess of shattered fibreglass, tubing, fractured black carbon fibre and a huge rear wheel bounding high in the air. I see the red glow. And I see the rising balloon of flame.

Then I am out of visual range and my car is hugely out of control. There is nothing I can do except sit there with my foot hard on the brake and wait. There is a change of pitch as the car leaves the pavement and slides along the grass, gouging up chunks of turf. The left front wheel catches the soft earth and the car is rolling over and over and I think this has to stop as the left rear wheel tears off and is flung up into the air.

The car doesn't want to stop but it does with a bang as

the nose smashes into the Armco barrier. But no, it hasn't stopped and the car spins around another time, righting itself to come to a stop with another bang, backing into the barrier again.

For a few cautious moments I go through my body checking for injuries and finding none. Still not sure, I move my fingers and toes. I switch off the ignition switch, take off my outer gloves, strip off my oozing Nomex gloves, and pull off my helmet and the woolly Nomex hood. A marshal puts down his fire extinguisher and unbuckles my harness.

Gripping the sides of the cockpit with my bleeding hands, I lift myself up, and I get out of the car.

Chapter 37

There was snow on the mountains and just above us the slopes faded into low, black and grey clouds. More rain before the end of the day.

This is another Italy; high, remote, and Alpine. As much Swiss as Italian, as much French as Swiss. The air is cold and thin and clear, the streets in the village precise and clean. Down below, the black snake of the new International Motorway glides through the bottom of the valley, but the roar of the cars and the trucks, tourists heading south, car parts heading north, the roar of the traffic is silenced by the distance. I turned away from the window and back to the nun who was holding the boy.

He looked fine. He had his father's black eyes, alert to every movement. And he had the delicacy of his mother's features. I don't know the difference between a baby's grimace from colic and a grin. I prefer to think he was smiling. The nun handed him to me and I held the soft, infinitely fragile bundle.

Babies need holding as much as breath. We know this because of a terrible experiment in the Second World War in London. It wasn't meant to be an experiment, that was the last thing it was meant to be. The nuns who ran a shelter for homeless infants orphaned by the bombing were working themselves to exhaustion trying to look after all of the children. There was an army of bombed orphans, many of them injured, and more kept coming in every night. So the nuns didn't have time to cuddle all the infants. There were some babies who were fed and changed and washed, but who were never held and never cuddled and they all died. Every little one of them died.

Aldo looked fine. He was obviously getting plenty of cuddles and plenty of love. I had been told this was the best home for him now. It was certainly the most expensive, but that didn't matter in the least. Expense would be the least of his worries.

"We are very grateful, you know," the nun said, wanting to say something as I held on to the child. "There are so many more things we will be able to do now. You have been so generous, with your gift. I cannot begin to express . . ."

"It was his money and it is his gift," I said, not wanting her to go on.

Little Aldo would not have it easy without a father or a mother. We would have to deal with the question of a foster home soon. He was not going to be an easy child to place. Thanks to a few well-chosen Italian inheritance laws and to a few billion carefully placed lire into outstretched official hands, Aldo was now one of the richest individuals in Europe. And thanks to the miracle of satellites, Aldo's money was safe in the Cayman Islands, Switzerland, Jersey and several other places where the tax man and his grandfather could not get it. Whoever his foster parents might turn out to be, the child was going to arrive with a lot of luggage.

"Yes, of course. His money. It is just that it is difficult for me to think of a little baby being so rich."

"I'm sure that's the way his father would have wanted it," I said.

On the way out of the main building, after I had finished signing the last sheaf of documents, a nun bustled across the floor and intercepted me just before the door. Her mild wrinkled face looked up at me, her eyes magnified by thick glasses.

"Excuse me," she said, laying a stubby white hand on my sleeve. "I don't mean to be rude, or intrude on your privacy. Goodness knows we all need our privacy. But I couldn't forgive myself if I didn't at least ask. I'm afraid I am rather a fan of motor racing and excuse me for asking, but aren't you Forrest Evers, the Formula One driver?"

"I was," I said.

Exciting New Mysteries Every Month

BERKLEY PRIME CRIME

__FINAL VIEWING by Leo Axler
0-425-14244-2/$4.50
Undertaker Bill Hawley's experience with death has enhanced his skills as an amateur detective. So when a blind man is found dead with an exotic dancer, Bill knows the death certificate isn't telling the whole story.

__A TASTE FOR MURDER by Claudia Bishop
0-425-14350-3/$4.50
Sarah and Meg Quilliam are sleuthing sisters who run upstate New York's Hemlock Falls Inn. Besides bestowing gracious hospitality and delicious meals, both find time to dabble in detection.

__WITCHES' BANE by Susan Wittig Albert
0-425-14406-2/$4.50
"A delightful cast of unusual characters...engaging."–<u>Booklist</u>
Herbalist China Bayles must leave her plants to investigate when Halloween hijinks take a gruesome turn in Pecan Springs, Texas.
 Also by Susan Wittig Albert, available now:
__ **THYME OF DEATH** 0-425-14098-9/$4.50

__CURTAINS FOR THE CARDINAL
by Elizabeth Eyre 0-425-14126-8/$4.50
"Sigismondo and Benno are captivating originals."–<u>Chicago Tribune</u>
A raging prince has murdered his own son. Now Renaissance sleuth Sigismondo must shield Princess Minerva from a heartless killer.
 Also by Elizabeth Eyre, available now:
__ **DEATH OF THE DUCHESS** 0-425-13902-6/$4.50